DEAD AND BACK AGAIN #2

SPIRIT OF SUSPENSE

C. RAE D'ARC

Cover design by 100 Covers

ISBN: 978-1-961733-12-1 (Paperback)
Library of Congress Control Number: 2026901103

Published by Bursting Box Publishing

www.burstingboxpublishing.com
www.facebook.com/c.rae.darc
www.instagram.com/craedarc/

Praise for the Haunted Romance Trilogy

Don't Date the Haunted

"Certain to have the reader laughing out loud."
– Readers' Favorite

"Sitting on my 'Best Books I've Ever Read' shelf."
– Gee Liz Reads

Don't Marry the Cursed

"Rating: 10/10 I can't wait for the next one!"
– Leyendo.Lina (Bookstagrammer)

"Don't Pass Up This Series."
– Jim Doran, author of Kingdom series

Don't Dance with Death

"Am I allowed to call this a perfect trilogy?"
– Valerie Evans, author of Wolves of Worsham series

"Exciting and engaging from the very beginning."
– *Libromancy Podcast*

Books by C. Rae D'Arc

HAUNTED ROMANCE
Don't Date the Haunted
Don't Marry the Cursed
Don't Dance with Death

* * *

Oz's Haunting Survival Book
From Horror with Love

DEAD AND BACK AGAIN
Specter Inspector
Visionary Investigations
Spirit of Suspense

DREAMING PRINCESSES
Dreaming Beauty
Fairest and the Frog
Little Red and the Lumpy Bed
Golden Locks and Riddles

To the thriller genre.
For mashing genres well enough to become official.

World of Novel

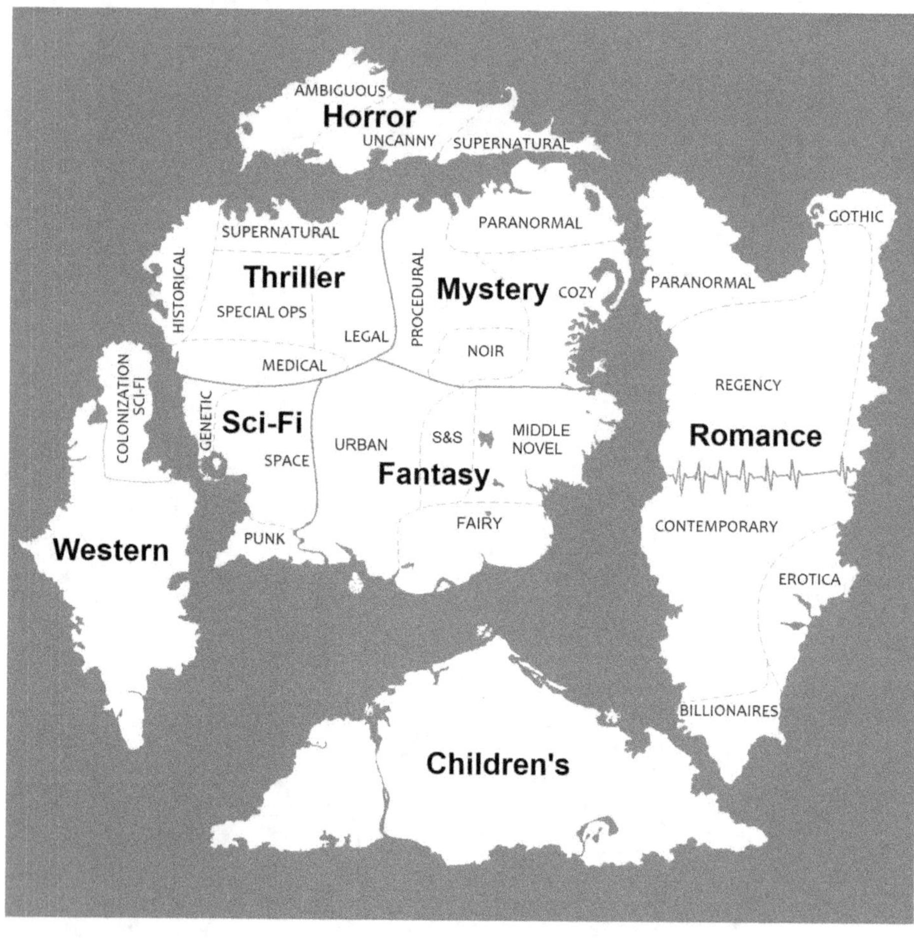

DEAD AND BACK AGAIN #2

SPIRIT OF SUSPENSE

CHAPTER 1

When Heroes recount their thrilling
Adventures, they often begin with the
ending of another.

- *Lemuel Gulliver's Travel Guide, Vol. 5: Thriller*

"You have no idea who I am, do you?" I asked my abductors. Despite my time in Mystery influencing my Fantasy-Horror accent over the last several years, I asked with more of a statement than a question. I doubted they knew my real identity. Besides, it was only fair since I had no idea who they were. They'd surprised me from behind, and having a white-ish pillowcase that smelled of cheap cigarettes over my head didn't help.

With my hands tied in cords behind me and crunched in the back seat of a vehicle, I had little to analyze for a criminal profile. Based on the rough seat fabric and stickiness of something near my left hand, I guessed I was in a base model sedan and my foolish abductors were not only drug addicts, but also slobs.

"We know exactly who you are," Fool #1 said beside me. "That's why we nabbed you."

"Then it's official," I said. "You're the dumbest crooks I've ever met."

That earned me a smack on the side of my head. Bare handed? Good to know.

"We ain't dumb! You're the dumb one for thinking you can stay in Shigaqua without anyone learning your true identity, Aeron *Frome* of the *royal family* of *Fairy, Fantasy*. This is our city, and we know everything."

I couldn't help myself. I laughed. It started as a chuckle but grew into a belly laugh until the hand met my skull with another smack.

"Ow. First of all, it's Fromm—meaning noble and honorable. The Fromes are a family of fly fishers in Vluz. Second of all, this city doesn't belong to you. I don't even know who you fools are."

"You will soon. We're the Underground, and we'll make sure you never forget us. The whole city will know who we are by the time we're done with you."

Idiots. Publicizing their group name simply gave the authorities a better target.

"Pish-posh. If it belongs to anyone, it's the city police force, with whom, I might add, I have major connections." The fools dropped my birth-given name but left out my occupational title as a private investigator. Jerks. I'd worked hard for that. "Also, my full Fantasy title is Earl Fromm, the *Haunted*, of Margen. Do you know why they call me the Haunted?"

Fool #2 snorted from the front. "We know you got some creepy magic that lets you talk to the dead, but you ain't in Fantasy no more. This is Noir, and magic don't work here."

"That's only half correct," I said, "but it's a common misunderstanding, so I'll let your stupidity slide into ignorance this time. Magic is a learned power that, yes, mutates outside of Fantasy. However, I don't have magic. In fact, it would be nearly impossible for me to learn it because of my *ability*. Abilities are birth-given traits, usually found among royalty and nobles—which, as you know, I am. But unlike magics, abilities transfer between countries without alteration."

"He's bluffing. Magic don't work in Shigaqua."

I settled back into my seat to get comfortable. "Oh, I'm going to enjoy this. And I haven't even told you the best part yet."

"What," Fool #1 asked carefully, "is the best part?"

"The best part is that the people you plan to contact for my ransom—my family—*all* have abilities. This isn't my first abduction, you know. The first time, I was taken to Horror. You know, home of Hauntings like serial killers and monsters of the worst sort. Only three members of my family came to get me, and they ended up massacring an army of Hauntings in the Valley of the Shadows of Death. You know the place? You think you're more dangerous than they are?" I chuckled again. "Dumbest crooks ever."

Another smack. I predicted it this time and rocked away to avoid most of the attack.

There was an uncomfortable silence until we hit a divot in the road and the fool from the front mumbled, "He's bluffing. There's no way anyone's that strong, and we'll be safe in our hideout."

"Ah, it doesn't matter," I said. "I doubt you'll even meet my family. You'll be caught by my local friends first. Unfortunately for you, they're just as dangerous."

As if on cue, a sound-bursting pop broke into the entertaining conversation. The vehicle swerved and screeched as the front left tire exploded.

The driver swore, and Fool #1 screamed next to me. A maniacal laugh slid through the vehicle as we drove through my poltergeist assistant. My abductors' screams shrilled at the un-embodied sound. I ducked and braced myself as best I could against the seats as the car careened to the side. As soon as we came to a stop, gunfire blasted, the windows shattered, and the fools screamed in pain. As expected, my local friends had come to rescue me. The living and the dead worked together on my behalf.

The gunfire ceased, but the screams continued. I deemed it safe to begin my escape. Scrunching my pillowcase against the seat's headrest behind me, I managed to shift it up and off of my head.

The fool next to me struggled to staunch the entry and exit wounds in his shoulder. The driver fool slumped to the side at an uncomfortable angle. He didn't move.

With a heavy sigh, I motioned my wrists to the remaining fool. "I can help you with that wound, but I'll need you to untie me."

"What?" he half screamed. "Like I'd fall for that! Garrett, help me with this! Get up, Garrett!"

"He's dead," a calm, cold, female voice said from my side of the car. A woman of about my age stood at my door, expertly aiming her gun at the other fool. "And you will be too if you try anything."

Fool #1 yelped and stared in shock at my investigating partner. Nita's sneaky appearances tended to have that effect on people.

The simplest way to define Nita was to say she was unde-finable. She wasn't blonde or brunette, but somewhere in between. She wasn't dark or light-skinned, but again, some-where in between. Every time I looked, her eyes shifted through every dark shade of the rainbow. She didn't cover her face with gobs of makeup, but neither was she entirely natural. She was plain and average, yet absolutely beautiful. Her hair was tied back in a low bun, and she wore all black military cargo pants and a leather jacket despite the summer night. I'd learned to stop gifting her with colorful clothes and accessories. She wore black the way a black cat wore its fur: unchanging and like she knew that danger lurked wherever she went.

Despite the last three years of working together, she was a mystery to me and herself. Everyone called her Nita Incog because she didn't even know her real name. A curse of amnesia had taken away her memories three and a half years ago. What little we did know was that she had been trained to be a special operative, and I trusted her with my life.

"Took you long enough," I said, smirking. "They got me in their car and on their merry way to their super-secret hideout."

"Your ghosts would have kept track of you," she said, keeping her steely sights on Fool #1 while opening my door. I slid out and gestured with my wrists.

"Are you going to cut me loose?"

"Loosening you could make me lose him."

I grunted. "No one else needs to die. You already shot his shoulder and accomplice. He's as stupid as they come, but I doubt he'll try anything."

Fool #1 seemed to go into a catatonic shock as he whimpered to himself. Nita kept her eyes on him, regardless. "There's a switchblade against my lowest left rib."

I didn't mind the excuse to study her muscled waist. "I don't see it."

"It's in a wrap under my shirt."

I blinked. "As much as I appreciate the insistence to follow my uncle's rules of surviving Horror, and I'm flattered that you trust me to be a gentleman, but do you really want me to wiggle my tied hands from behind my back up your shirt to find your switchblade?"

Her face remained stoic except for the speckling of red across her cheeks and nose. Yes, I considered her beautiful, but we were partners, and she kept an extremely annoying no-dating rule until she rediscovered her past. She was also incredibly stoic in the most extreme circumstances, making it all the more fun to shamelessly flirt and test her breaking point.

"You're impossible," she muttered, shifting her gun to her left hand. I had no doubt that she was equally skilled with her nondominant hand…if she had one. Then she reached under her shirt to deftly retrieve a hidden switchblade and toss it to the ground without removing her sights from Fool #1.

"You couldn't hand it to me like a normal person?" I asked, lowering my whole body to the ground to reach for the blade. Her stony expression cracked again as her lips pinched back a teasing smirk. "Are you going to help me?"

"Well, the officials will be here soon enough. I expect you to free yourself before they arrive. There will be paperwork, after all."

Grumbling, I maneuvered the blade to saw against my bindings without cutting myself. Flashing lights whirled in the distance by the time I'd freed my hands.

"How did you know I was missing?" I asked Nita. "Did Neil contact you?"

"Eventually," she said. "I stopped by the office, and your poltergeist had left a message for me. He was the one who blew the tire."

"I figured. Why were you at the office?"

"You called me after hours and didn't leave a message. When I called you back and you didn't answer, well, I knew something was wrong."

I grinned. "You were worried about me?"

"At first, I was confused. It was the first time the phone rang longer than a minute, and I realized you always answer my calls. The fact that you hadn't meant something was wrong."

"What can I say? I like the sound of your voice. And you hardly ever call me, so I know it's important when you do."

"And you frequently call me, which is why I often let your ringing become a pacer for my exercising."

"Hey, it was important this time! Not only was I about to be abducted, but I scored a VIP visitation at Arrowhead."

"What?" She jerked toward me, taking her sights off of the fool for the first time.

Arrowhead was a secretive independent contractor and training facility for special operatives in Thriller. Based on Nita's mastered skills in their forms of combat, we had a theory that she was trained there or somewhere like it before her amnesia-inducing accident. We managed to corner one of their operatives last autumn during a Case. Over the winter and spring, I'd slowly pulled strings to score a tour of the facility. I was allowed to bring a single escort, and I hoped to jog Nita's memories with the tour.

"How?" Nita asked.

I grinned back. "If I told you, I'd have to kill you."

"That's too ambitious, even for you."

I laughed. "They finally contacted me as the Earl of Margen, thinking I was in need of their services. Instead, I offered them an alliance deal to train recruits from my family's duchy, but first, I want a tour. Before I was abducted, I was calling to tell you to pack your bags because we're going to Thriller in a few days."

Her lips went micro-thin as she bit back her excited smile. She did nothing to restrain the eagerness in her eyes.

The cops arrived and took over the situation, cuffing Fool #1 and declaring Fool #2 dead on arrival. Unfortunately. That meant questions for Nita and me. We gave our statements a dozen times, and I warned them to be on the lookout for a gang calling themselves The Underground. If there were more than the two of them, failing to capture me probably meant they'd try to abduct another big name for ransom.

Finally finishing our reports, Nita insisted on accompanying my taxi ride home.

"Thanks," I said, "for rescuing me before those fools contacted my parents. My family doesn't need another reason to want me home." Every weekly call ended with a question about when I'd visit again. My parents didn't love the idea of me chasing crooks so far from home, but this was my life, not theirs. I'd never admit that I was growing tired of Noir's international prejudices and dating pool of femme fatales.

The taxi pulled up to my rambler house in the northern suburbs of Shigaqua. Nita asked for the taxi to idle as she followed me from the vehicle.

"Walking me up to my door?" I teased her. "My my, Nita. Are you always this chivalrous with your dates?"

Her cheeks darkened enough to be noticeable in the moonlight. "If that was your definition of a date, I'm concerned for those you've taken lately."

I simply laughed. Yes, I'd dated a lot this last year, but nothing serious. I felt like Goldilocks, dating women who were too hot, too cold, too soft, too hard…never finding my "just right."

Lost in my memories, I habitually walked up my driveway and waved to my invisible friends before noticing that Nita was no longer beside me. She stood frozen, only three steps from the sidewalk, wide eyes darting at everything and nothing around her.

"Is something wrong?" I asked. "Or are you afraid of a little ghost?"

She glared at me with clenched teeth. "There's a lot more than one little ghost whispering unintelligible words in my ears right now."

I grinned. "They don't call me the Haunted without reason." Addressing the air around us, I asked, "Fellas, could you back off a bit? I've never been walked to my door by a woman before, and the idea entertains me."

Nita scowled at me and then visually relaxed as I assumed my spiritual friends left her alone. I beckoned her to join me down the pathway.

"Come on. I can't get a doorstep goodnight kiss if you don't come to the door with me."

She narrowed her eyes at me, but something seemed to snap in her. She marched up to me, grabbed me by my shirt collar, and then twisted, forcing me off balance. My back landed on my lush lawn (I'd have to thank my spirit friends again for their landscaping) with Nita kneeling on my chest, still holding my collar.

"Oops," she said, as if she was some innocent schoolgirl who hadn't effectively pinned me.

The streetlamps sparked her eyes with gold, and I lost myself. I reached up and tucked a loose curl of hair behind her ear. She stiffened, and her golden eyes went wide with fear. As if she was the one pinned, trapped, and without control.

"Please, Aeron," she whispered. "Stop doing this to me."

"What, you're allowed to torture me, but turn around isn't fair play?"

Her answer was to stand and retreat. I released a heavy breath before regaining my feet. I'd pressed her buttons enough for one night. Tired in more ways than one, I raised my hand to wave goodbye when—

"*Aeron!*"

A single voice rang through my head and washed over me with a chill. It wasn't the subtle voice of a spirit trying to nudge me, and it wasn't the chill of a spirit entering the space of my body. It was the clear voice of an almost seventeen-year-old young woman, speaking directly to my mind. My sister.

Lady Samantha Fromm, The Silent, of Margen had never spoken a word aloud in her life, but she had her own way of communicating. Her one-way telepathic ability allowed her to speak directly into people's minds. She'd never contacted me while I was in Mystery before. I hadn't known that she could. It required a lot of mental energy and focus for her to speak farther distances. That meant that whatever she had to say was important enough to push herself to the brink of exhaustion and migraines.

Curses, what happened?

I thought it couldn't get worse, but it did. One more word was all it took. She spoke it between half of a sob.

"Grandfather."

No. Cold dread filled me.

"Aeron?" Nita stared at me, confused and worried. "I'd say you look like you've seen a ghost, but, well, you see ghosts all the time, so…"

"I—" I paused, finding it difficult to breathe. "I need to go home."

"Oh-kay?" Nita gestured to my rental house ten feet away. "I'll see you tomorrow then?"

"No, I mean *home*. To Margen. My grandfather is dying."

"Did a spirit tell you?"

"No, my sister did." I stepped back to lean against the brick wall of my house for support. It wasn't enough. I slid down onto the grass. Curses, his health had been failing for the past few years, but my parents had never asked me to come home with this urgency.

"Aeron," Nita said, "I'm sorry about your grandfather. We can tell our clients you need emergency leave. How much time will you need with your family?"

"Nita," I said, my throat dry. "My grandfather's the Duke of Margen. Even if my parents accept my abdication after all these years, my presence will be expected for the month of mourning and the coronation of my parents."

"A whole month?"

"That's *if* my parents accept my abdication. If not, I'll have my own ceremony as marquis and there is no coming back. My time as a private investigator is over."

She blinked, and it became her turn to find stability by sitting beside me on the grass. She stared at her feet and even took my hand in hers. As much as I wanted the motion to be romantic, I recognized it as simply a gesture of comfort. Was it meant to comfort me or herself? I wasn't allowed to think of her hand-holding as anything else. Not anymore.

"First Truth left," Nita said in a daze, "to care for her dying mother. Now you too? What will happen to the investigation agency? You're the best investigator in Noir. Who else can solve the cold Cases?"

"You flatter me. I didn't do it alone."

She scoffed. "You think I can solve those Cases without you? You talk to the dead. No one else can do that. I can't just pick up another partner—" She paused as the full reality hit her. "Aeron, no one else knows me like you do. Sometimes, you know me better than I know myself. What do I…what am I supposed to…"

"Truth knows you," I said. "Maybe you can convince her to come out of retirement."

Nita shook her head. "No, she's too busy helping her ailing mama."

I swallowed. "I may be back. I just need a month to be with my family."

"Liar." She gave me a sad attempt at a smiling stink-eye. It sagged back into a somber version of her usual dead stare. "Well, will you, um…need support? Like, emotionally?"

I blinked at her a couple of times. "You want to go with me to Margen?" Curses, if the mood wasn't so somber, I would have teased that she wanted to go home with me.

"Only if you need me," she added in a rush. "I don't want to be in the way or anything."

"No, no, you'd be… I'd really like you to come. Besides, we still have an appointment with Arrowhead to keep."

CHAPTER 2

As the youngest genre of Novel, Thriller is
an Action mix between Mystery and
Horror with some gadgets from Sci-Fi.

- *Lemuel Gulliver's Travel Guide, Vol. 5: Thriller*

I didn't sleep well that night, meaning I didn't visit my spirit friends as much as I wanted or needed. Giving up on sleep around five in the morning, I packed my personal items. Technically, I didn't need to pack anything since I was simply returning to my childhood home where I already had a closet of clothes and hygienic supplies that were appropriate to Fantasy, but a gut dread said that these were my last days of truly living in Noir.

Regardless of my location, I strapped on my Hauntings holster, including my Colt Detective Special and utility pockets for a matchbox, wooden stake, and other survival tools. After a surprise run-in with a vampire last autumn, I wouldn't take any chances, even in Noir.

I met up with Nita at Visionary Investigations to finish the other preparations to leave. We called our clients and my friend

Detective Kenneth Ross of the Shigaqua Police Department to pass on our Cases, then locked up the office until further notice.

Before heading out, Nita ran upstairs to change and grab her pack from Truth's penthouse. Nita house-sat for our former investigating partner and her husband while they spent more and more days with Truth's cancer-fighting mom in Cozy, Mystery.

To my surprise, Nita returned in a long-sleeved cream underdress beneath an ankle-length dark-red overdress with front-facing laces and a leather belt supplied with several pouches and a dagger. She'd blend right in with Margen's casual Adventurers, but I was willing to bet that she had more weapons hidden on her person. Had she borrowed clothes from Truth's Fantasy wardrobe, knowing she'd meet my family today?

She carried only one suitcase and a duffel bag.

"You packed light?" I asked. "We don't know how long this will take."

"I have everything I need," she assured me, hefting her duffel. By its weight and shape, I assumed it was filled with weapons.

I raised an eyebrow. "You realize that anything more technological than a single-shot pistol won't work in Margen, right?"

"Yes. Most of this bulk is blades and vials of Fantasy herbs—courtesy of Truth's collection."

I chuckled to myself. "I think you'll get along with my mom."

We made good time to Fantasy's border thanks to my six-cylinder roadster. I stored my growler of a car in a garage and had the pleasure of giving Nita the tour around the border crossing that I knew by heart. Apparently, Nita had a fake ID that was accepted by the patrol officers with hardly a hiccup.

As soon as we crossed into Middle Novel, I pulled out my traveling candle. We were still two days away on horseback from the capital city of Eimad. However, we were on Fantasy soil, which meant that magic worked.

"Travel candles are a rare magic," I explained. "They require a lot of magic to create since anyone—including non-magicians—can use them. They extinguish faster with longer distances, but it'll save us two days of travel."

"It's instantaneous?"

I nodded. "Just hold on to me, and I'll do the work."

She narrowed her eyes at me.

I replied by rolling mine. "Come on, it's not just an excuse to make you hug me, though I'll admit—"

"Shut up," she muttered, and wrapped her arms around me. We technically only needed to be touching, but she didn't know that. Hmm, the sea salt scent lingered in her hair, contrasting with her sweet perfume. It was a different scent than usual.

Focusing my thoughts, I concentrated on a mental picture of the city of Eimad with its blue-gray stone buildings, thatched-roof homes, and cobblestone streets. I narrowed on the rising path to the front gates of Ruezdad—the castle I called home. With Nita holding onto me, I fished out my matches and lit my candle.

As soon as the candle wick caught, a loud whooshing noise filled our ears. It was over in a flash with a fifth of the candle extinguished, but Nita's arms tightened around me.

"Nita?"

She opened her eyes and let go of me. Unfortunately. She gaped at our surroundings; thumb-sized fairies dancing in a water fountain, steel carriages rolling down the cobblestone streets—pulled by magic—and fully clothed rabbits and foxes walking on two legs and shopping in the bustling gothic buildings of Eimad. Ahead of us, a great castle of iron gates and blue-grey stone walls sat on a tall mound.

"Welcome to Ruezdad," I said. "My home."

Together, we passed between the two gates, beneath the murder holes, and through the barbican into Ruezdad Castle. I knew the pathway well enough to enjoy watching Nita's eyes zip side to side, analyzing her new surroundings. We stood in a large courtyard. Yards of grass stretched on both sides: training grounds, stables, and knights' quarters to our left, then gardens, servants' quarters, and the royal chapel to our right. Straight ahead, the keep rose several stories high, with knights standing on guard at turrets on every corner. Every resident within the castle would know of our approach before we even entered.

This was proven true as the door opened before we finished climbing the twelve steps to the keep. Master Bahr, my personal guard and self-defense tutor, greeted us with a bow, stepping back to let us inside.

Nita took a quick intake of breath at Master Bahr's appearance. He was a seven-foot brown bear, after all, wearing a Sensei's Gi.

We stepped into the main entry hall decorated with an elaborate rug, a winding staircase that went up three more levels centered by a magnificent chandelier with twinkling fairy lights, a six-foot marble fireplace, thick wooden doors (not hollow like Mystery's doors), and a grand archway that led to a stone corridor of more rooms beyond. From our entry point, we could spy into the next room across the corridor with its own open archway to a sitting room for guests with couches comfortable enough for sleeping, surrounded by masterpieces of art, warmed by yet another oversized marble fireplace. The fireplaces were stocked with magical logs that emanated light and warmth without decay or smoke, creating a clean and welcoming atmosphere. The entry hall smelled of morning dew and the lingering embers of a campfire.

"Earl Fromm." Master Bahr's voice was somewhere between a bass and a growl. "Welcome home. How long may we expect your stay?"

"He talks?" Nita hissed, her expression terrified and amazed at the same time.

"Thank you, Master Bahr," I said, escorting Nita past the bear and inside.

She mouthed at me, *"That* is Master Bahr?"

I nodded to confirm the stories and finished addressing Master Bahr. "Please have a guest room prepared for my companion, Miss Nita Incog. Depending on the duke's health, I have plans to take Nita on a quick trip to Thriller tomorrow. I'd like to see him at the earliest convenience. Any chance I could have my quarters cleaned?"

The bear's lips twitched upward. "The servants prefer to respect the earl's privacy."

"Meaning no one living has stepped foot in the entire east end of the second floor since I left. Gotcha," I scoffed. When spirits haunted my bedchambers, I did my own dusting and sheet changing.

Master Bahr waved for a servant to take our bags to our respective rooms as the door to the private west corridor swung open to reveal a young woman with black hair, brown eyes, and a creamy complexion.

"Aeron!" My younger sister ran to me. Despite her sixteen years of age, she was still small enough for me to pick up into a twirling hug. She laughed in my mind and breathed with excitement. *"You received my message? My heart smiles to see you. Who is your friend?"*

"It's good to see you too, Sam. This is my partner-in-crime—I mean, combat specialist, Miss Nita Incog." I gestured as an introduction to Nita.

"You work together in the crime department, after all." Sam smirked.

"Whoa!" Nita twitched. "Her voice echoes."

Sam turned to my partner fully and simply blinked.

"She's telepathic?" Nita squeaked. Fear was the common first response to Sam's ability.

"Only half telepathic," I said. "She can speak to minds but doesn't read them."

Nita glanced between Sam and me, probably listening to two conversations at once.

"Hey, Sam," I said. "Do you want to include me in your conversation?"

Sam's eyes flicked to me— *"No"* —then back to Nita.

Nita's shock at Sam's ability wore off, and she flushed with embarrassment. "No, no. It's not like that."

"Sam! What are you saying?"

My sister had the audacity to smile mischievously. *"Come on, Mr. Investigator. Can you not try to deduce our topic with half of the conversation?"*

"Supernaturals," I swore and turned to Nita. "Please don't listen to my sister and whatever stories she tells about me."

Nita smirked. "Well, it's kind of hard to ignore someone who speaks directly to your mind. But don't worry, she asked less about you and more about me."

Before more was "said," the western doors opened again to welcome my mom. The Marchioness of Margen wore her long black hair up in an elegant bun with jeweled hairpins. Knowing my mom, the hairpins also doubled as tools and weapons if needed. Her dress demonstrated the height of women's fashion, which recently took a turn for the more comfortable side. Possibly because of my mom's influence. I wouldn't put it past her.

"You came." She smiled in welcome. "And brought a guest?"

"Yes, Mom." I bowed respectfully and waved Nita over. "This is Nita Incog, from Noir, Mystery. Nita, this is my mom, Marchioness Pansy Fromm, the Unsettled, of Margen."

Nita quickly joined my side and slipped into a graceful curtsy.

My mom's eyes twitched with confusion and suspicion. "You're from Noir? But your curtsy is perfect," she scoffed. "It took me months to learn the correct posture. Please, stand. My ankles hurt just looking at that stance."

Nita smiled and straightened.

My mom continued, "Welcome. We can give you the tour after you pass my husband's test."

"Test?" Nita's eyes darted to me, suddenly nervous. "From the marquis?"

"You'll be fine," I said, eager to place a reassuring hand on her back. "It's just his ability to see your aura."

I wanted to say more, but the full truth about his ability was a family secret. While it was widely known that the marquis could see auras, and many acquaintances understood that the auras revealed when a person was in danger, only family and confidants knew the second part, that his auras also revealed when a person had dangerous intentions. Even fewer people knew about his possession of a legendary wand that gave him the magics of a wizard, complicating any rumors and theories about the true nature of his birth-given ability.

"Come on." My mom beckoned us all to the door. "He should be finished with the reports now." She paused to look at Sam. "Yes, but only ten more minutes. Your grandpa will be anxious to meet with Aeron home."

Sam smiled and skipped back into the library as my mom led Nita and me down the corridors with guards at our flanks. Nita stared wide-eyed at everything, as if the tapestries and wooden walls were the most fascinating sights. The corridor opened into another enclosed courtyard with a large white tree commanding the grassy center.

My mom used her speed ability to go five times faster than time itself, blurring into motion then solidifying at the end of the hall, knocking at the duke's study. We were halfway down the courtyard when my father emerged, gracing my mom with a quick kiss.

Even with that personal gesture, he managed to do it with an air of exemplary perfection. He hadn't inherited the title of Marquis until age twenty-six, when his older brother died, but my father carried the position like the poster child.

He was an inch taller than I was and fair-skinned, but otherwise, we were mirror images with the same facial features, blue-green eyes, and dark brown hair. He wore a classy blue-grey tunic over a pure white long-sleeved shirt. Ever since grandfather's health started to decline, he'd taken on more responsibilities and worn his tunics a little straighter. He followed Mom's gestures toward us and froze in terror. Then, his face shifted into confused wonder.

"Theo?" Mom snapped into a defensive stance and glanced between Father and us.

"Who is our guest?" he asked.

"Father," I said, "this is my combat specialist partner, Miss Nita Incog, from Mystery. Nita, please meet my father, Marquis Theodor Fromm, the Trusted, of Margen."

She curtsied again, extra careful in her presentation under his bewildered eyes.

"It is an honor to meet you, Trusted Marquis," she said.

Father responded with a curt nod. "Welcome to Margen. I appreciate your working partnership with our son. Aeron has many acquaintances, though there are few whom he *trusts* enough to bring to Ruezdad."

That was…unexpected. My own alarm spiked a little at my father's subtle warning. What did he see in Nita's aura? Was her aura dangerously long or dark?

His calm posture and friendly smile made me question the subtle warning. He whispered something to Mom, and with the subtlest of movements, she conveyed her understanding.

With a little confused expression to me, my mom asked, "You said she's a combat specialist? Didn't Master Bahr and I teach you enough to handle yourself in Noir?"

I smirked. "I'm not bad, but Nita's better. She was trained in Thriller."

"Really?" Mom's dark Horror eyes glinted. "Are you open for a quick sparring match?"

"Pansy?" Father asked, slightly worried.

"What? Are either of our auras dark?"

"No, however—"

"Then let's go." She grinned at Nita eagerly. "It's been too long since I've sparred with a Thriller. We can spar right here in the courtyard."

Nita eyed me for direction, and I nodded with encouragement. I was curious as an investigator to watch. Father sighed as if he knew that arguing would lead nowhere.

Mom removed her outermost layer and stepped onto the grassy area. Nita likewise removed a couple of her outer layers, revealing a surprising number of hidden weapons on her. Instantly interested, Mom asked for a show-and-tell of each weapon.

"Hey," I interrupted Mom as she pointed out her favorite style of daggers. "Are you going to spar or not?"

"Ohhh." My mom smirked. "Let women have their fun. But what do you say, Nita? Rules of combat?"

Nita tilted her head as if unfamiliar with the idea. Had there been no rules during her training? After a moment's thought, she said, "Fight with honor."

Mom smiled back.

They took positions on the grass and bowed to each other from the waist. Mom fell directly into a defensive position while Nita went on the offensive. My mom was a fighter because she had to defend herself against monsters before hacking them to pieces. Nita was a fighter because she'd been taught to attack first, neutralize enemies or eliminate if necessary.

As I expected, Nita advanced first, throwing a jab at Mom's right shoulder. She managed to graze her, throwing another punch for my mom's left waist—the natural direction to dodge from the right jab. To my surprise, my mom anticipated that and took a step back to pivot away, at the same time bringing up a hook with her right. Every move by both women was almost faster than I could follow. I would have lost to either of them within the third exchange, but after two more sets, they stepped back to reassess.

Nita bounced lightly on her feet as my mom stretched her arms. Both women grinned with exhilaration.

"You've been partnered with Aeron for how long now? Why haven't we done this before?" Mom asked. "You're fast, and I'm realizing how rusty I've become."

Nita rolled her shoulders loose. "Well, you aren't using your speed ability. You're going easy on me."

"You want me to use my—"

Before she finished, Nita charged her, sliding on her knee to kick with her other foot at my mom's shins. She was too late. My mom blurred and reappeared behind Nita. She held one of Nita's hidden daggers at her throat.

"If you were an actual enemy," my mom said, "your eyes would be gouged out and your jugular slit. I commend you for keeping a few more weapons on hand, even in a fistfight, but beware, any weapon you have can be used against you."

Nita smiled secretively. "I could give you the same warning."

My mom's whole body twitched with an electric shock as Nita ducked and twisted out of the threatening hold. Nita retreated, twirling my mom's Vulgur Knife. "How do you have a functioning Fulmen Dagger in Fantasy? I thought they were Sci-Fian weapons."

My mom gaped. "When did you—" She patted her skirts for her blade, but must have come up empty as she looked back to Nita. Her smile accepted Nita's challenge.

I cleared my throat and explained, "The Marchioness's Vulgur Knife has magical enhancements to mimic the electric functions of the Fulmen Dagger. Nita, you're trained to wield Sci-Fian weapons too?"

"Ah—pparently." Nita shrugged and then offered my mom's blade back to her. "Thank you for the sparring match, Your Highness."

Mom grinned and pulled away. "Oh, we're just getting started. And I think you've earned the right to call me Pansy." She tossed Nita's dagger and blurred with her speed ability to swipe back her knife. A new match began. My mom dropped her speed, letting it be a fair wrestling match that Nita won after twenty seconds.

With the entertaining fight, I didn't see my father wave his arm for the spell but heard his voice in my head like a message from Sam when he touched my arm.

"A word. In private."

"Sure," I said, then turned to Nita, who was in the middle of a twisted wrestle with my mom. "Will you be okay if I take a moment with my father?"

She spared me a glance and a wild smile. Yeah, she'd be fine.

Father clapped my shoulder and turned me up the stairs and into an empty side room. I was fairly certain this room had once been Oswald the Tyrant's bedroom. Now, it was a mere storage closet.

Father closed the door to seal our privacy, then exhaled a heavy breath. "Curses of déjà vu."

"Father?"

He ignored me to stare at the corner by the door. "Neil, may I have a moment with my son?"

I followed my father's gaze to turn behind me, assuming Neil stood in the vicinity. My father couldn't see regular spirits, but he could see the auras of living, undead, and cursed beings—including poltergeists. I had assumed my father's desire to speak privately was to discuss Neil and his gradually lightening aura since my mom shuddered at any reminder of my poltergeist friend.

I asked, "Is his aura lighter than last time?"

Father narrowed his eyes to study my invisible friend. "I cannot say if his aura is growing lighter or just more translucent. He is less of a black spot in my vision than when we first met. With that said, some privacy, Neil?"

I rolled my eyes. "Father, just because you can't see my other spirit friends doesn't mean they aren't here. There's no such thing as privacy among the dead."

"Fine." My father huffed. "Then I had another person of interest to discuss. Who exactly is that woman you brought here?"

"My combat specialist and investigations partner, Nita In-cog. Why? Is something wrong with her aura?"

"You mean to say—" he pointed at the door "—that you spent the last three years in Mystery working beside and trust-ing your life with a poltergeist *and* that woman?"

"Yes, Father," I said, starting to panic. "What did you see in her aura?"

He groaned and massaged his forehead with his fingers. I mentally cringed to think of how many times my actions or words had caused that reaction from my father.

"She is," he said, "the second most complicated woman I have ever seen."

My panic twisted with confusion. "Meaning?"

"Aura shades of danger may fluctuate between light and dark by changing rooms during adventures; however, only *once*—" he met my eyes "—have I seen someone's aura *lengths* fluctuate as hers do."

I squirmed. That meant… Hoping to clarify, I asked, "She has dangerous intentions to hurt you? But only sometimes?"

"My auras have never been wrong, Aeron. The longest I ever saw was Duchess Abadda's as she devised to destroy me and those I loved. The shortest ever remains as Pansy, who would put herself in danger before endangering me. Your partner takes every range between them within a single sen-tence. She either wants to kill me or protect me and does not know which to act on."

"She doesn't know…" I repeated. "Ah, that actually makes sense."

"It does?" Father frowned. "Please explain."

"She suffers from amnesia and identity loss. I've seen her shift personalities in the blink of an eye, but she's always fair to me."

Father eyed me, his expression concerned, and didn't say anything for a few breaths. Then he nodded. "Her aura projection is determined by her intentions towards me, not others. If you trust her, I will trust your testament to her character. The one other person I have known to fluctuate so much was your mother."

"Really? I thought she was always your shortest? Wait—Mom frequently considered *killing* you? Didn't you experience Love at First Sight with Mom?"

Father raised both his eyebrows and gave a half smile. "Yes, except it had been one-sided," he laughed.

"Ah, right." I'd forgotten about that part. As a Contemporary, Horror, my mom had no experience with Love at First Sight and little experience with love in general. I leaned back and pondered our conversation. Sure, Nita had fluctuating intentions toward my father, but so had my mom once. What were Nita's reasons? How could I help her to be less dangerous to my family? Let her spend more time with them and attend social gatherings that spotlighted my family's goodness?

I tried and failed to imagine Nita in a ball gown and fancy up-do. She was too Contemporary, too independent. If only that wasn't what I liked most about her.

My father rubbed his left temple. "Aeron. Please tell me that your relationship with Miss Incog is entirely work-related. Your bringing her here implies a certain…closeness."

I winced. Despite my many flirtations… "Nita is my investigation partner. I trust her with my life. Even if we were romantic, why would it matter? Mom was a commoner from Horror."

"Was," the marquis snipped. "I will not have you speak of your mother that way. Pansy proved herself worthy to Duke Konrad and Margen by defeating a destructive mountain giant and a terrorizing speed goblin. She gained a unique and powerful ability—a mark of nobility in Fairy. She also proved her loyalty by saving my life and risking her own to vanquish other tyrants of Margen."

The readiness of his response and commanding voice of authority spoke of an underlying tale of the many times he'd needed to defend my mom's status. I frowned to realize that the people of Margen still struggled to accept "the Horror commoner" as their future duchess.

Father released a calming breath. "As long as you two remain professional, your Mysterious Miss Incog only needs to earn our trust, the same as your mother did. Until then, I must urge extreme caution. Someone who is trustworthy for just a day is not trustworthy at all."

"I understand, Father." Though I only partly agreed. I could trust Nita. Hoping to end on a light tease, I asked, "Should we rejoin them to make sure they don't kill each other?"

Father opened the door to exit as his affirmative. "If anyone can handle a suspicious someone, it is your mother. They should all be fine. Their auras were light enough when I suggested that we talk separately. All the same, I will warn you against developing any feelings for such a woman, especially if my father makes the request of you that I expect."

CHAPTER 3

- Lemuel Gulliver's Travel Guide, Vol. 5: Thriller

Leaning over the second-floor railing, I smirked at my mom and Nita in the courtyard below. Both collapsed onto the grass, breathing heavily, but not quickly. Sam had joined to watch from the sidelines.

"Are you done?" I asked, amused, but I got the feeling that they were enjoying this more than I was.

Across the corridor, the duke's guard approached my father with a simple message: "His Highness is awake if you wish to see him."

Father thanked him with a nod, and then shouted down to the women below. "Miss Incog, if you will excuse us, we have a family matter to attend. The duke will be anxious to meet now that Aeron has arrived. Shall we?"

Mom stood to redon her outer layers and give Nita an apologetic smile. "Sorry to say 'welcome,' then run away, but only family and medical healers are allowed to visit the duke's rooms right now. If you'd like, a servant can show you to the entertainment hall and attend you while you wait. Is that alright?"

"That should be fine." Nita smiled and started toward the opposite end of the corridor with a servant, but her eyes lingered on me.

When Sam made to follow Nita, my mom beckoned my sister. "You too, Sam."

Sam exhaled loudly through her nose with reluctance. "*Do I have to go in that room again?*"

Mom turned to give Sam a hard stare. She didn't need to speak for Sam to hurry and follow us. Mothers had their own version of telepathy.

My family and I went together to Duke Konrad's chambers. It was the largest bedchamber, situated on the easternmost side of the private rooms on the second floor. The room was almost an exact mirror of mine—the largest bedchamber on the westernmost side of the guest rooms on the same floor.

While my room was extra cold, dusty, and sparse in decorations, the duke's was cluttered with a bale of hay in one corner, medical tools and supplies against the wall, and rolls of reports within reach of the massive bed. Two white doves sat on the duke's wrists, softly chirping with his steady pulse. While I preferred minimalist patterns, the duke's curtains, rugs, and bedding were made of intricate pictures and vivid colors that gave me a headache.

My father winced for other reasons as we stepped through the doorway. The room had a spell on it to negate abilities. While the spell had no noticeable effect on me, my sister, or my mom with our intermittent abilities, it had turned off my father's constant ability to see auras. The spell was commonly used in prisons to hold creatures and enemies with birth-given powers, but in this case, the spell was to negate a curse that forced my grandfather to use his ability to turn into a horse. Instead, he lay in the large bed as a wrinkly and weak man.

Curses, he looked hollowed out, like his spirit was already halfway out the door.

"Father, do you have enough energy for a visit?" My father spoke loudly over the birds and to compensate for my grandfather's hearing loss. To compensate for his poor eyesight, Father said, "We have Aeron and Sam here. Di and Dunstan are on their way and should arrive by tomorrow evening."

"Aeron?" With my grandfather's attention directed at me, I approached and knelt at his bedside.

"I'm here, Grandfather."

"Aeron," he scolded as much as his frail voice could muster. "Where have you been?"

"Forgive me, Grandfather. I've been busy in Mystery."

He grumbled. "If you had come sooner, we might have had time for pleasantries. I am not long for this world, and I worry about you. When will you leave Mystery alone and settle here? Surely, Princess Sayer wants you home."

I cringed at his false memories.

Thankfully, my mom spoke up for me. "Konrad, we made a deal, remember? We postponed the marriage arrangements for Aeron and Sam. They have until their twenty-fifth birthdays to marry for love."

Only a year and a half away for me. My gut twisted.

"No, no." My grandfather tossed his head back and forth, and the heart monitoring birds chirped with increasing alarms. I stepped back as my mom and father rushed to his side, but he spoke over their attempts to calm him. "Aeron's place is here. He is the Earl of Margen. I will name no one else as my future heir."

I started, "But Sam—"

"No!" Grandfather's frail voice shouted. "She will live in Erebor when she marries Prince Thunderhelm. Aeron must carry the Fromm legacy in Margen and marry Fantasy royalty."

I turned to Sam for support, but she answered me with a stink eye. Curses, we were in an ability-negating room. She couldn't speak to our minds, and she'd never spoken out loud.

"Sam," I said, "if ever there was a time to speak up, it's now. Say something! You can't let him decide our futures like this!"

She simply bowed her head and sighed.

"Father," my father said, "let us handle it. Margen and our people will be protected for as long as Pansy and I shall live."

On his other side, my mom softly massaged the duke's hand for comfort. "Aeron and Sam are still young with many choices ahead. Please trust us with them."

After a few more minutes of coaxing and reassuring, the duke's heart rate returned to a safe pace. He asked about the citizens, and my father gave a report. The rest of the conversation passed me in a blur.

I followed in a daze when we left the room. As soon as the door closed behind us, I snapped.

"I'll abdicate the duchy to Sam."

Father frowned. "People have fought wars for the privilege you scorn. Do you plan to forsake the family name and continue to live in Mystery under the name of Spade?"

I grimaced at his wording. My father never said he was disappointed in me, but there were signs. "My Mystery alias was toasted last autumn and might be burnt to ashes now."

"Probably for the best," Father said, missing or ignoring how much it hurt me to lose my Mystery alias. "Fromm is the royal name, passed down from my grandfather King Fromm. Half of the work of being an earl or marquis is earning the respect of the people, and using his name will help."

I rolled my eyes. "You're supposing I want the respect of the people. Sam knows them all better than I do."

"*Aeron,*" Sam said, *"I cannot serve as Margen's duchess when I marry Erebor's prince and become queen."*

I raised a confused brow. "You don't need to marry Prince Thunderhelm. We can both marry for love like Mom and Father did."

I'd mentally thanked my parents a thousand times for arguing against the political schemes to arrange me with a daughter of King Aneirin of Fairy. Princess Sayer and I were second cousins. Our ages were appropriately close, but our heights were not. She was half human, a quarter dwarf, and a quarter fairy. I'd courted her anyway a few years back as a political ploy to show camaraderie between Margen and Faenor.

It had worked…apparently too well. The people called us "adorable," and the king loved the idea of strengthening the two Fairy duchies.

Sam bit her bottom lip and shyly avoided my eyes. *"I may be content with Reignac."*

I blinked. She'd said, "with Reignac." Not "as queen" or even "with Prince Thunderhelm." She'd used the intimacy of his first name. Curses, she actually wanted her betrothal to the deaf half-dwarf. She would go through with her arrangement and become Queen of Erebor, leaving Margen…to whom else?

With a near whisper, my father asked, "Aeron, do you mean to defy the duke's dying wish?"

"What's the phrase?" I glared back. "He should be more careful about what he wishes?"

"Aeron!" Mom snapped. "Now isn't the time. We're here to support your granddad in his last moments, not to argue about the future that can easily change."

I scoffed. Supposing he didn't go directly to the Unknown Beyond, "Grandfather will be easier to talk to after he passes. He won't be hindered by his weakened body and mind."

"Aeron!" she snapped again with an extra scolding. "Don't say such things."

"I'm not afraid of death, Mom! And Grandfather shouldn't be either! In fact, he should welcome it! I can be Duke of the Dead but not the Duke of Margen. I know how to help the spirits, but I don't know the first thing about your people. How am I supposed to rule them?"

"The people of Margen are your people too," Father said. "They are still your responsibility, no matter how much you neglect them."

"Stop, both of you!" Mom broke through my retort. She glared with her dark Horror eyes at each of us. "Konrad knows he can speak with you after his death, but he specifically asked for your presence so we'd discuss this together while he's still the duke. Even if he dies tonight, I'm not planning on dying anytime soon, which means you're not allowed to go anywhere either," she added with a point at Father. "We have plenty of time to figure out our succession."

Father seemed less content to leave the discussion unresolved as he ground his teeth. Landing his stormy eyes on me, he said, "As second eldest, the title of Marquis was thrust on me when I was twenty-six, when my brother Greggory died. You were born with this title and educated for it your entire childhood. Additionally, you have your degrees in law, experience in civil service, respect from the people, and a lifetime of understanding your ability. I had only the first of those four points. I expect you know more about ruling a duchy than you think."

"Great," Mom said, stopping my response. "Now, I don't want to hear another word about this until it needs to be said.

It's Aeron's first day back in a while. Can't we simply enjoy this time together?"

"Maybe another time," I grunted. "I have an appointment to meet in Thriller tomorrow."

My mom's shoulders sank with her expression, but she didn't stop me as I turned away. Curses, I'd disappointed her again. But I wasn't like her. I couldn't live my life one day at a time because, as a Horror, she never expected tomorrow to come. I couldn't join them for a horseback ride into the sunset as if my whole life hadn't just been forced aside by the blade of fate. I needed to sort it out my own way.

Nita joined my family and me for an awkward dinner in the great hall. I didn't mind the excuse to look out the giant windows instead of facing my father as he casually remarked on my accomplishments and accolades. Was he trying to prove my worth as an earl or say that I was too good for Nita? I subtly argued for Nita's worth by referencing the many Cases where her help had been pivotal or the many moments where she'd saved my butt.

"Then, there was that time we met the Thriller agent in the woods—" I cut off as all light disappeared. A small gasp escaped my sister as my mom cursed. My breath hitched, and I struggled to ground myself.

"*Aeron?*" my sister asked, patting the table, searching for my hand. Bless her. I grabbed her hand and held tightly to the comfort of her presence, willing my mind to stay out of my memories, out of the Valley of the Shadow of Death, out of my childhood experience of dying.

"Aeron?" Nita whispered across the table. "Stay in the present. How do you have a power-outage without electricity?"

"It's never just a power-outage," my mom muttered darkly.

My breathing quickened, and I squeezed my sister's hand.

"Dunstan!" Father shouted his brother's name like a curse. "Aeron is here."

"Oh, even better," a playful and deeper version of my father's voice said from the doorway. "How are you, Aeron?"

A chair scraped against the floor from Nita's direction.

"Dunstan," my mom hissed. "You know what this does to him—"

"It's okay, Mom," I said through gritted teeth. Nita's chair slowly eased back into place. "I have Sam beside me. I can feel that I'm sitting at our dining table in Ruezdad. I'm not in Horror's valley." That didn't stop my heart from racing or my shaking grip on Sam's hand.

"*Aeron, please relax,*" my sister asked with a little whimper.

Light returned as if it had never left, revealing a man who was a near replica of my father (trimmed beard included), but he had a narrower facial structure, rounder nose, lighter and longer hair tied in a low tail, and emerald-green eyes. Lord Dunstan Fromm, the Night Shade, wore the black pattern of my father's formal tunic and attire. Somehow, my uncle made the outfit look more adventurous, like he spent his days spelunking through caves rather than sitting at desks and thrones. With his ability to absorb light, he loved the dark.

"Sorry, Aeron," he said with his typical teasing grin. "I didn't know you were already back in town. But you've improved a lot in facing your fear."

"I know how you like to make an entrance." I released my sister's hand and gave my uncle a doubtful smirk. "Good to *see* you. Sam sent me a message about the duke."

He turned impressed eyes on my sister. "You can reach all the way to Noir, now? Fantastic!"

"Dunstan," my mom warned. "You know you're still banned from requesting Sam's ability for your own uses and nefarious pranks."

My uncle responded with a playful eye-roll. Father gave me a look of warning before he excused himself from the table to "share reports with Dunstan." His warning was a silent reminder to be on my guard around Nita's variable aura. My mom seemed content to sit and chat all night with Sam, Nita, and me, but I expected that to turn into another awkward interrogation about my support for the duchy or partnership with Nita.

I stood and gave our excuses to retire, leading Nita back to the main entrance with Master Bahr padding along behind us.

"Sorry," I grunted. "My family can be a pain."

"You have no idea how lucky you are."

"Excuse me?"

"You have a family who loves you very much. The main reason I want to remember my past is because I want a family like yours. I want a sister who adores me, a mom who worries about me, and a dad who's proud of me."

"My father? Proud? Of me?"

"Yes, your dad's very proud of you—"

"Are you sure we're talking about the same man? Marquis Theodor Fromm, the Trusted?"

"Aeron, even I can tell he loves you. Maybe he doesn't know how to connect with you, but, well, all he talked about tonight was your accomplishments and capabilities to help people. He really believes you'll make a fine duke someday."

I snorted to the side. "If you say so. Feel free to borrow my family whenever you want. They seem to like you." Mostly.

"Really?" Nita's smile lit like a timid bulb.

"Yes. I'm not the only one who's glad you're in my life."

She pinched her lips inward as if to suppress her blush.

Yes, they liked her, but my parents wouldn't trust her as long as her aura fluctuated. If I'd brought Nita home as a serious girlfriend, I imagined my parents would have tripled the number of cautionary glances.

We stepped outside to the guest quarters that rimmed the palace wall. I stood at the doorway as Nita stepped inside. Instead of spinning around to admire its decorations, she fingered the bottom edges of the furniture and checked under the bed.

I chuckled. "It's not bugged. Even if it was, magic bugs work differently than those you're used to."

She grunted softly in acknowledgement. "Well, am I supposed to stay in here for the rest of the night? I'm not tired yet."

"Right. Eimad is an 'early to bed, early to rise' city, so there isn't much to do around here after nine unless there's a festival. What would you like to do on your first night in a castle?"

"First night in Fairy, too," she said, her eyes wandering toward the ceiling crowning. "Well, I'd like to go over your notes about Arrowhead, if you have them."

"Sure," I said.

Master Bahr helped me to prop her door wide open with a potted plant before stepping inside. He took a position against the wall by the doorway.

Nita shivered. "Did your ghosts come with you?"

"Probably."

She raised an eyebrow. "Do they ever leave you alone?"

"Yes, in one place," I said. "Wherever I reside, I always have a spiritually crowded bedchamber and spiritually vacant personal lavatory. There, and only there, I can change clothes, bathe, or simply think and enjoy solitude."

"Your lavatory, meaning your bathroom?" she asked with a raised eyebrow. She shook her head and turned her focus toward the research papers. "You and your dead friends. Well, let's review what we know. We know I was trained in Special

Operations. What do we know about Special Operations and the Arrowhead Complex?"

I chuckled and allowed her change of the subject. We went over our plans and the social expectations of Thriller until the moon brought its misty chill through Nita's open door. My bear guard urged me to find my own bed in the dimming fairy lights.

"If all goes well," I said in parting, "we should have a better clue to your past by this time tomorrow."

CHAPTER 4

Few enemies are more terrifying than the one you do not know, yet Thrillers often run from nameless foes controlled by a bigger foe.

- Lemuel Gulliver's Travel Guide, Vol. 5: Thriller

After saying goodnight to Nita, I went up to my grandfather's bedchamber. I wanted to talk to him again before leaving for Thriller and wasn't sure if there'd be time in the morning. Maybe I could convince him that I wasn't the best option for an earl. Maybe he would have suggestions of someone else to be my father's heir.

The guards let me into his room, but the cracking of the door and my footsteps didn't wake my grandfather. I stared down at Duke Konrad Fromm, the Horse, of Margen, younger brother of the late Queen Alóvera, uncle to King Aneirin of Fairy.

He looked tired even as he slept. Recalling his history, I could guess why. He'd grown up as a prince, son of a self-made king, with the ability to transform into any breed of horse—an animal that carried others. His first wife died while giving birth to my uncle Dunstan. Then, he'd married Abadda, who was beautiful but conniving to the point of being downright evil.

A small piece of Abadda's treachery had twisted the duke's ability, forcing him to remain in his horse form outside of ability-negating rooms. One step out of his bedroom, and he'd turn into a thoroughbred or Andalusian of choice. One by one, she'd tricked and manipulated everyone around her until she nearly completed her schemes to become an immortal queen and empress of the world.

Margen didn't need to look far for a bad example of royalty's influence.

While I was a far cry from Duchess Abadda, I worried that even the smallest issues could have grave consequences. One didn't need to be power-hungry to be a bad leader. A ruler with any one of the seven deadly sins could destroy my people.

I couldn't stand the thought of messing up and becoming their next bad example.

I took a seat in the padded rocking chair and hoped to catch my grandfather when he woke. In the meantime, I picked up a book to entertain myself while waiting.

Without even realizing it, I fell asleep, and for the first time I'd ever known, I dreamed. My ability was negated in the duke's room. I didn't float from my body to wake among the spirits. Instead, I dreamed of Father being crowned as Margen's duke with Mom and Sam by his side. Somehow, my brain filled in the gaps, and I understood, Grandfather was gone…and so was I. Maybe I was dead or maybe I was in Mystery as an investigator, but it didn't matter. I wasn't there. I wasn't the heir.

The people celebrated their new duke, but then my dream shifted to another time and celebration. Sam's wedding day. It wasn't in Erebor to Prince Thunderhelm, but to a blurry-faced man. My stomach twisted as I remembered her timid smile when she'd said Prince Thunderhelm's first name. She had feelings for him. Instead, no one truly smiled at her wedding to

Prince Blur. Not Mom. Not Father. Not Prince Blur, and especially not Sam. They smiled and waved, but their smiles were fake.

The falling flower petals drifted away, and so did everything else that was beautiful. Scenes of possibilities flashed by. Prince Blur neglected my sister, treating her simply as a child bearer for his legacy. She became more silent than ever as Prince Blur took control of the duchy, lumbering away the forests, forcing labor at the mines in Divinity, and hoarding his wealth from the citizens.

Master Bahr was whipped like an abused animal. My favorite pastry chef sobbed at the grave of her husband, wearing rags covered with more weevils than chocolate, and the markets were empty save for the nobles picking through the meager goods. Kids ran through the streets with soot on their faces, gangs with magically enhanced repeating crossbows rode down alleyways, and the only reason good citizens left the safety of their homes was to add to their piles of uncollected waste outside their doors.

Just when I thought it couldn't get worse, I recognized one of the gang members. A woman turned her weapon on her fellow criminals and let loose. Every living creature dropped around her, dead. Then, as if noticing me watching in horror, she turned to me. I woke with a jolt as Nita shot me with a crossbow through my heart.

My sudden movement and screeching chair caused my grandfather to cry out from his bed. I hurried to his bedside, nearly tripping over my feet in the dimness of the night.

"Who is it?" he panicked. "Friend or foe? Who are you?"

"Grandfather, it's me, Aeron." I tried to calm him even as my own heart continued to pound from my dream. What a weird and traumatizing experience. And that was supposed to be normal? I highly preferred my nights with the dead. "I'm sorry that I woke you."

"Oh," my grandfather said, gradually slowing his panic. "Aeron. When did you arrive? I have waited to speak with you. You need to accept your place as future duke."

A sick unease dropped into my gut. He didn't remember our earlier conversation. His words didn't help settle my unease from my dream. If I didn't accept the duchy, who would? How could I guarantee its growth through peace?

Swallowing hard, I gripped his hand. His skin was too leathery, too wrinkly, and too loose on his bones.

"We'll talk later," I said. "Just sleep for now."

He moaned and quickly returned to sweet slumber. No way was I going back to sleep, at least not in that room. After a lifetime without dreams, one was plenty for me. As soon as my grandfather's snores were steady, I quietly left the room and returned to my own chambers across the castle.

Neil and several other spirits waited to greet me and welcome me to Fantasy's Spirit Kingdom. I did my usual rounds, asking after the welfare of their living descendants, checking on projects, and (since I was back in Fantasy) listening to their news and jokes of how they used their various gifts and abilities to affect the living.

I woke up as the sun dawned over Divinity's mountainous horizon. Neil had left a note on my desk, detailing my night.

Grabbing my usual dress slacks, button-down shirt, and suit vest, I hesitated to put them on. Maybe I didn't need to rebel against everything my parents wanted. I set aside my modern clothes and pulled out my Margen-made trousers, long-sleeved white undershirt, Fromm-blue tunic, and a matching sleeveless cloak. They smelled a little stale and felt tight. When was the last time I'd worn them?

Master Bahr met me at the end of the hallway to follow me to the dining room, catching the tail end of Sam's breakfast. I did my best to remain calm as Nita entered with the escort of her assigned chambermaid.

Supernaturals, she looked gorgeous. My Mystery partner wore a long creamy under-dress (I forgot the official name for those things) with sleeves that draped to her knees. Her over-dress was maroon with laces to taper its shape around her body. Fine golden embroidery made leafy designs around her neck-line and down her center.

I said a quick, "Good morning," then filled my mouth with oatmeal to distract myself.

"Morning," she returned. "Well, our appointment with Ar-rowhead isn't until later today. What's on our agenda?"

I swallowed and grinned. "I have some ideas."

After breakfast, I escorted Nita out to the stables for the coach with a single bench, which would force Nita to sit next to me and Master Bahr to take the footman's bench behind. What could I say? I was feeling a little devious that morning. That dress wasn't helping.

"Good morning, Straub," I said to our stable master. "How are the mares doing? Could I take one of them around town for a tour?"

"Crossfire's already been exercised, but Ginger and Spook could use the stroll."

I grunted. "I'll take Ginger." Spook got her name from spending too much time around me as a foal. She was a fine horse, but she had a second sense for the spirits around me and…spooked easily. I stepped up to Ginger, admiring her beautiful red-brown coat, black hair, and white stripe down her nose.

"You look good for having given birth a few months ago. How's the foal?"

Ginger bowed her head in sorrow. "He didn't make it."

My expression and shoulders dropped. "Oh. Ginger, I'm sorry. Would you like a hug?"

She took a deep breath and nodded slowly. "Thank you, Earl Fromm. It was a tough time at first, but I'm doing better with the warmer and longer days. Keeping busy helps, so I appreciate your excuse to go out today."

I offered her a sympathetic smile. "I'm so sorry for your loss. Would you like to grab some spark-apples while we're out? My treat."

She neighed pleasantly, and Straub grabbed the hitching gear from the posts. Once Ginger was hitched, Nita and I set off with Master Bahr sitting on the back bench, riding through the front gates of Ruezdad and into the town, which was bustling with its usual late-morning activities.

I pointed out the monuments and summarized their histories, including the Sword of Videliz, which was stuck in an anvil until a worthy warrior would draw it in a time of need. Nita studied the weapon with its lightning patterns of yellow and white.

"It looks like it's made of multiple grafts."

"Silver, gold, and white oak," I said with a nod. "It was originally created by a dwarf in Middle Novel as a magically enhanced sword, but then my parents infused it with elements to behead an immortal witch. They tell the story better than I do. In the meantime, there's a fantastic gourmet chocolate shop that you simply must try."

Nita's eyes glinted with interest. "You almost know me as well as Truth."

"I'm serious," I said despite my grin. "Everything they make, put into your mouth."

Prestigious as it was, the shop kept hold of a location in the city's market center.

I pulled Nita into the shop as a little bell sounded at our entrance. A grey-haired, human-sized badger with a permanent smile and twinkling eyes greeted us.

"Welcome—oh! Haunted Fromm! I didn't know you was home. What can I serve you with?"

"Thank you, Mrs. Becker. I trust Mr. Becker's doing well?"

"He broke him leg from a fall off the ladder last winter. The healers say is all better now, but he still complains like a leprechaun that lost him treasure." She whooped with a burst of contagious laughter.

"Good to hear nothing's actually changed." I grinned back and gestured to Nita. "My friend needs to try one of everything."

Nita balked. "Everything?"

"Of course, m'lord." Mrs. Becker smiled and began filling my usual order.

"Like I said, 'Everything they make, put into your mouth.'"

Mrs. Becker giggled with glee as she deftly picked a piece of each style of truffle and placed it in a paper box. "Oh, you flatter me, Haunted Fromm."

"You deserve it," I said. Turning to Nita, I explained, "The Becker family has branches all over the city—even a few in Vluz, right?"

"Three now. After Abraham married, he and him wife started a shop. Them's due to have a baby this fall."

"Abraham started a family and his own shop?" I asked. "Good for him. I thought he'd spend away his life as an Adventurer." Turning back to Nita, I said, "Anyway, the Beckers do more than chocolates. They've been making the most delicate pastries for as long as anyone can remember, but when chocolate made its way into the fairylands, the Beckers added it to their pastries."

"It was a real bitter flavoring, it was," Mrs. Becker said, picking up the history, "but we experimented with it. We purchase us cocoa beans from Childrens and use local Fantasy flavors to refine them with."

We continued to chat as Mrs. Becker finished our order. With the skies clear and the cool summer breeze, we took our bag of goodies to the park. I spread my cloak like a blanket across the grass for us to sit at the edge of the field—currently crowded with weekend market tents and shoppers.

I wanted to play a game of guessing the chocolate interiors before taking bites, but Nita cheated by reading the description page. Even knowing the fillings, she seemed pleasantly surprised by the variable flavors and textures.

With a quarter of the box devoured, I asked Nita what she wanted to try next. Her glazed eyes stared at nothing as she faced the market and throngs of people.

I took her hand in mine. "Nita?"

She blinked and snapped her attention toward me. "Sorry, what did you say?"

"I asked which treat you wanted to try next. What else is on your mind?"

"No, I—" She cut off as she looked down at my hand on hers. Her eyes glazed with dreams again. "I was just thinking about how everything can change so quickly. Even if nothing changes for me at Arrowhead, you'll be reinstated as earl and 'promoted' to marquis. This, for instance—" she squeezed my hand for emphasis "—probably won't be acceptable. I'm torn. I want to know my past, but I don't want anything in the present to change."

My father's warnings and reprimands echoed through my mind, but I held on to her hand. I wanted to internalize the brush of her skin, the curve of her fingers, and every line of her palms against mine. I slid closer to her on the cloak, ignoring Master Bahr's warning growl.

"I know. But the future isn't set in stone. Who says anything needs to change?"

"Nature," she whispered. "We are all constructions of our pasts. Who we are is molded from our social spheres, experiences, and attitudes. Other than my experiences and social connections of these last few years, the only part I have is my own attitude."

"And your attitude is what defines you," I debated. "Regardless of your past, you could choose to still help me with Cases and we could—"

"Aeron, I have responsibilities," she interrupted. "I don't know what they are, but there's this nagging feeling that I'm forgetting something important. Aeron, even you can't ignore the responsibilities of your past."

I gulped. She knew better than anyone how hard I tried. I pretended to be someone else by working on Mystery's unsolved Cases, but in the end, I was the grandson of a duke. I knew that nagging feeling all too well. Every day, I felt the pressure of responsibility looming over me, especially now that my grandfather was dying and my time of pretending was running short.

She was right, though. As soon as she remembered her past, she would remember her parents, siblings, friends, and relationships. She would return to whatever job she'd been working on before and whatever connections she had. I'd need to stop pretending and fantasizing that we could ever be more than what we already were.

With a heavy sigh, I said, "I understand. I don't like it, but I get it. I don't want anything to change either. Though I can tell you this…" I paused and waited for her eyes to meet mine.

"No matter what happens to each of us, I care about you, Nita. That won't change."

Her currently purple eyes widened, and her chest rose slightly with a small gasp.

Before I could do or say more, my ears were diverted by someone using my title.

"Is that the Haunted Earl?" a young lass asked with hushed excitement.

Voices whispered through the market air like promptings from my spirit friends. I groaned, realizing my rookie mistake. By removing my hooded cloak, my face and embellished tunic announced my identity to the whole market.

"I believe the bear behind them is his guard." An older voice smoldered, "My, he's grown up."

"Who's that he's with?" more voices asked.

"Are they on a courtship outing? They're sitting awfully close."

Nita eyed them and gestured to two other women whispering behind a tent of silks. "Are they talking about us?"

From the corner of my eye, I spied a bunch of young maids crowded around a market tent, feigning interest in a vendor's set of handcrafted knives.

They squealed with embarrassment and delight at being caught. "It's him!"

"Curses," I growled low. "I almost forgot what it was like. Come on."

I stood and stashed our belongings, planning our getaway. "Master Bahr, I may need you to divert their attention." He nodded curtly and eyed our eavesdroppers. To Nita, I asked, "Do you know how to lose a tail?"

Noticing my hurry to leave, Nita frowned. "Of course. Why? They seem harmless."

"They're far from harmless. They're gossips," I said with a low growl. Supernaturals, there would be rumors about us before nightfall. "I'm sorry for bringing you into this."

I led her back toward the throng at the market. People made way for me, but Nita became clogged in the crowds. I reached back to take her hand and slip through the currents of shoppers. My name drifted around us in soft murmurs.

As a seven-foot brown bear, Master Bahr easily gave away our position. He parted down another aisle to distract half of the group in another direction, and I yanked Nita behind another tent. We dashed between the market stalls, taking quick corners and cutting through stands. Calls and giggles followed closely behind.

"Good heavens," Nita puffed, "they're everywhere?"

"They're like the worst kind of Haunting. The further you go, the more they multiply. When you think you lose one, two more follow." My mind went through different methods of losing a tail and smirked at one option.

"I have an idea," I said, wrapping my cloak's darker reverse side around my shoulders, "but you probably won't like it."

"What is it?"

I ducked into the next hat shop and grabbed the largest one I could find.

"Kiss me," I said.

"What—no!"

Gleeful footsteps pattered closer. There wasn't time to argue.

"Just pretend," I whispered, pulling my cloak hood over myself and placing the giant red sunhat on Nita's head. I pinched the edge of the large red brim and pulled it to cover our faces. Nita went rigid.

"We look like we're hiding," I whispered. "We need to look like we want privacy."

I wrapped my arm around her and made a show by rubbing her back, as if we were lovers about to get crazy in the market. Nita slowly raised her eyes to mine. When her dark rainbow locked onto my blue-green, her wide-eyed fear shifted into a confident smile. She smashed her body into me until she pressed me against the wall. I grunted in surprise and analyzed her hat.

Oh, curses. Did I recognize that red sunhat with the large cream flowers attached? I'd forgotten that those were all the rage in Fantasy lately.

The scampering giggles passed a second time, but Nita held me to the wall, pressing every curve of herself against me. She stretched her neck so our noses almost touched. The cursed hat shaded her sultry, now-burgundy eyes.

"I only have one question for you, Aeron," she whispered across my lips.

"Just one?" I asked, thinking of several as I struggled to breathe and remain focused as her leg grazed around mine. Around the edge of her hat, I spotted one of the gossips scanning for us in the alleyway.

Completely oblivious to the scandal she'd create if we were caught, Nita purred, "Well, if you wanted me to kiss you, what were your other two wishes?"

I laughed nervously, weighing the risk of getting caught by the gossips versus allowing Nita to continue. I raised my hand to her face and brushed my fingers up to her overgrown bangs. The gossip dashed down the alley and out of sight. I sighed with relief and then flicked off Nita's red hat.

The magical release was instantaneous. Nita's eyes went wide with shock, and her abdomen tensed against my own.

I smirked. "So, now that you've made your true desires known, did you want to try that again?"

She shoved me against the wall and pushed herself away. Looking around herself in embarrassment, she found the red hat on the ground and glared at it.

I laughed nervously. "Sorry. I should have known better than to grab a Romantic Hat of Confidence. It's infused with confident magic, slanted toward romantic inclinations. Sorry. My mistake. But at least we escaped the gossipers."

She blushed and wrapped her arms around herself. "Don't let it happen again."

Someone coughed nearby.

Nita jerked around, and I pulled my hood lower over my face. The hat vendor eyed us. "Do you plan to buy that hat?"

"Oh, no," Nita stammered and cleared her throat. "Well, do you have anything magically attuned for hiding?"

The hat maker raised an eyebrow at her Mystery accent. "You on holiday?"

Nita cleared her throat again, with subtle glances at me. I smiled to think she was distracted from our moment. Did she want to resume it as badly as I did?

The vendor offered a few other options, including a farmer's sunhat.

We bought a smaller, less ostentatious hat to hide my face, then peered down the aisles for remaining gossipers.

"Come on, we should be clear now."

I took her hand and led her toward the side of the long market. We purchased a few more trinkets and some spark-apples for Ginger on our way back to our carriage. I dropped Nita's hand before Master Bahr spotted us, and we headed toward the castle for lunch. I struggled not to steal glances at Nita in Fantasy garb, including her new gold-chain bracelet that let her disguise her appearance like a common spell. For her supposed first time in Fantasy, she wore it well, changing her hair color and style every time I looked.

"Well," Nita said as Ginger trotted us through Ruezdad's gate, "even though you haven't been around, the people still respect you like you're the heir."

I smirked. "Naw, their treatment of me isn't because of my Earl title but because of my Haunted title. I think you're mistaking respect for fear. I talk to their dead gods in my sleep. That scares people. Or, in some cases, makes them want to worship me."

"I don't think so," Nita said. "You're genuinely friendly—it's your nature—and you care about these people. You know their names, businesses, and histories. Deny it all you want, but I think you'd make a good duke."

I frowned, unsure of what to say about that.

CHAPTER 5

Everyone has a secret base,
super villains and heroes alike. These are
places to train, find teams, and hide.

- Lemuel Gulliver's Travel Guide, Vol. 5: Thriller

After lunch, I grabbed my Hauntings holster and packed for a weekend trip. Checking on Grandfather, I said quiet goodbyes before heading out with Nita. I tried not to enjoy her embrace too much as we traveled by candle to Crossover, Urban.

The Fantasy city was close enough to the borders of Mystery, Thriller, and Sci-Fi that the ability to use magic or teleporting technology changed year to year. As a result, the airport was a mess and almost as unpredictable as Children's. Almost. It had stations for charging gadgets while also adding question marks to the ends of their exit signs. It was the kind of place where you never knew what was going to happen, but it somehow always worked out. The flight itself was only two hours, but we arrived early for customs and security. I had to admit, being the grandson of a duke had its perks with the VIP lines. Nita's fake ID let her through without even a second glance. I had expected Urban to be more cautious than Middle Novel. Apparently not.

Despite my many travels, neither of us was terribly familiar with airplane rides. I gripped my armrest during takeoff and enjoyed Nita leaning over me as we both pressed our faces to the little window.

"Wow," she said, looking down at all the shrinking streets and cars. "To think, they all have their own Cases and Adventures."

"That," I said, "would be the definition of a sonder. Congratulations. You've recognized how small we are. Puts life into a new perspective, doesn't it?"

"Huh," she said, leaning slightly back. "Makes it feel a little meaningless."

"Yet grand and beautiful at the same time," I said. "Because every day can be a mysterious adventure full of thrills."

She smiled at me, and I wished to live in that moment.

When it came to landing in Londinium of Special Ops, my hands returned to gripping the armrests. This time, Nita's hand joined on top, pressing down until my hand became imprinted with the edges. She didn't release me until the plane came to a slow drive toward the terminals.

"Sorry," she said. "I realized that my life was in the hands of our pilot, and if he'd been drugged or taken out, there was little I could do about it. I don't know if I have the muscle memory to fly a plane."

Gathering our limited bags, we stepped down onto the tarmac, finding a man wearing a suit, black tie, and sunglasses with a sign for "Earl Fromm."

I cringed. "Looks like my Mystery alias isn't an option here." I walked up to the man and gave him an uptick nod. "You can put that sign away. I'm Aeron Fromm."

He lowered his sign but didn't bother with pleasantries of a smile or handshake. "Thank you for confirming your first name. Your client hired me to welcome you. I have just a few more questions to confirm your identity before directing you to them."

Thankfully, he talked as he walked, as I expected a long and personal quiz. He asked me to verify my employer, "Visionary Investigations and the people of Margen"—my birthday, "January 25th," and mother's maiden name, "Finster."

We were almost to a private hangar when I asked, "Are we done? Because if you ask any more questions, I'll wonder if you're trying to bypass some email password. If so, the joke's on you, because living in Margen and Noir means I don't have an email." I'd deleted my student account in Procedural after graduating from Spyglass University.

He turned to grace me with his first tight smile, then punched in a security code to open the hangar. Inside were a private jet and a jet-black car as sleek as an icicle.

"I hope," he said, "that you still use new age vehicles."

I gaped at the beautiful luxury sportscar before me. Every angle of its low-riding body was crisp enough to cut into my heart with desire. With a click of a key fob, our escort opened the two doors upward instead of sideways.

"I-er, I drove an LXK120 Panther in Noir."

He nodded appreciatively. "A classic. This year's Vae Sport model by Castellus may suit your needs, Earl Fromm."

To my side, Nita muttered, "All we needed was four tires and an engine. Why did they think we'll need a racecar?"

"A car chase?" I guessed.

Nita's eyes widened. "What kind of trouble are you planning for this trip?"

I grinned back. "When in Thriller. I told you this was a VIP trip. Arrowhead must really want to impress me. Come on, let's check it out."

"Right," she agreed. "I'll do a bomb sweep."

I opened my mouth to retort. They wouldn't possibly blow up a magnificent vehicle like that, would they? Simply looking through the doorways gave me a good indication of its luxuries. Bright red leather framed the black seats and dashboard with an electric console for temperature control, music, GPS, and phone connections.

Nita opened the trunk and hood to check for bombs while I gawked at the engine. Beautiful inside and out. My partner finished her sweep by holding up a small device. "A tracker? No thanks."

She dropped the tracking device to the ground and then stomped on it. The shaded man sighed. "Forgive me for not requiring the paperwork first." He passed me a file of terms and conditions, non-disclosure agreements, and contracts.

"In case it escaped your notice, Earl Fromm, my employer doesn't accept many visitors. The terms of your visit are set up for a request for hire. If you represent yourself and your duchy well, you may hire their agents. In return, they will open submissions from your people to become trained agents. If you represent well."

With that warning, he accepted my signature and then tossed over the car fob to let us climb inside. Yes, I'd agreed to this arrangement, but his words drew out a deeper meaning. I was there acting as Margen's Earl. They wouldn't have accepted Aeron Spade, PI of Noir, so to accept this VIP tour was to accept my position as Earl Aeron Fromm of Margen. At least temporarily. Though, for some reason, the idea didn't terrify me as much as it once did. Heavy thoughts.

Running my hands around the steering wheel of the luxury sportscar, I oriented myself in the new-age vehicle with its many buttons.

Nita rolled her eyes. "Do I need to give you some time alone with the car?"

"Maybe," I teased. Couldn't I appreciate a beautiful piece of art and engineering? I was in love, and I hadn't even turned her on yet.

With the simple touch of a button, she came alive with a pleasurable purr. I sank into her seat as if it was a massage chair. The GPS lit up with our destination already plugged in. I was tempted to add a few stops along our trip for excuses to drive longer, explore more of Thriller, and enjoy more time with Nita. Unfortunately, we had an appointment, and they were expecting us.

Driving out of the airport involved a bit of a learning curve as I familiarized myself with the power and upgraded gears. My experience of driving the classic in Noir kept me from stalling completely, but it had also taught me expectations and habits that weren't necessary for this modern marvel. I became comfortable and confident enough to test her around the tarmac before driving onto the main roads. The fancy sportscar turned more than a few heads in the daylight, making Nita whisper gratitude for our tinted windows.

The Londinium airport sat at the edge of a metropolis. I needed to remind myself to focus on driving as half of me wanted to count the skyscrapers and their floors. Londinium was easily larger than the cities in Procedural, Mystery, where I'd attended university. It also had twice the number of law enforcers as lights flashed every mile, helicopters swarmed overhead, and getaway cars sped around us. I thanked them for the reminder to drive carefully, despite my desire to test this beautiful machine's capabilities.

"Does anything look familiar?" I asked Nita, who stared through the windows.

"No," she said, twisting her head this way and that as if to capture every single sight.

"Huh," I mused. "Let me know if that changes. We should arrive at Arrowhead in about forty minutes."

She didn't ask about our plans after our visit to Arrowhead, but if she did, I would have responded that, "I thought we could play the rest of the trip by ear." Because who knew what would happen if (or after) Nita remembered her past. Would she decide to stay and work in Thriller? Would she leave to reconnect with other people from her past? Or…would she possibly stay with me?

I had a hard time imagining a scenario where she remembered her past but decided to reject it to continue on the path I was paving. With that analogy, I'd be paving a cobblestone street according to my grandfather's preferences for Nita to drive over with a Thriller motorcycle. It would be a bumpy and hazardous ride.

"Are you nervous?" Nita asked.

"What? Why would I be nervous?"

She pointed at my leather bracelet. "You were fidgeting."

Curses, I thought I'd broken that habit. I exhaled but didn't share my concerns. This was supposed to be for Nita's benefit. I wanted her to be happy. If rejoining those of her past would make her happiest, then I needed to support her in that decision. Helping her find herself and her purpose would allow me to focus on Margen as a future duke.

We drove around the belt of the city, continuing to turn heads from simple sedans and turning our own heads at the speeding motorcycles and following cops. We even spotted a few parachutists jumping from helicopters and buildings.

Our GPS navigated us away from the capital city, but the neighboring cities were just as developed. After skirting around five major cities, we passed a thin band of suburbs before breaking into wild woods. Even within the groves, Nita spotted a car chase with dirt bikes and four-wheelers. I was too busy enjoying the drive to play "I Spy" with spies. The deciduous forest surrounding us reminded me of eastern Margen's Notting Forest.

After about half an hour into the drive, we were instructed to take a turn-off. It came almost out of nowhere, like a secret passageway with no marker and barely a break between the trees. The new road was flat and even for our low-riding vehicle, but I took it slowly. With our new pace, it took us an extra five minutes than planned to arrive at our destination: a small log cabin. It had a desolate front porch with leaves and moss covering its roof. Its sparse windows were dark, and a few decayed pieces of broken furniture leaned against the side. A rushing creek splashed with shallow rapids within a stone's throw of the cabin's back wall.

I frowned. "That's Arrowhead?"

Nita pressed her lips into a flat line. "Why not? It's unassuming. It could have a basement with underground training facilities."

"Curses," I swore. "If so, my mom would never let me go in there. It breaks every single rule of Horror. A cabin in the woods, with basement lairs, no cellphone service, and no help for miles? The only benefit we have is that we came during the day."

"Only one way to find out," she muttered.

Grumbling, I turned off the car and moved to get out, but Nita stopped me with a hand on my arm.

"Hold on." Opening her window just a finger's width, she shouted at the house, "We have invitations to be here. Why are you threatening us?"

I blinked. Who was threatening us?

The little cabin's front door opened, and a person stepped outside to greet us. They wore black clothes from head to toe, including a headscarf and shaded eyewear to completely cover their face. Their gear and padding made it impossible to distinguish even their gender. They tilted their head like a curious alien.

"Earl Aeron Fromm, of Margen," they said with a voice-altering speaker. I cracked my window to hear them better. "Who said we're threatening you?"

Nita explained, "Call off the four agents surrounding us."

I searched the surrounding woods, seeing no one—or, no. Was that a person in that tree?

The stranger's head-tilt angled upward…with respect?

"Five." With this announcement, five camouflaged operatives emerged and dropped from the surrounding trees, confirming the one I'd found. "But it's impressive you spotted even the four. You brought an interesting companion with you, Earl Fromm."

"Your invitation allowed me to bring a plus one," I said.

The person grunted. "Unfortunately, even with your invitation, this is as far as you go without an escort. Arrowhead is not a government base, but a private and secure training facility that recruits from and lends its agents to many nations, meaning no nation may know our exact location. If you wish to tour to the facility, you must be sedated for the rest of the journey."

Nita muttered, "I don't like this."

I didn't either. I shouted back, "You did your research on me, right? Then you know of my ability. Sedating me will only send me to the spirit state where I may watch you carry my body to your location."

Nita shot me a questioning glance. She knew that my ability required two hours of sleep to kick in, but that was a secret she only learned from working with me for three years.

The person at the cabin door stood silently for a moment. Was their chin moving under the mask? Were they talking to someone through a mic?

"If you wish to continue to Arrowhead," they said again, "you must ride in the back of a truck."

A small utility truck, decorated in camo, drove out from behind the cabin. It pulled in front of us, and one of the agents opened the back doors for us. There were no windows at the back.

Nita cringed. "They're basically asking for permission to abduct us."

"Essentially," I grumbled. "But they're our best clue to discovering your past. I'll feel safe as long as I have you and Neil with me, but it's up to you."

Her suspicious eyes flicked between the agents before us and the truck. With a deep breath in and out, she nodded. "They obviously trust us about as much as we trust them. I won't let any harm come to you, Aeron."

I gave her the best smile I could manage between my nerves. "I believe you. Come on."

We stepped out of the sportscar and voluntarily stepped into the cell on wheels. They closed the doors behind us, and a sliding click sounded like a lock.

"No turning back now," I said, and the truck began to roll us away. Rather than attempt to keep my balance during the bumpy off roading ride, I sat with my back to the wall. "Let's just hope the rewards are worth the risks."

"Yeah," Nita agreed, sitting beside me. "I know it's the whole reason we're here, but I have this gripping fear that someone will recognize me."

"That's only natural," I said. "You've been waiting so long for this moment. It's natural to be nervous."

"Not just that," she said. "I have this ingrained sense that I should disguise myself or hide, anything to keep myself from being recognized."

I thought about that one. "That's normal too, at least for you. You've been trained to go undercover. Recognition blows your cover, so you've been trained to avoid it at all costs."

She angled herself to grace me with a smile. "Thanks for understanding."

"Of course."

Our ride continued for at least another half hour, and we could have been driving in circles for all I knew. Even Nita seemed to lose track of the bumps and turns we took. We finally came to a stop, and the back doors opened.

Nita and I stepped into an enclosed concrete bunker garage. The place was large enough to store three fighter planes and two helicopters, not to mention dozens of other off-roading vehicles.

A dozen more disguised operatives stood at perfect parade rest, lining our path forward. One of them stepped forward, the only one not wearing a full-face mask and sunglasses. Even still, the short haircut and features left me clueless as to their gender.

Speaking in a high tenor or low alto, they said, "Welcome to Arrowhead."

CHAPTER 6

One common use for undercover operations is for blending into enemy organizations.

- Lemuel Gulliver's Travel Guide, Vol. 5: Thriller

Despite all the rules about surviving in Horror that screamed against it, I followed the mysterious figure dressed all in black through the hidden underground bunker in the woods with no cell phone service. Along with the helicopters and planes, the massive garage showed off several four-wheelers, motorcycles, cars for speed or blending in. The perfect line of operatives who welcomed us stood still enough to make me question their breathing. Were they statues?

The ambiguous maskless one bowed in greeting. "My name is Agent Brown, head of the Public Relations department for Arrowhead. I'll be your host and guide as you tour through our facility."

I asked, "Are these all of your operatives?"

"No," said Agent Brown, already guiding us at a quick pace beyond the welcome procession. "We have several who are currently deployed."

"What's with the disguises?"

Brown tilted their head slightly. "Our agency depends on anonymity. You may have heard of our organization as Treadstone, Guardians, or even the Destroyers. We have a proud history with many names since our establishment sixty-five years ago. Whichever it is, our goals are the same: protect those who cannot otherwise be protected, secure information that cannot otherwise be secured, and eliminate those who cannot otherwise be eliminated."

"Can you give an example?" I asked.

They turned to me. "Not specifics. But if an undercover agent from any of our clients has been compromised, one of our agents provides the extraction team. On the opposite end, if a covert operation might fray national allegiances, such as escaped Hauntings or loose Experiments, our agents are trained to fulfill Missions without leaving any trace of any specific nation's influence."

I grunted. "I'm more impressed by your capabilities to deal with Sci-Fian Experiments than Horror's Hauntings. Every day people destroy Hauntings."

"Ah, yes," Brown scoffed. "With your experience in Horror, I assumed you'd play hard to get."

Nita coughed back a laugh. "That'll be a first."

Our guide turned down the garage and curtly beckoned. "This way."

Leaving the line of operatives in the garage, we entered a brightly lit locker room. It was the cleanest locker room I'd ever seen, with nothing hanging out and fancy keycode locks. Even the connected bathrooms were pristine, without an overwhelming smell of bleach.

"During your drive in," our guide said, "you passed several stations, including multiple ranges for guns and bows. We even have a bombing zone where our agents can safely practice and experiment with explosive devices. This locker is where many of our operatives keep their training gear, uniforms, and 'disguises' to change into before going on exercise Missions. As you will see, our facility is arranged for optimal efficiency."

Taking one of the exits, we started down a wide hallway but took a quick turn into a new room. Inside was a line of hospital beds and posters I'd expect in a health class. A full skeleton hung in the corner, and a CPR dummy sat on one of the empty beds. It smelled like a Procedural hospital with sterilized bedsheets and tools.

"Here is one of our hospital rooms. We have two more situated by our gymnasiums. These also serve as classrooms to teach our agents first aid, paramedical training, and how to find locations for off-the-books medics. Rest assured, all of our agents are provided with the finest medical attention and instructed on how to appropriately help themselves when necessary. Follow me. We have a lot to see and only so much time."

I'd hoped to compare some of the medical tools to those kept in my mom's lab, but our guide hurried me with a stern gesture to keep moving. Back in the hallway, we passed some administrative rooms, and I realized what struck me oddly about the place.

"Where is everyone?"

"Again, anonymity. All of our agents are currently either deployed, training on the ranges, or in town. With quick access to Londinium, we frequently train for real-life experiences among the crowds of skyscrapers and suburbs. Our agents are careful not to interact with others in the city, though. If any one of our agents is recognized, it blows their cover."

Wow, and I thought Mysteries liked their secrets.

"And what happens when their cover's blown?" I asked. "Are they reassigned? Removed from the field? Terminated? *Exterminated?* When my partner caught one of your agents and I later tracked him down with supernatural help, what happened to him?"

Brown hesitated ever so slightly before offering a political nod. "Our agents live to see Missions fulfilled, to whatever capacity that requires. Training our agents takes years, making each one more priceless than life itself. We do not consider them expendable. Far from it. We care for each of our agents as gun enthusiasts care for their most prized piece. The agent you caught, who was employed by Sponsor, was punished according to the law of his nation and our contract."

"Meaning?" I prodded.

"He was encouraged to take early retirement."

"Encouraged?" I repeated. "I'm sure you people know all sorts of methods to…encourage. And I shudder to think of your definition of retirement."

"He no longer works here. That is all I can divulge."

I grunted with dissatisfaction, passing Nita a knowing look. If she was considered an AWOL agent, they might force her to quit too. I hoped that wouldn't mean exterminating her, but instead would allow her to continue working with me.

Our tour continued into various simulation rooms that mimicked buildings and settings of airports, hotels, and outdoor streets.

"Explain something for me," I said as we returned to the barren hallway. "What exactly are your agents? Spies? Mercenaries? Ninjas?"

"Our agents are whatever they need to be. Learning defensive and lethal maneuvers is only a part of Arrowhead's training and operations. As you will see, we have many classrooms where our agents are taught thoroughly on matters of math, science, engineering, history, and even the arts. Our agents may be whomever you need them to be. Though if you have any special requests with specific needs, we may require extra time to train the appropriate agent for your needs."

I frowned. "I have a hard time imagining what you mean by that. Do you have an example?"

"For instance, if you needed a six-year-old girl to enter and win a sculpting contest in order to gain access to the judge, that might require a few months to appropriately train one of our agents who might pass for that age."

Only a few months? Did that mean that they already had children in the program?

I was almost scared to ask, "How young do you begin training your agents?"

"As early as possible," said Brown.

Nita must have seen the horror on my face as she shrugged. "Well, how young were you when you began learning to be a duke?"

That was…a fair point. From birth, I learned to wear clothes appropriate for a duke's grandson. From my first step, I was taught posture and grace. From my first word, I was taught formal grammar and articulation (which I'd mostly ignored the past few years while living in Mystery). I'd had private tutors who were professors of mathematics, science, and histories. I'd likely have learned many of the same classroom lessons, but outside of the classroom…

I returned Nita's shrug. "I don't have their fighting or espionage skills on top of it all."

Continuing down the hallway, we briefly entered various classrooms for a maximum of twenty students. They had obvious age ranges and subject matters such as those mentioned earlier plus languages, computers, puzzles and codes, and art (or forging for identifications, documents, and signatures).

The scale of it all was admittedly impressive.

We reached an area that seemed slightly more homey with a large cafeteria and industrial-grade kitchen. There was no staff, but there had been three plates left on warmers for us as a late lunch. Our guide explained how the agents took turns cooking and cleaning, allowing the facility to remain independent of outside employees. The meal included a balanced diet—a "regular meal provided to keep our agents in good health."

Continuing to the bedrooms, I was surprised to find no decorations or personalizing.

"Are you raising robots?" I asked. "Even military bunkers have more character than this."

"Our agents are allowed mementos, but they tend to be small and kept on their person. It's a popular…activity to attempt to steal one another's mementos. While we discourage bullying, these minor thefts teach them necessary qualities for security and stealth Missions."

I still found it difficult to believe that no one even kept a frame of their family.

I asked, "What about their families?" Was it even possible for Nita (or anyone) to have a family outside of this facility?

"Although Arrowhead has a large influence in Thriller's government, we are a private contractor, meaning we can recruit and receive clients from multiple genres across the globe and even from Sci-Fian planets. Because of this, we must eliminate conflicting interests. Anyone who trains through us has given up their original identity. They give up any sense of family or loyalties outside of Arrowhead. They are no longer people, but weapons, tools to be used for our clients. Nothing more, but far from anything less."

Nita frowned and whispered to me, "Then what was I doing in Mystery? Truth was certain that I wasn't a native. Had I blacked out during a Mission?"

I shrugged. "That might explain your innate sense that you have a Mission to complete."

She shook her head. "It still doesn't make sense. While this place seems familiar, I don't feel like this is who I am. I wasn't simply a tool for a company. I sense a greater loyalty to people than to any organization."

"To people…" I mused, "like me?"

"And Truth," she admitted. "And I think to someone from my past I've forgotten."

I gulped, wondering and worrying about who that could be. A family member? Friend? Lover?

Since the bathrooms were empty, all three of us walked through the men's and women's. They were the sort that my mom would have liked: community, clean, frosted glass shower doors, good ventilation, and no bathtubs to accidentally drown someone.

Continuing down another long hallway, we toured a few padded rooms for hand-to-hand combat, melee weapons, and throwing weapons.

"We train all of our agents with conventional and un-conventional weapons. They also have access to open mats, weights, and machines for strength, cardio, and physical ther-apy. Naturally, all of our weapons are blunted for practice. We train our agents to fight against dummies when handling lethal weapons, though…in the manner that we train our agents, *anything* can become a lethal weapon."

I raised an eyebrow at Nita. Was that true for her? Could she turn a paperclip or houseplant into a lethal weapon? She pointedly did not meet my questioning stare. That was as good as a confession.

"In that regard," our guide said for my attention, "we have reports on your people in Fairy, Fantasy, that some of you are capable of retaining your magics *outside* of Fantasy. You are one of these people, correct?"

I blinked, wondering why this was a sudden concern. "Yes, I have an ability, which is different from magic, and isn't altered by land boundaries."

Our guide nodded as if confirming a theory. "Because magics and abilities look largely the same within the boundaries of Fantasy, we have mixed reports regarding how common abilities are. Would you agree that they're on the rare side?"

"They're very rare among commoners," I said, "but common among royal and noble families. Why do you ask?"

Their head straightened with resolve. "All of our agents are human and therefore susceptible to standard injuries. If your kingdom has someone with a healing ability, for instance… well, you can imagine the benefits they may serve with our training. I assure you; your duchy would be fairly compensated for such an agent recruit."

I narrowed my eyes at them. So that was Arrowhead's angle. They hadn't accepted my request for a tour simply because I'd impressed them by catching and threatening an agent. They wanted Fantasy's abilities to strengthen their agents.

"Aeron," Nita whispered from my side, "they lied earlier. Their agents *can't* become *anyone*. They can't become someone with an ability or magical trait."

Right. Any Arrowhead agent would have a Horror of a time trying to imitate Master Bahr or my father's fairy lieutenant. This was why they wanted to impress me. Because Fantasy had something they didn't.

CHAPTER 7

Agent Brown talked about a lake on the premises where the agents supposedly practiced swimming, scuba diving, and even working on submarines.

They'd really thought of everything. Were these really all skills that Nita knew?

The list kept growing as we toured a few laboratory classrooms for learning about, creating, and experimenting with electronic gadgets. Our guide listed off various patents and inventions including (but not limited to) tools used for stealth, communication, hidden weapons, armor, and other wearable gadgets.

Brown ended our tour by returning us toward the entrance from where we'd come. With the end in sight, I began to worry. Nita hadn't given any indication of remembering anything. Had this all been a waste?

"Excuse me," I called to our guide. "I'd like a moment with my companion to discuss…logistics."

Brown gave another head tilt. "You will have two weeks to form your agreement with us."

"Yes, thank you." I didn't have a good excuse for prolonging our stay. "Can I have just a moment in a room? I know you have cameras, so I promise not to touch anything. I just want to talk alone with my companion to make sure we haven't forgotten anything."

Our guide nodded to one of the hospital rooms. "You may have five minutes."

"Thank you," I said, then pulled Nita into the room with me. She blinked at me with her wide and curious eyes.

As soon as the door closed behind us, I asked, "You didn't recognize anything?"

"If I've been here before, I don't remember any of it." She shook her head and whispered with barely any lip movement. Hiding our conversation from even the cameras? Smart.

I tried imitating her methods to ask, "Nothing?"

"Not the rooms, or the hallways. Not even the smells from the kitchen or bathrooms. But I had to come here, right? You deduced I was from this state, and Truth caught similarities between me and the agent we interviewed from Arrowhead."

I pursed my lips in thought. "You could have been trained at a similar facility elsewhere. I wish we knew what your name was. Then we could ask if you were in their system, talk to your trainers, or find your quarters. Who knows if you scratched your name on a wall saying, 'I was here.' Something or anything that could prove you were here or jog your memories of this place."

Nita shook her head. "Even if I remember my name later, I won't get another chance to come here, will I?"

"Probably not," I admitted. "I needed to pull a lot of strings to arrange this tour. They don't let just anyone in, and I technically need to report to my father about the possibilities of future operations with Margen citizens."

"Well," Nita sighed with a sad smile. "Thanks for making this happen. I really thought it would work. Sorry for putting you through any trouble."

I shrugged. "It's no trouble. I also want you to rediscover your identity. You refuse to date me until you do, so it's in my best interest too."

Nita rolled her eyes. I winked to show my teasing, but a nagging thought stole my humor. Accepting my place as Margen's earl would add to the reasons I couldn't date Nita.

I started to head back to the hallway when award plaques caught my attention through a side door's window. Were those awards given to the facility or its personnel? Wouldn't that be part of the tour? Why were they behind a locked office door?

"Nita?" I asked and gestured at the door handle. With no further explanation, she immediately set to picking the lock. She had it open within the minute.

The room beyond had all the appearances of an administrative room. Computers and a circular desk sat behind a standing counter, and the wall on the far side was completely covered with small wooden plaques. But they weren't awards. Each plaque had a single name, a date range, and a location, but no more.

What were they? Graduates? But the plaques printed their full names. What about anonymity? Maybe that was why this room wasn't included in the tour. But what did the dates signify?

"Aeron," Nita hissed. "We shouldn't get caught in here."

"I bet they already know," I said, gesturing to a camera in the corner. "As long as you have me covered, I'm not worried."

She grumbled as I continued to analyze the plaques. At first, I'd thought the arrangement of plaques was chaotic because they weren't organized by first or last name, or by the first date listed. No, they were organized by the end date. Some years were missing, while one particular year had a large group. The ranges in between varied.

"These aren't graduation dates," I whispered as the truth dawned on me. "They're years of service…ending with their deaths."

I stared back at the wall of tombstones. Could I find any of these people as spirits? Would they be any more or less open about their occupation than the other Arrowhead agent I'd interviewed?

I really wanted to know why dozens of plaques had the same death date. I pondered aloud, "What happened on December thirty-first? About three and a half years ago." Only days before Nita had been found unconscious in Lake Mishi. "Nita, is it possible you were here and declared missing or dead?"

Nita's eyes shifted between me and spots on the floor like she was chasing a memory that kept zipping away.

"What are you doing in here?" Agent Brown barged in, their expression upset and scared as it landed on Nita. They glanced at their phone before pocketing it and pulling out their gun with one swift motion. "Agent Moreno?"

Nita's attention snapped to the agent.

Blurs.

It was almost like watching my mom activate her ability to move five times faster than time itself. Brown and Nita moved almost too fast for my eyes to follow. They must have clashed, because the next thing I knew, Nita stood between the agent and me as my would-be attacker stepped back, gripping their bicep. Was the agent injured? How? When? Just now by Nita?

Nita stared, her eyes wide and pleading. "What did you call me?"

"Why is she here with you?" our guide hissed at me and then turned back to Nita. "Who are you?"

Nita gave a full scoff. "That's what I'd like to know."

The agent tilted their head. "No, you can't be her. Every agent trained at Arrowhead is kept tightly under surveillance. They report regularly, and all are accounted for. He must be mistaken. The bodies were identified after the attack, except…"

Except? It was a common rule in Horror and throughout Novel that if a body wasn't identified as deceased, they were often still alive.

"Agent Brown, do you recognize my partner?" With a glance at the room cameras and the agent's pocketed phone, I wondered if someone *else* recognized Nita.

The agent answered with another quick skirmish against Nita. Metal clanged as a small weapon was tossed across the room, and fabric ripped with a gasp. Brown stepped back again, applying pressure to a bleeding wound on their thigh.

If Nita was trained here, she was a master. She seemed to have the skills to beat Brown if necessary. Could she have graduated from a rival organization?

The agent's breathing grew labored, and their voice strained. Slight head tilt again. "You can't be… Agent Moreno? You survived?"

In a flash, she grabbed their arm, and they grabbed back, expecting a fight. She breathed in, as if taking in the essence of her name. "What's my first name?"

Agent Brown rocked back and muttered, "Amnesia? You remember nothing? Nothing of the tragedy?"

Nita/Agent Moreno didn't say anything. She continued only to breathe heavily and hold the agent's arm.

"What do you mean?" I asked. "What happened?"

The agent didn't look at me but kept their focus on the woman holding them. Nita's eyes widened as if…she remembered something.

"What happened?" Brown spat. "Ask *her.* She knows more than we do."

"No," Nita whispered, frightened—truly scared for the first time since I'd known her. Then she looked at me. Her face contorted with pure terror. "No—no, I—"

The agent shrugged Nita off, and she let go easily. She backed toward the open door, staring at our guide, at me, at everything around us. Whatever had happened, it terrified her.

She turned and ran for the exit.

"Nita!"

"Stop!" the agent called out. Running back to the hallway, they shouted, "Intruder alert!"

I followed Agent Brown and Nita through the hallways as they spoke quickly into a radio and smacked an alarm. The lights switched to red as we entered the garage, and sirens erupted from every direction. An engine roared as Nita sped out of the garage with a hijacked dirt bike.

"Nita!" I shouted. Her face half turned toward me before she squared her shoulders and disappeared through the exit. I chased after as Brown mounted their own bike.

"You! Stay here," Brown demanded.

"Who is she? Who's Agent Moreno?"

"A traitor," they spat.

Nita was a double agent? No, they had to be mistaken. My legs lost their strength, and I leaned against the wall for support.

Agent Brown barked orders into their communicator. Six agents erupted from the garage doorways as if out of nowhere.

They hopped onto bikes, four-wheelers, and even the helicopter. All these agents to chase one woman?

A shorter one paused to give me a second look. "Earl Fromm? It'll be safer for you to stay inside."

Safer? I ignored them and ran like a lost soul to the exit where Nita had disappeared. "Who is Agent Moreno?"

The agent breathed sharply with the name and kept on my heels. "She's one of the best and most dangerous spies this agency has ever known. Half of our winning records have her name on them. Reports said they'd found her unrecognizable remains among the casualties, but…I wouldn't put it past her to fight her way out and fake her own death. She proved to be our best and most dangerous agent by spying on *us*. She betrayed us all and blew up the agency. To think she'd come back…"

I continued running toward the exit but became lost in my memories. Meeting Nita for the first time near the Shigaqua Police Department. Nita discussing Cases with Truth in our own little agency. Nita in a park, surrounded by food trucks. Nita in my car. Nita with Sam. Nita in my arms. Nita…

I reached the top of the garage ramp exit and then skidded to a stop. Agents lay scattered and crumpled on the forest floor, groaning in pain, gripping wounds, and struggling to regain their footing. Capsized vehicle wheels spun, camouflaged hideouts were overturned, and bullets rattled in the distance.

"Where did she go?" Agent Brown shouted from atop their dirt bike.

One of the agents managed to point in a direction, past the array of more injured agents and chaos. Agent Brown gave chase while I remained, shocked at the scene before me.

Nita did all of this? She was just one woman against these highly trained and skilled agents. Yet none could stop her?

I gaped openly at the dozens of agents as they struggled to stand and call for aid. The shorter one who'd followed took me by my arm.

"Lord Fromm? We should get you to a safe room."

I wanted to argue that it wasn't necessary, that Nita wouldn't hurt me. The scene before me made me doubt. I nodded and let them guide me to a small office within the bunker facility. I sat on a chair and fidgeted with my leather bracelet, the only sign of the war raging inside me.

I lost track of time. All I knew was it passed. Maybe half an hour, maybe an hour, maybe a few hours passed before the two agents who'd spoken to me directly entered my little saferoom with a third. They all removed their masks and their voice-altering devices.

"She escaped," Agent Brown said. "They lost her at the edge of the compound. Like she knew exactly how to escape!"

They slammed a fist against the table, and I slumped in my seat.

She'd slipped away from even the snakelike operatives. She could be anywhere now. Nita…

"Tell us, Earl Fromm," the tallest one said in a silky baritone and with the face of a hardened officer, eyes like thunderclouds. He was the new one. Maybe a higher-up to deal with the visiting loose string? He asked, "What do you know about Agent Moreno?"

"What's her first name?" I asked.

They looked at each other. He answered with a snarl, "Linda."

"Linda Moreno," I repeated. "About her, all I know is what you've told me, but that's not the woman I know. Nita Incog is a different woman who—"

"Moreno has played the long game before," the shortest one said with a raspy soprano. A woman? "She trained at

78

Arrowhead for five years before she betrayed us. How long has she played you? A year or two?"

"I've known her for nearly three years," I defended. "We worked together, solving Cases and—" and *almost* dated. Instead, "We went on a day trip and did stakeouts together. I dare you to do all that with a stranger and tell me you don't know everything about them in the end. I know the woman she is now, and I promise she's changed."

"You think he's in on it?" the tall agent asked the others. "How else did she access this building? Maybe he provided some magical escape for her."

"What?" I rocked back. "Are you kidding me? Ask any of the Shigaqua Police Force, they'll tell you I'm the worst liar they've ever known."

"We should keep him, just to be sure," the short agent said back.

I raised a challenging eyebrow. "I've been abducted before. Taken to Horror of all places. You really think you can keep me here against my will?"

She shrugged. "It's worth the risk."

"No," Agent Brown said. "He's the heir to half of Fairy. His family are people we want on our side."

"Not to mention," I said with a sneer, "you'd have a horror of a time keeping me awake. Wouldn't want me to fall asleep and talk to the skeletons in these closets."

I gave them all a nice cheesy smile. The woman tilted her head, confused. She obviously didn't know about my ability. Agent Brown and the tall one squirmed. They knew. Our tour guide actually seemed close to hyperventilating. They knew there were secrets in this building that were meant to stay secret. Maybe I'd visit the place in my sleep even if they let me free.

"No," the tall one said. "We don't need to keep him. He's fallen for her ploys, maybe even fallen for *her*. He won't know anything she wouldn't want him to know."

Was that possible? I knew that Nita could act and go undercover, but for three years? No, she had no idea who she was. She did have amnesia. The surprise on her face with Agent Brown was genuine. But why did she run? What did she remember? After everything we did and shared over the last three years, did none of it matter?

No, it did matter. Whoever Nita was, whether she was a real person or an idea of a person, she was worth holding onto.

That thought led me to a rather frightening realization: I loved her.

Then, my chest clutched painfully. And I'd lost her.

CHAPTER 8

Car chases are not limited to
automobiles. Motorcycles and tanks may
be involved.

- Lemuel Gulliver's Travel Guide, Vol. 5: Thriller

Arrowhead agents escorted me out of the building and back to my VIP car. I hardly noticed getting in and out of the napper-van with my mind in a fog of realizations and lost futures. I sat in the borrowed sports car, unable to move.

Between Truth and me analyzing Nita and the Arrowhead agent we met last autumn, I'd given Arrowhead a fifty-fifty chance of renewing Nita's memory. Even still, I'd expected a clue, not a full revelation. I'd imagined gaining a hint of her employment history, not a full condemning résumé. I'd hoped Nita would earn a conclusion to her past, not a sequel.

I sat in the driver's seat of the luxury vehicle that could transport me anywhere I wanted to go...but I felt stationary and stuck. Was I supposed to return to my life and work in Noir as if losing my partner was just another Monday? No, with this incident, Visionary Investigations was officially dissolved. We'd scraped by since Truth left, but now I was all that remained. Nita had worried about carrying the investigations agency by herself, but it seemed equally impossible for me to carry it alone. Sure, I had the credentials and network to be an independent investigator, but I'd enjoyed the teamwork.

Also, there was my family matter. I was needed at home. But again, it felt impossible to whistle on my merry way back to Margen as if I wasn't worried about Nita.

My mind kept replaying moments with Nita—Agent Linda Moreno. Who was she really? She had run away too fast for me to ask. Arrowhead seemed to know everything about her, but they'd called her a traitor. Maybe Agent Moreno had been a traitor, but Nita wasn't. Why had she run away from me, too?

I needed to know what had really happened. That meant talking to the spirits.

With a goal finally in mind, I put the sportscar into drive and made my way off of the property.

I hadn't known what would happen if or when Nita regained her memories, but I'd assumed the tour would take most of the afternoon. I'd researched vacation rental houses for lodging but hadn't booked anything yet. As much as I would have preferred to book us in a double-room hotel, my royal reputation and spiritual visitations vetoed any shared options. I'd hoped to enjoy dinner together while we discussed whatever discoveries we'd made.

Now what was I supposed to do? I could technically catch a last-minute and late-night flight back to Urban, but I wanted to stay local to find the spirits of Arrowhead. Considering that wall of plaques, they were bound to have a few spirits lingering around.

I was about to beeline for a researched and preferred vacation rental house when Neil blew on the back of my neck with short warning bursts. I was being watched. No, followed. A silver sedan two cars back kept pace with me. It was so non-descript, I nearly lost it in the traffic, but I mentally tagged the front license plate.

Why would they follow me? Nita wasn't with me. Did they think I'd know where to find her? I didn't. But if I wanted Nita to feel safe reaching out to me, I probably couldn't have Big Brother looking over my shoulder.

The vacation rental that I'd researched was in a suburb of Londinium, but I passed the exit to go deeper into the city. I needed to shake off my tail first. Casual as a commute, I signaled over to the far lane for faster speeds. The silver sedan sped up to keep me in its sights.

"Alright," I muttered to any spirits with me. "Let's see what this baby can do."

I floored the gas pedal and shifted gears to zip through a break in the traffic. I barely made it over in time for the exit, cringing and holding my breath as the metal divider whistled by.

"Let's hope that's enough."

It wasn't. The sedan had slowed to make the exit, but with only four cars between us, they gunned the engine to catch up.

Curses. I'd hoped to turn back and find my way to the lodging on the backstreets. Time to get creative and commit some misdemeanors. How much could my diplomatic immunity cover?

I ignored the stoplight at the freeway exit to take a squealing right turn into the city. City speeds were painfully slow, forcing me to speed or stomp on my brakes to avoid collisions. I weaved around cars, taxis, and city buses, but that cursed silver sedan kept haunting my rear-view mirror.

A red light forced me to stop behind stalled cars, but my shadow dared to dart into oncoming lanes to leapfrog closer.

Gutsy. Could I... There was an opening. I gritted my teeth and gave a yawp for courage. Twisting my wheel, I sped into oncoming traffic.

Honks and horns loudly proclaimed my idiocy as I cut right, through the intersection. I took the turn a little too wide and forced the car in the next lane to swerve. They overcorrected and teed into the car behind me.

"Sorry!" I shouted. As if they could hear me over the screeching tires and blaring horns.

I also wanted to thank them, as their little accident blocked others on the street. I lost sight of the silver sedan. Did they lose me too?

I took the next left turn and stayed straight for three blocks. Then... No, it couldn't be.

That cursed silver sedan was back on my tail.

I swore under my breath and jerked my wheel to turn down the next street. Except it wasn't a street. It was an alleyway between the backsides of townhomes, like many I'd seen in Shigaqua.

"Curses-curses-curses!" I swore as my beautiful rental sportscar bashed into trash bin after trash bin, scattering litter and questionable garbage in my wake. Papers caught in my windshield wipers, and leftover food splattered across the glass. Thanks for the reminder that I was hungry for dinner.

I smashed into toys and even a bike that had been left out. Sorry, kids! Did Thrillers have insurance for these types of incidents? Could I look up their addresses later to compensate them?

I finally cleared the alley and sped back into the chaos of city traffic. The silver sedan slipped into view again.

Curses, how did they keep finding me? Was the car bugged with a second tracker? They could have easily tagged it again while I toured Arrowhead.

I grumbled with the engine. I needed to ditch the car. Besides, it deserved better than my recent abuse.

Skidding around a corner, I spotted some small tents under a bridge. Fantastic! I'd finally reached a less populated area of town where I could take full advantage of the sparse streets. Testing my turning speed capabilities, my tires burned with another quick right. The sedan fell behind as I went all the way around the block. Once, twice, thrice… After six times, the sedan slowed their pursuit. Did they think I was playing with them?

"Joke's on you," I muttered, pulling left at the next intersection. During my rounds, I'd noticed a dark alley nearby. I pulled my car into it but was forced to immediately stop. It was a dead end.

"Fine," I snapped, yanking off my seatbelt. Leaving the keys in the ignition, I stumbled from the car and ran. I didn't get far before the silver sedan pulled around the corner. I ducked behind a trash bin, praying they hadn't seen me. They drove along as if they hadn't, but I wouldn't take my chances. As soon as they disappeared, I bolted for the tents beneath the bridge. A few homeless people huddled around an open fire and gave me curious stares as I ran to them.

"Hey!" I called out to them. "Who wants some nice clothes?"

I didn't wait for them to respond before hiding behind a tent and shrugging off my suitcoat and kicking off my shoes.

"Who ya runnin' from?" a man asked like this was just another Thursday. This was Thriller, after all.

"Just a stalker," I fibbed, slipping off my slacks. "They don't want to kill me, just keep an eye on me. Who's willing to trade clothes?"

One man eyed my suitcoat. "You got good taste. I'll trade."

"Thanks. Even if they don't fit, you can sell them for a pretty coin."

With a nod, my volunteer handed over his patched coat, beanie hat, and a spare set of holey pants. I wouldn't have minded if he put on my duds to parade down another street as my decoy, but he smartly folded my suit and hid it in his grocery cart. Probably to sell it later.

I tucked my shoes behind my "new" coat to add some bulk to my belly. They were too nice to fit this outfit, but my mom taught me to always wear shoes good for running, and these were no different. I'd need them if this disguise wasn't enough.

Properly dressed, I grabbed ashes from the fire to rub across my face and create the appearance of a beard.

"Thanks," I said, standing beside them with my hands to the fire. The silver sedan passed right by without a second glance. I smirked. No one expected to find someone like me under a ratty coat and unkempt beard. I hadn't been trained as a special operative, but I'd learned a lot as a private investigator over the last few years.

I asked my new friends about the public transportation routes. Thankfully, the buses were still running this late in the evening. One took me most of the way to my preferred lodging, but I took the stop after to ensure that I'd truly lost my tails. I stopped by a fast-food burger restaurant for a slippery version of a hamburger and "locked and loaded" fries. At least I didn't need to decipher the menus like Mystery foods. Just in case, I walked around the block of my desired vacation rental house to canvas the area. I trashed the coat and beanie and found an outside hose to wash my face, attempting to appear presentable when paying for my room with cash. At least my button-up business shirt was mostly clean.

I loved my ability to visit the dead, but they complicated my lodging accommodations. I would have loved to stop at the closest hotel, but I needed a place with no shared walls or floors.

This little vacation home was perfect. The build was considerably newer and more updated than my Noir house, but the layout was similar—particularly with its main bedroom lavatory located near the center of the home. It was my single sanctuary to be completely alone.

Hoping to be sneaky, I went in through the back door and began to close the curtains. The summer sun was on the cusp of setting, blaring through the windows and granting me some light even after they were closed. Still, I used my emergency flashlight from my Hauntings holster before closing the last curtain in each room. Walking around a strange house with only my flashlight tested my limits as the darkness threatened to consume me. It didn't help that my spiritual friends had already arrived, creaking the floorboards, making faucets leak, and whispering their welcomes. Windows and doors secured, I flipped on the lights with a breath of relief.

"Spirits of Thriller," I called into the house. "I look forward to meeting you. If you haven't met Neil yet, don't worry. He's one of—er, he's my partner." I caught myself from my standard phrase. Could I still count Nita as one of my partners? "He knows the drill, so please listen to his instructions. Don't let anyone living enter this house and please stay out of my lavatory. It's been a long day, and I could use some quiet time to think."

In the main bedroom, the doors swayed, the drapes waved, and the floor creaked. I even caught a glimpse of Neil as he passed through the window light. He stared at me with impatience in his eyes. The spirits waited for me, and they were agitated. I could figure out what was happening in the Spirit Realm after some "living" research.

I searched for a classic radio before remembering that Thriller used television to broadcast its news. After a minute of button mashing, I found a news channel and let it play in the background as I rummaged through my daypack to begin my nightly routine.

"Up next," the news anchor announced from the TV, "the nightly reminder and commentary of the public BOLO list."

Of course, it went to a commercial break and forced me to wait another five minutes before the news returned. They began with photos of eight suspects "still at large," for various crimes, then, "We received reports of two more people of interest. A Fantasy Earl went missing two hours ago, last seen in West Londinium near the distillery district. It's believed he's been captured by a known fugitive and terrorist, Linda Moreno."

"Terrorist?" I balked. Even if half of the plaques on that wall were her fault, she hadn't attacked innocent civilians. I grumbled as they posted a high-angle camera still of Nita and me in one of the many nondescript hallways of Arrowhead.

"They were spotted together at a private facility earlier today before a mass attack resulting in dozens wounded. Both are heavily armed with long and short-range weapons. If seen, do not approach—"

I turned off the lies. Yes, I carried my revolver and stabbing stakes in my holster, but I wouldn't call myself "heavily armed." Even if parts were true, the facts were spun in a way to cause suspicion and fear.

Speaking of incomplete information, there was a note from Neil on my nightstand, saying, "Here."

How vague. Did he mean "here" as a location or "here" as a motion to give me something? Was he simply telling me his location so I could request his aid if needed? Even after three years as my note-keeper, he needed to work on his clarity.

I had a feeling that I'd learn more about Agent Moreno in my sleep, but the pit in my stomach warned me that it wouldn't be good.

CHAPTER 9

The privacy of the center lavatory lured me in with relief. Ah, solitary silence. I didn't look forward to the "told you she was trouble" stares or lectures from the ghosts.

With reluctant and lethargic movements, I rewashed my face to remove any remaining ash. I still felt dirty and worn, like change from a Shigaqua street vendor. My "new to me" trousers needed to be cremated.

Prepping a towel beside the bathtub, I untucked and then unbuttoned my shirt. I was about to shrug it off my shoulders when a voice said, "Don't move."

I spun toward the noise but saw no one. "Please, spirits, I asked you not to come in here."

"Which is why I did," a strong voice said from the cupboards beneath the sink. A living voice. The ajar door opened to reveal a silencer in a black-gloved hand. "I said, 'don't move.'"

I raised my hands in defense, then almost charged at my offender. "Nita!" I started forward, my heart screaming for an embrace. She was safe! She was here! And she had a gun trained on me?

"Stop!" she shouted, keeping me back. "Please." Her voice shifted to desperation. "Please, Aeron. Don't make me shoot you."

I stepped back and returned my hands to the air. "Nita?"

"I…" Her breath stuttered until she took a long inhale, deep and calming. "I need your travel candle."

My heart dropped. "Is that the only reason you came—"

"Yes."

Her clipped reply made me wonder, "Is it?"

Silence.

"You could have gone anywhere in Novel," I said, "and you chose to hide under my lavatory sink? How did you even know I was staying here?"

"I saw your research on this vacation home," she said, curt and practiced. "I made an educated guess you'd come here. I need a speedy and far escape, and your traveling candle is perfect. I knew your residence would be private because you said your haunted housing is always avoided by the living. Aeron, even for a rental in Thriller, your living space is freakishly haunted."

I chuckled. Despite the fear in my heart of staring down a muzzle, the rest of my heart was elated to find Nita and have this chance to talk with her. The cupboard door opened wider. Nita crawled out and straightened like a rising cobra, all the while keeping her gun aimed at me.

"Then I remembered," she continued, "that your bathroom was your only place for privacy."

"So, you came here," I concluded, "and waited for me to undress?"

Her eyes flickered to my open chest and the homeless-man's trousers. She sucked in her cheeks to remain stoic, though her face reddened slightly. "Nice pants. I needed to make sure you were unarmed and unwired."

"I swapped clothes with a homeless chap in order to lose a tail. Losing a tail would be pointless if I was wired."

"Well, I need your travel candle."

"Yes, you've said that." I dared to step closer.

"Aeron," she warned, tightening her hold on the gun.

"You know what I think?" I said, testing another step. "I think you don't really want a candle. The Nita I know wouldn't find me just to threaten me for transportation. She wouldn't zip around to different magic-capable places for no reason. No, she would have escaped the agency to grab her get-away stash, then she'd realize that no matter where she went, I would find her anyway, and no matter where she went—" I gambled my next words and another step "—she'd *want* me to find her."

She stared at me with wide eyes. One more step put my chest against her barrel.

"I know you," I said, and slowly raised one hand to hers on the gun. "The Arrowhead agents claim you're a traitorous ter-rorist. If they were right, you would have shot me already. If you want to prove those jerks right—that you're no more than a cold-blooded double-agent—" I lifted her hand to place the muzzle over my heart "—then aim true. My heart is useless if the woman I love is too heartless to love me back."

Her mouth opened in a small gasp at my confession, and her grip loosened.

"However," I continued, "if you have any feelings that make it difficult to kill me, talk with me. Please?"

Her bottom lip trembled, and she blinked away a shimmer from her eyes. Finally, she stepped back and lowered her gun. She let out a deep breath and leaned against the sink counter.

"Well, you're right about one thing: I wanted you to find me and not the others, so I came here and waited." She grimaced to herself and shook her head. "I'm sorry; this was stupid. I shouldn't be here."

"I'm glad you are, but yes." I grinned nervously. "My investigation partner of the past three years is in my rental bathroom. This puts our reputations into question." Forget the gossips in the market; if we were caught together like this, the rumors would never end.

Careful not to spook her, I reached for her free hand to guide us out to the bedroom. At least there we had spiritual chaperones. The lights flickered as a reminder.

"Aeron, wait." Nita pulled my hand to keep me from exiting to the main room. "I can't let them find me. They'll kill me for sure. The things I did—I...I can't. I deserve to be—"

"Tell me what happened, Nita. Arrowhead told me their side of the story, but I want to know yours."

"They told you?" She paled. "And you still say you love me?" Her wide eyes rapidly blinked away tears. "No-no, you can't—I infiltrated Arrowhead for the sole purpose of destroying them."

"Why?" I asked. "Was it for someone's justice? Were you following orders?"

"Orders?" she echoed, and somehow the thought of her commander made her pale even more than the fear of me knowing the truth. "Don't ask me about him. The less you know, the safer you are."

Then she hadn't worked alone. That fact leaked in far too many questions. "Who? Why—"

"I'm serious, Aeron. He's dangerous," she said, as if she wasn't already one of the most serious women I knew. "Forget about him. He doesn't exist. Besides, it doesn't matter. I was the one who pulled the trigger, lit the fires, and set off the bombs. I *killed* people in cold blood. I *betrayed* my own team-mates. You can't love me—you hardly know me! I remember it, and I hardly know *myself!*"

"Then you hardly know me if you think I care about that," I argued. Yes, it hurt to hear her confession and confirmation of Arrowhead's accusations, but the repentant tears in her eyes hurt me more. She hated the person she'd been. Also, the fear in her expression gave me clues about her situation. Had she been forced to betray Arrowhead by her commander? Or maybe she simply hadn't known any other way of life…like the life she had with Truth and me…

"I know who you *are*," I said with a heavy step forward, "and I love you as you are."

"You can't mean that. If you actually thought—"

"I mean it, Nita," I said, taking her by the shoulders. I wanted her to believe me. I *needed* her to believe me. "My uncle, Dunstan the Night Shade, once destroyed an innocent town and was known as the Night Terror. Then he became a priest and used his ability for good to save me in Horror. Then there's Neil, my poltergeist assistant. Nita, he tried to choke me the first time we met, and now he's my best man. People can make bad choices, but people can change. If we don't allow second chances, then we're all doomed. You had the ultimate second chance at a new life, and I love what you did with it. I love the person you became, the person you chose to be—the person you are."

She didn't say anything, but breathed heavily, calming back her tears.

"You don't need to be Linda," I continued and pulled her close. "You can be Nita: a PI partner or master actress who can be anyone in the world. Linda is a woman from the past. I'm not the same PI Aeron Spade I was last year. I could go back to pretending to hide from my inheritance, or I could accept my place as Earl Aeron Fromm of Margen. Who do you *choose* to be?"

She didn't respond immediately. She calmed her heavy breathing and then looked up at me with glistening eyes. "You're sure you can ignore my past?"

I slid a finger across her cheek to wipe away a tear. I'd never seen her cry before. Her tears were beautiful and heart-wrenching at the same time.

"I'm not ignoring your past. I'm just choosing to focus on the present; right now, with you in my arms, vulnerable and open. They claimed you were a heartless death machine. The woman I see before me is full of passion and possibilities, if only she chooses."

"Well," she said, "I don't know what to choose…other than you."

She pressed her lips to mine.

Yes-*yes*-*YES!*

Some spirit knocked on the wall, and Nita jumped away.

"Let them see," I said, pulling her back and recapturing her mouth. I finally had this woman in my arms and would never let go, especially now that I'd tasted her. I was already addicted to her touch and craved to go deeper. I wanted to grip her close to me and express more passion than usual for a first kiss. Besides, this wasn't some woman I had courted a few times and simply found intriguing. This was Nita. I'd been falling for her every day since we met three years ago.

I broke away to change the angle, and she leaned back, staring at me with pure wonder.

"Is something wrong?" I whispered above the growing white noise of our specter spectators. Supernaturals, were they cheering?

Nita blinked at me. "You have no malicious motive. Your kisses aren't meant to lower my guard or distract me for an attack. I can trust you, and I do trust you. It's a weird feeling."

Curses, what did she mean by that? She might be older than I was, but we'd clearly had different experiences with romance. "This isn't your first kiss, right?"

She blinked up at me, nervous. "It's my first kiss that matters to me."

My lips drew up in a smoldering smile. "Good, because you're already too good at this."

A spirit hummed, providing a soundtrack as Nita pulled me back in. Her lips landed on mine with determination and force. She held on to me and seemed to dismiss our unseen audience, to forget her worries, her past, and just think about now, about us, about a possible future.

I remembered that my shirt was unbuttoned as her hands tickled around my back. My craving for her reached a new level.

Hands yanked us apart at our shoulders. Nita yelped and staggered, searching for the imposer, but saw no one.

"Was that your poltergeist?" she asked, her hand to the spot where someone had pushed her.

"Most likely," I confirmed and glared at the place I figured Neil was hovering.

"Well, shoot," she swore, and leaned back against the dresser to hold her head in her hands. "My life's taken a turn for crazy today. I remembered I'm a murderous double agent, I'm now a fugitive in Thriller, and I'm in love with a duke's heir who lives half his life with ghosts."

I grinned at her casual love confession. "Naw, I only sleep for seven hours. That's less than a third of my life."

She laughed nervously as her eyes darted toward the various spiritual disturbances in the room.

"Right," I said, "that's why I came here in the first place. Curses, I'd rather be with you, but I have work to do in my sleep."

"A phrase only you can get away with," she said with an uneasy smile. "Do you have to go back to work?"

"Did we ever stop?" I joked. "Look, feel free to stay here for the night. I can take the couch, and we can figure things out in the morning."

"I'd rather take the couch," she said. "I doubt I'll sleep much in this haunted house, anyway. Probably for the best. Since we toured Arrowhead together, well, they know we're connected somehow, and it's very likely they'll put a detail on you."

"Yes, they tried to tail me here," I muttered. "All the more important that I sleep while I can."

"Aeron." She paused my return to the bathroom by grabbing my arm. She looked at me with big eyes, like she had a million things to say. Instead, "Well, goodnight?"

"Goodnight…Linda?"

She shuddered.

"Alright, a new name then. Step one in running away from special operatives: take on a new identity. Who do you want to be?"

She caught my eyes and held. "Well, I want to be the woman you see in me."

"I see Nita. But that's a nickname. Anita then?"

She gave me a small smile and a nod. I combed her hair back with my fingertips and whispered across her lips, "Goodnight, Anita."

She shivered with an anticipating smile. "Yeah, I can get used to that."

I bent down to kiss her, but my lips met cold dead skin when I was still a centimeter away.

"Gagh! Neil?" I shouted into the air around us. "Was that your hand? Please tell me that was your hand and not some other part of you."

A maniacal chuckle echoed through the room, and I groaned. "Fine! We'll be good little children and go to our separate sleeping spaces without so much as a goodnight kiss! Happy?"

Anita's expression balanced between amusement and fright as she stepped out of my bedroom and closed the door behind her.

CHAPTER 10

*Beware the double agents. Unlike disillu-
sioned agents, these always straddled the
line between loyalty and betrayal.*

- Lemuel Gulliver's Travel Guide, Vol. 5: Thriller

My spirit rose from my body to find only a couple of
ghosts waiting for me. It seemed that Special Operations, Thriller, wasn't a place where spirits
lingered. I suspected their powers were limited here, like those
in Noir, encouraging them to move on. Neil stared at me with
a raised eyebrow.

"You're welcome," he said.

"Excuse me? For what?"

"For stopping you before you went too far."

"I—" I stumbled on my words. I wanted to deny the possibility and say that his precautions were unnecessary. That could
also explain why there were so few ghosts around. Most of our
specter spectators had left to spread the gossip.

"You're a terrible liar." Neil smirked. "You can't even argue
it. Does Margaret know?"

"Probably," I guessed, referring to the ghost I attempted to
date three years ago. "She kept track of my dating life better
than anyone else, and she suspected my desire to be with Anita.

98

Either way, Margaret deserves to move on. We both do. I haven't been the keeper of her heart for quite some time now."

"Three years isn't 'quite some time' among spirits who dwell for eternity."

I grunted. "At least she pretended we parted on good terms. Undoubtedly the rumors are flying around already, so there's nothing I can do about that."

"Undoubtedly," Neil echoed with a chuckle. "It's not every day the Duke of the Dead gets smoochies from a harbored fugitive in his vacation Presence Chamber."

"'Smoochies?' Who says that anymore? And this is my *bed*chamber."

His eyebrow went higher.

"I know that doesn't make it less scandalous!" I flustered. "Tell me what else has everyone agitated?"

"First of all, you finally got somewhere with *A*-nita. A lot of bets and debts will be settled tonight."

"I asked what *else?*" I groaned. I'd hoped to keep a positive attitude from Anita's affections. Now, I just felt chastised. "Nothing? Fine. I need to go back to Arrowhead for more information about what happened on December thirty-first. Any dirt on Arrowhead to make them hesitate about chasing Anita and me will also be helpful. Unfortunately, I don't have the exact address, and I couldn't tell exactly which direction we went. All I know is we met at a cabin south of Londinium. Neil, were you able to follow me?"

"Yeah, but you know my sense of direction isn't reliable." Unfortunately, true.

"The Arrowhead facility?" One of the spirits drifted forward. He offered a spiritual handshake with his introduction. "Agent Renolds of International Relations. We employed Arrowhead agents occasionally, so I searched out their location after my passing."

I scoffed with a smile. No secrets among the dead. "Can you take me there? I don't know how much time we have."

He smiled. "With my job, I traveled a lot. As a spirit, I was given the gifts of teleportation and location awareness."

"Fantastic. Can you take Neil and me there now?"

"I would need to take two trips. I can only teleport one person at a time."

"That's fine." Such were the limitations of this land.

Agent Renolds closed his face with concentration as he passed his hand into my core. I squirmed at the sight, but if I closed my eyes, I wouldn't have noticed anything happening. His eyes flicked open to mine, then the house disappeared, replaced with the woods of Arrowhead. As a spirit, I saw the world as if the full moon was directly above despite the clouded skies and leafy canopy. The operative grounds weren't much different at night, but then we floated through the ground entrance.

Three people dressed in black went about cleaning the machines, hypothesizing about how someone could escape the compound. Were they still searching for Agent Moreno? I floated right up to them, analyzing them without their masks. They seemed more…human. A boy and girl were barely teenagers with acne and lanky limbs. They snickered over a crude joke until the older third glared death at them. Their faces became stone like the stoic expression Anita often wore when I'd first met her.

Curses, was this Arrowhead's training? Control and no emotion even during downtime?

Hoping for more information, I continued into the nearby medical room. Every bed was filled with injured agents, but there were no moans or complaints. They slept in fits, gritted teeth, and did breathing exercises to suppress their pain. Had the medical facilities run out of pain meds or was this another method of Arrowhead training to turn their agents into flesh robots?

Muffled voices in the administration room next door took me in that direction. A short man in black scrubs stood behind the counter, talking on the phone.

"I see. Thank you. We'll send someone by to pick them up." The nurse hung up and sighed.

"Agent Collins didn't make it?" a man from the corner of the room asked. I hadn't noticed him sitting in the shadows. He was taller than I was and spoke with a familiar silky baritone. He'd been one of the people to interrogate me after Anita fled.

The nurse shook his head. "I suppose it could have been worse. The first time Agent Moreno fled this compound, she killed every agent here."

Being a spirit didn't keep my heart from stopping at his words. Every agent? I stared beyond, to the wall of plaques. Dozens listed the same death date. Dozens killed by Anita—or Agent Moreno.

The nurse continued, "Considering the dozens of wounded she left behind this time, we were lucky to only have one casualty."

The tall man grunted. "Can we confirm it was actually her? It seems odd for her to come back after all these years and then to spare her attackers as witnesses. It was sloppy. Not the way she was trained."

The nurse raised his brows. "Or it was on purpose. Agent Brown said she'd suffered from amnesia and regained her memories while standing in this room. From analyzing the wounds she left, she demonstrated incredible skill, knowledge, and precision in her attacks. The severity of Agent Collins' wound came from his foolish attempt to drive the motorcycle back to the garage after having his tendons sliced. Director Lister, I don't think—"

"That's enough for today," the tall man said. Director Lister? This was the man in charge of Arrowhead? He dismissed the nurse and tapped on a tablet to wake up the device. His eyes scanned the screen as his finger slid slowly upward. I drifted over to read over his shoulder.

"Located in Noir, Mystery, the Visionary Investigations Agency has no online presence, but our local research found most of the Shigaqua Police Department open to discussing them with variable opinions."

Supernaturals, he was investigating our investigations agency. There were several quotes about our Cases and team from newspaper clippings, policemen we worked with, and policewomen I'd dated. I grunted as the first two sets were more favorable toward us than the third.

Detective Celso Montgomery had called us, "Suspicious and a bunch of lucky hand-wavy freaks." I scoffed. He wouldn't have arrested Sponsor last autumn without our help. On the other hand, Detective Kenneth Ross was quoted as saying, "They do good work. They use unconventional methods, but they always find proof of their findings. If I ever have a Case I can't solve myself, I reach out to Digger."

I smiled warmly at that, wondering how Ross would react to our agency dissolving. I smirked a little when the Arrowhead report admitted that they couldn't determine which person in our agency was "Digger."

The report continued with side notes.

"Last autumn, Agent Lysenko was spotted by Truth Locke Johnson and apprehended by Earl Aeron Fromm of Margen (AKA: PI Aeron Spade), both from Visionary Investigations. Agent Lysenko has thus been terminated. It's believed that Johnson and Fromm had the help of a partner—an amnesiac woman trained in stealth—with an alias of Nita Incog (real name: unknown). Our intelligence petitioned them for a minor Case of a stolen item but never spotted the third partner."

There were detailed profile pages of Truth and me, but Truth had discovered more about Nita than Arrowhead's intelligence agents had. They didn't know what kind of person she was.

The weakest of chimes made Sergeant Lister's eyes scan the room and then flip out a burner phone. He pulled up a sparse text thread.

ARROW'S HEAD

Why am I only now learning that Linda Moreno survived and is touring the facility like a VIP?

LISTER

She escaped, but we're on the hunt. We tagged her partner's vehicle and put out a BOLO.

ARROW'S HEAD

Take care of it before I do. Or else.

Curses, that couldn't be good. And who was Arrow's Head? Was the director not really the one in charge?

LISTER

This was her partner.

Attached was my PI profile. Beneath the "unread" bar was a longer text.

ARROW'S HEAD

The director didn't respond, but hid the burner phone in his pocket and began a new search on the tablet for a vacation rental. Curses, it wouldn't be long until they found my location. I needed to acquire information about Agent Linda before I was forced to wake up and warn Anita. I turned away to continue my search for lingering spirits when the director spoke into his watch.

"Agent Moroz?"

"Yes, sir?"

"Send agents to the homes of Aeron Fromm and Truth Johnson."

Panic froze me in place. Truth was currently caring for her dying mother. If they sent agents to her home, they'd endanger her parents.

Also, he'd said "Aeron Fromm," not "Aeron Spade." They wouldn't go to my empty haunted house in Noir but to Ruezdad.

Sam! I needed to warn my parents!

"Aeron." Spirit agent Renolds floated into the room. "I found some spirits you'll want to meet."

Curses, there were too many things to do! But there was little I could do for my family while I was in Thriller.

With a quick decision and plan, I said, "Take me to the spirits."

He nodded and led me to an auditorium with a stage.

"Of course," I scoffed. Ghosts sure loved the theater.

Unlike the spirits of the Regal Theater where I'd met Neil, this theater wasn't occupied with over-the-top dramas and melodramatic directors. This theater was alive with the strange and bizarre acts of modern art. One spirit had multiplied herself a dozen times over to create a group that synchronized jerking movements with poignant speeches. Another spirit created ghost images of animals for their wild dance representing…a hunt? The remaining couple of spirits practiced a scene that I could only describe as guerrilla theater.

Neil chuckled beside me. "Takes you back, doesn't it?"

I shared a smile with him before addressing Agent Renolds, "I need you to go back to my body. There should be some spirits available to spread the word to Margen. The marchioness needs to be warned that Arrowhead is coming for them."

I trusted my mom to take a mysterious warning seriously, even if it was given by the Fantasy spirit who had a gift to appear to the living and called himself the God of Random Advice.

As for Truth and her family… "Neil, I'll need you to write a note for me to call Truth about Arrowhead. I have a feeling that I'll need a lot of notes after tonight."

He shrugged as if it was nothing unexpected. I gave him a grim smile of thanks before turning to the spirits on the stage.

"Excuse me," I called to them all. "Did any of you know Agent Linda Moreno?"

My question was met with a series of glares and narrowed eyes. A handful of people raised their hands. I pointed to the entire group of agents on the stage, and they collapsed into a single female spirit. Yep, the gift of multiplying themselves.

"Hello. My name is Aeron—"

"Fromm," she finished. "Arrowhead doesn't have many tourists, so several of us followed along and researched you. This is what they meant by your visiting the dead in your sleep?"

"Yes. What's your name?"

"I choose to keep that to myself."

"Agent…A? B? C?" I offered.

She rolled her eyes. "Agent B will do."

"Agent B, do you mind if I ask you some questions?"

"You've already asked three," she scoffed. "Ask whatever you want, but no guarantees I'll answer how you want."

"I only want you to answer honestly. Based on your comments so far, that seems to be your style, whether people like it or not."

Her scoff carried a smile this time. "Fine. What do you want to know?"

"How did you know Linda—or Agent Moreno?"

"She was my roommate."

I made a quick glance at Neil as my cue for him to listen. I'd likely need him to remind me later about the details of this conversation. "How long were you roommates?"

"About four years. She excelled in classes and training. She was both innocent and secretive at the same time."

"In what ways?"

The agent shrugged. "She was one of Arrowhead's oldest recruits, but she didn't need much catching up. She claimed she'd been trained by the military, but seemed…socially naïve. Like she'd never had friends before or had never shared living quarters with others. I thought that was why she was so keen on talking with everyone and why she studied so much. I thought she loved learning, especially about people and the agency. I didn't know she was stocking knowledge to turn it against us."

"Did she give you any reason to suspect her?"

Agent B shook her head. "Not really. She obviously had a hard upbringing, but so did all of us."

"Please explain?"

"We were trained in special operations from our youth," she said, giving me a downward stare. "You don't get here by having a cookie-cutter home and family. Whatever families we had left were given our death-certificates when we signed up. We were ghosts. Some of us were so deep in witness protection that it was easier to fake our deaths. Others had nowhere else to go. I assumed Linda had been part of that second group—no family or friends, and nothing left to lose."

Except if she'd had nothing left to lose, why would she spend years here only to betray teachers and friends? Why follow a command that destroyed all connections and resources she'd built over four years?

I prodded, "Then the attack. What happened?"

"No one expected it," Agent B said. "It all happened so fast. The power-failure, the bombs, the fires… Half of us died before realizing what was happening. The other half were convinced it was some kind of drill. Only as spirits did we make sense of it all. We didn't know it was her. Most spirits around here don't linger, so we'd figured Linda had gone straight to the Unknown Beyond like the others. By the time we pieced it together, it was too late. Linda had disappeared. It was only when Agent Brown called her out that Agent A here recognized her." She nodded toward a male spirit who was dressed like someone on the stage crew. "He spread the word about her return, but she's disappeared again. Good thing too. I know more than a few spirits who want to haunt her for the rest of her miserable life."

I grimaced. So, Anita was running not only from the living but also from the dead.

"Please," I said, "if you find her, don't haunt her. She's a changed woman and a good person when given the chance."

The spirit eyed me for a long second. "So, the rumors are true then? You're sweet on the traitorous murderer?"

My shoulders slumped.

Neil answered for me. "They were partners for over three years. They worked together, and I can stand as witness: the woman never showed signs of malice or ulterior motives."

"Thanks," I whispered to Neil.

"Huh, go figure," Agent B snorted. "The Duke of the Dead is in love with the angel of death. That's what she is, you know? She's a murderer, a trained killer, a death machine."

I shook my head. "She's better than that. She returns my love."

"You're lying to yourself. We were covert operatives; trained to spy, lie, and fight."

I opened my mouth to argue, but Agent Renolds returned and called my name.

"You need to wake up," he said. "There are operatives surrounding your body's location."

Curses. I hated waking with an alarm, but this was no time to hesitate. I pointed at the poltergeist. "Take Neil back to my body. Neil—"

"I know what to do."

I really didn't like the smile and glint in Neil's eye as Renolds teleported them back to my rental.

Returning to Nita's murdered souls, I asked, "Is there anything else I need to know?"

The woman gave me a dead stare. "Don't let her kill you. But if she decides to, there's probably nothing you can do about it."

Before I could sarcastically say, "Thanks," a stinging pain jolted my soul back to my body. I woke up with a shout and hand to the little hairs on the back of my neck.

"Ouch!" I sat up and waved my arm around as if I could make Neil leave me alone. But there wasn't time to complain. One urgent bit from my dream screamed from my memory.

My door burst open with Anita standing in the shadows of early dawn. "Good, you're awake. We need to go."

I nodded. "They're here."

CHAPTER 11

- Lemuel Gulliver's Travel Guide, Vol. 5: Thriller

A paper note fluttered between us.

Neil's writing. "Duck!"

"Get down!" I shouted and fell to the floor. Not a moment too soon. Bullets pelted the windows, shattering their glass across the floor. "Seriously, people?" I muttered. "Are they trying to kill us? This place is a rental. I hope they plan to pay my fees for cleaning and damages."

With my face to the floor and my elbows restricting my vision, I didn't notice Anita crawling to me until she tapped on my shoulder.

"They broke windows on every side. They have us surrounded and will close in while we're pinned down. Do you need anything before we go?"

Did that mean she had an escape plan? This was not how I'd hoped to check out of my rental. I army-crawled to my nightstand and grabbed my revolver and Hauntings holster. Securing my side pack was difficult on the floor, but I managed. Since my spirit always appeared in my current clothing, I always wore sleeping pajamas that could pass for daily wear.

110

Still, I grabbed my long coat to cover my cotton button-up and drawstring bottoms. Meanwhile, Anita was decked out in black leather and gear like she didn't know the meaning of comfort clothes.

She analyzed the spray of bullets and cursed. "Shoot. They must have heat-sensor vision, meaning there's no hiding from them. They're mostly aiming at me, but, Aeron, they're targeting you too."

"Me?" I gulped. "Curses, they're trying to kill us both? They didn't shoot at me yesterday."

"I wasn't with you yesterday. If they kill you by accident now, they can stage it to look like I'd killed you instead. Blame the 'terrorist' for attacking a foreign earl. It's a believable story."

Especially with her variable aura. My parents would possibly believe the lies and spare Arrowhead from retaliation. Curses, I'd be murdered without justice.

"Then we run?" I asked. "How?"

"What happened to the VIP car?"

"E-eh," I stumbled between my cringing memories. "It might be currently sold for parts."

Anita scoffed. "Figures. We'll use my car then."

"Your car? Last time I saw you, you rode away on a dirt bike."

"I traded up for something that wasn't tracked. It's down the street at a park, though."

"How are we supposed to reach a car at a park when we're pinned here? Wait, you say they're reading our heat signatures?"

"Most likely. You have an idea?"

"I need two spirits," I called through the room. "Envelop us."

Neil's creepy chuckle announced his status as a volunteer before a bone-shivering chill settled into me. Anita shuddered with a "Burr."

The firing halted.

"It's working." I grinned. "Let's go."

Anita shook her head. "They'll be watching the doors and windows. By eliminating our heat presence, they're likely to move closer for a visual."

"Then we can't stay here. We need a distraction to create an opening. Spirits, I need someone to replace Neil in covering me. Neil, scream around the agents watching over—"

"The dining-room window," Anita finished, catching onto my plan. "But how will we know when we're clear?"

"We'll know," I promised.

Sure enough, only a minute passed with us huddled beneath the dining room window before a stomach-curling scream echoed through the morning neighborhood. Anita didn't need my signal to move. She had already unlocked the window with a pole and oiled the track during our wait. With Neil's scream as the signal to go, she threw open the window and hopped out, landing soundlessly in the garden bed below. My landing wasn't quite as silent, but Neil's scream woke the whole neighborhood of dogs and their masters.

Anita passed smile to me. "Go figure. Dogs are a bane to spies. With this commotion, we should make it to the festival."

"Festival? For what? At this time of day?"

"It's 7:45. They're setting up in the park for a car show. This way."

She took my hand to pull me into the neighbor's lot. They were one of the houses with a dog, which began a new rhythm of barking at our intrusion. Yep, dogs were a bane to spies.

"Shoot—hurry!"

Anita pulled me faster as voices called to one another.

"Over here!"

"They're getting away!"

My ears bounced between a distant bang and a nearby smack. Looking toward the nearby smack, I found a sharp impact of a small projectile in the house wall less than a meter from Anita's head.

Supernaturals, a headshot? Did they want Anita "dead or alive" or just dead? They answered "dead" when a second hole embedded the wall closer to my head.

Anita didn't give me the time to rationalize their actions as she tugged harder. I didn't need more motivation. I ran alongside her, ducking, crouching, and crawling between shelters. We weren't sure which direction our enemies were coming from (it seemed like every direction), so our best defense was to keep moving.

Laughter, engines, and crowds of voices announced our destination ahead. We were so close to escaping into a thin crowd, but an empty street lay between us and safety.

Anita poked her head out to check the road. Gunshots forced her to retreat. She whipped out a pistol and fired both ways up the street. I'd never seen that pistol before. When had she upgraded her weapons technology to Thriller's?

Claiming that the coast was clear, we ran together into the open street. Anita fired twice more in each direction to scare off our pursuers, but these operatives weren't easily spooked.

"Shoot!" she cursed, jerking me past her. Her hand twitched in mine as she yelped with their return fire.

"Anita!"

She froze like a deer in headlights, staring at a wildlife reservoir more than a hundred meters away.

It was my turn to yank her to safety, ducking between the vendor canopies. "Anita?"

She crouched, sinking into a near-fetal position as her eyes darted around like a spooked puppy. "Shoot—he's here. We're dead—there's no escape."

"Anita, they'll find us if we hide." Blood spread around her ripped sleeve near her shoulder. I palmed her cheek and directed her eyes toward mine. "Can you run?"

With a shudder and blink, she nodded.

I grabbed her uninjured arm and tugged her back to her feet. "We'll make it out, but I don't know which car is yours."

"This way," she said through gritted teeth and frantic breathing.

We turned into an alleyway of vendor canopies, which wasn't nearly as crowded as I would have liked for hiding. We allowed ourselves to slow to a stroll, like we were simply there to browse the stalls, except most of the vendors were still setting up their displays. We were too early to act like shoppers. I spared a few glances as we sped-walked past teenagers carrying banners into the park.

Gunfire shot through the air, making pedestrians stop, drop, and cover. At least, that was the normal thing to do. Three other people on the sidewalk cursed and reached for their concealed weapons. One dared to fire back, though the other two relaxed as we ran past them, realizing the pursuit wasn't for them. I could have sworn every tenth person in Thriller was an operative or fugitive.

"Affirmative, it's them!" someone called.

"Curses," I swore under my breath.

Anita also cursed and started running again. Whoever had spooked and shot her from the street was now an after-thought.

"Move in! Move in!" another one shouted.

"Don't let them escape!"

"Out of the way!" yet another voice said from behind. "You there, freeze!"

Despite the terror of being caught, I remembered our chase through the market, days before.

"You want to hide with a real kiss this time?" I chuckled between puffs for breath.

"Good idea."

"Wait—really?"

Shouting footsteps pounded closer. Anita grabbed me by my jacket and then pushed me into a spin, tearing my jacket free. She slipped out of her own overcoat and then ran to the side where a couple was already heavy into a make-out session. Anita hung our jackets on each of them, gave them a thumbs up, then grabbed my shoulder to pull me in a new direction toward the lineup of automobiles.

"Oh." Yeah, I was disappointed.

She rolled her eyes and ran faster. "We aren't running from gossips in the market. These are trained professionals who expect clichés like that."

She darted into another stall of vests and jackets with car labels and brand names. Most of the clothing matched her style of black. With no explanation, she swiped a men's leather jacket from its hanger and tossed it at me. I didn't have time to check for the prices before she slipped off a plain zipper jacket for herself and then dashed out.

I was pretty sure diplomatic immunity wouldn't cover stealing. I dropped two gold coins onto the table before we ducked out of the market stall. Considering the exchange rate, I definitely overpaid, but I hoped the extra tip would go into buying the vendor's silence about our quick visit.

We managed to reach the first line of cars with their hoods propped for viewing when the shots chased after us again. Car alarms sounded as bullets threatened their safety. I cringed with each alarm, imagining the damage to these beautiful machines.

"Over here," Anita said, pulling me toward a car that was significantly less impressive. She pulled down the hood and clicked a fob to unlock the doors.

"This is your car?" I asked, incredulous. It was a tiny two-seater called a Minor Coup. "I don't know if I'll fit."

"Get in or get shot," Anita said.

With those options…

I hunched, crouched, and wedged myself into the little vehicle as Anita put the keys into the ignition. The little beast growled with far more power than I'd expected.

To answer my questioning stare, Anita shrugged with a little blush. "I added a few upgrades."

Before I could ask for details, she slammed her foot on the gas and jolted us forward. Voices shouted with alarm as Anita sped through the lanes to the exit. We skidded slightly as the tires spun over the grass, but Anita seemed in control even as we swerved. Breaking onto the road, we jolted again with more speed.

"Is this necessary?" I asked. "I think we lost them—"

Police cars screeched on the streets ahead, lights flashing.

"Wait," I said, "those are everyday policemen. Maybe they can help."

Anita barked with a laugh. "Arrowhead might be a private organization, but Agent Brown said it has influence in the government. We're not running just from Arrowhead."

Staring down the cops ahead, she had the nerve to smile. Oh, Horror. What was she planning?

"We're running from Thriller."

She floored the gas to zoom through traffic, treating all signs and lights like advice from a younger sibling. Cars and my life flashed before my eyes as every intersection made me believe in miracles.

Every time I thought we'd lost our pursuers, two more seemed to gather around us. Two sedans careened onto our path ahead. One had its windows down for someone to poke out their face and—was that a machine gun?

"Curses!" I tried to duck, but that little car didn't give me much room. I thought the car chase to my lodging had been intense, but this time, they burned my diplomatic immunity!

Gravitational forces shoved me to the side as Anita twisted for a sharp turn.

"Hold on," she calmly warned.

I shouted back, "To what?"

A glance up at our future path revved up my anxiety. We were off-roading toward a downward set of stairs. I palmed the ceiling and clawed my armrest. Supernaturals, don't let me die this way!

We were airborne for a terrifying second before we landed with a crunch on the stairs. I let go of the armrest to grip my jaw as it chattered violently with each step. Anita hardly seemed phased as she continued to analyze our path and options ahead.

We burst onto the next road, right in front of a city bus. Its horn could have deafened me. Anita yanked us to the side again to align us with traffic. Were we finally safe?

A glance at the stairway we just survived dashed my hopes. Two motorcycles followed, and the bus's horn had alerted the whole city of our location.

We were stuck on a one-way street and in a construction zone, causing congestion. Apparently, that wasn't enough to hold Anita. Eyeing the oncoming motorcycles, she pulled into the closed lane for construction.

"Anita?"

Gunshots answered me as bullets shattered the back window. I ducked in part from the bullets and in part to brace myself against Anita's next bumpy ride as she sped toward the construction cones.

I never would have thought to be glad that I'd ditched that sports-car, but I was immensely relieved we weren't using it now.

Anita blew over the construction cones like they were toys. She drove directly at the giant light-up sign warning about the closed lane. The motorcycles followed us, shooting at our other windows and side mirrors.

"Anita?" I repeated, louder.

Too close to the sign, she jerked the wheel to clip its edge and drive onto the sidewalk. Pedestrians leaped out of our way. One woman picked up her little dog to scamper before us. I was unsure who screamed more, the woman or me.

Anita crashed through the wooden lane barrier, sending chips flying as we exited the construction zone. Somewhere in there, we'd lost one of the motorcyclists, and only one remained.

We hit an empty stretch of road, but our car slowed. Was it low on gas? No, we still had half of a tank. Was it mechanically damaged? Considering what we'd just put it through, that wouldn't surprise me. The motorcycle behind us seemed fine as its rider gained on us.

I ducked again as they fired, each shot closer than the one before. A glance in my cracked side mirror claimed that objects were closer than they appeared, and the motorcyclist looked ready to jump on our back end.

"Eat this," Anita muttered before stomping on the brakes.

Metal crashed into our bumper as a body tumbled over our hood. I cringed as they landed on the street before us. Anita swerved around them and floored the gas again as the cyclist somehow still had enough strength to shoot at us. A back tire popped and dropped us into an imbalanced lean, but Anita didn't stop. She did, thankfully, slow down and obey traffic laws again. With a few more turns, she drove into a parking garage. Going down two levels, she finally killed the engine. She winced as she unbuckled her seatbelt.

"Right, you were shot. Let's take a look—"

"We're not out of the red yet," she said, pulling out two pairs of sunglasses, a beanie, and a ball cap from the glove compartment. "After we switch vehicles, we'll be safe to check our injuries. We're only a few blocks from where we need to be."

Holding back my grumbles, I followed her out of the car and up the parking garage stairs. According to me, "where we needed to be" wasn't merely blocks away, but countries. Personally, I wouldn't feel safe again until I was behind the castle walls of Ruezdad.

CHAPTER 12

Passing a small grocery store, I called Anita to a stop. I wasn't willing to starve for the next few days until we reached Fantasy. If we even made it that far. It would be a long few days on foot, but maybe if we found horses somewhere, it would cut the journey in half, or even to a third. I hoped with our disguises, we wouldn't be recognized as I purchased a few fruits and vegetables with long shelf lives and that were good to eat raw. Meanwhile, Anita bought another wig and some creams to change our skin tones.

She frowned at my bag of groceries. "That bag makes too much noise. How do you plan to carry all of that?"

"I can loop the handles through my belt like a classic Adventurer. Maybe you've trained to go days without eating, but I need food," I said, biting into an apple. After a swallow, I added, "We can use my teleportation candle as soon as we reach a realm of magic, but we're at least a couple of days' drive away

120

from Urban. Please tell me we're not walking all the way back to Fantasy."

"We're not walking," she said.

"How are we getting back then? Do you have a second getaway car or something?"

She didn't answer as she pulled me back to the street and into an alleyway. Instead of walking onto the open streets, she picked the lock of one of the alley doors, taking us through a side entrance into a large apartment complex. We weaved through the hallways until exiting on the other side. Directly across a narrow street was a storage facility with a back area for loitering vehicles.

"You're not going to steal a car, are you?" I asked, having no doubt that she'd have the knowledge and skills to do so if she wanted.

"You're aiding and abetting a fugitive, and you're worried about stealing a car?" she asked with a teasing smirk.

"I haven't committed any felonies if I can clear your crimes."

She shook her head at my ridiculousness, but was it ridiculousness for believing she could be cleared or for drawing lines at certain laws while breaking others?

Reaching a back corner of the storage complex, she asked me to keep watch while she picked the lock for one of the units with a tall garage door. Inside was a 16-foot walk-in van. Sure, it wasn't the fanciest, but the white and boxy utility vehicle would blend in with many others on the long roads.

"Keep watching for spies," she said as she did a sweep of the van and then picked at the lock.

A click echoed through the unit as Anita unlocked the front door on the passenger's side.

"Okay, let's go," she called to me with a whisper, and I joined her at the van. She took the wheel and slid out a bucket seat for me.

Climbing into the passenger seat beside her, I said, "What are the chances that the carrier's empty in the back? I'd feel guilty if we stole not only the owner's van, but their merchandise too."

Sweeping her hand under the seat to find a pair of keys, she said, "Don't worry. It's mine."

"It's yours?" I repeated. Even as she turned the key in the ignition, I had to ask again, "This van is yours? How? When did you buy it and put it here?"

"Seven years ago, when I first enrolled at Arrowhead. That's why I asked you to wait on the side. I had to make sure there weren't any extra cameras or devices added in my absence."

I gaped at her. "You actually have a getaway car. What's in the back then?"

Her cheeks shaded. "Living quarters."

"You're serious?" I looked back even though it was blocked by a steel sliding door. "What exactly do you mean by 'living quarters'? Like a cot and a toilet?"

"A bit better than a cot, but not much. They're military beds with a three-and-a-half-foot clearance, but it's more than you'll get on a sub. There's also a shower, kitchen, and my bike back there."

"Okay, this I have to see." I reached to unbuckle my seatbelt, but stopped at her shaking head.

"Sit down. I didn't say you were free to walk about the cabin. First, we need to make sure we're free and clear of the city."

Her words made me antsy for two reasons. Not only because I was eager to explore her off-grid mobile home, but I was also nervous to escape the cop-filled streets. I pressed my-self against my seat as if to duck behind the edge of my window while also scanning for any police or other authorities. Nita turned on the radio for news reports, listening for any updates or alerts about our situation.

The city stretched longer than I remembered seeing from the airplane. It was a good hour with typical traffic until even the houses and fringe businesses dwindled into wild acres. The news took a break for some music. I'd grown up with the folk music of Fantasy and occasional listens to my mom's favorite raps from Horror. Noir had blasted big band jams and blues from their jukeboxes, twisting my mind with Thriller's…alternative? I wasn't sure of the official name for the male singer's pop lyrics, hip-hop beats, and combination of synthesized and real instruments.

Loving you is…
Dangerous!
They're coming after us
Don't know who to trust
Yeah, it's win or bust.
Been shot through the heart by Cupid's arrow
Took the leap for the faith that I don't know
Falling hard toward the ground, will I make it?
Can I take it?

It feels like I'm falling in love
For the last time.
To love you would be a crime
Of passion, yeah, a crime of passion,
'Cause the only way I'll leave you's in a coffin.
Write a eulogy to my single life.
Yeah, I think I need you as my—

"—rifle and grenade launcher," a female reporter interrupted as Anita changed the station.

Thank the Supernaturals. That song had started off a little too close to reality but had been on the verge of becoming awkward.

Half an hour later, the station was interrupted with "an urgent alert to beware of two fugitives. A male and a female. The man is from Fantasy with magical capabilities including telekinesis, and the female is a highly trained terrorist. Officials are seeking information about these individuals, either dead or alive. If spotted, we warn citizens not to approach. Both are heavily armed and considered highly dangerous—"

"Lies!" I jabbed the power button. If they had my father's ability to see dangers, the story would be flipped. I sighed and rubbed my temples. I needed to reach my family, to warn them and tell them the truth, before they heard Arrowhead's version.

Checking the fuel levels, I asked, "Will we find a gas station out here?"

She shook her head. "We couldn't fill up in the city. I have an emergency two-gallon tank for situations like this. We can make it to the next small town that won't recognize us, but we still better wear disguises. I have a couple of wigs and a change of clothes in the back. Are you comfortable paying cash in the shop while I fill up?"

"I can do that," I said, eager to help and return home as safely as possible.

"Also," she added, "could you grab the first-aid kit? It should be mounted on your door."

"Sure." Hidden beneath my bucket seat, it took some finagling to release the kit from its mount. Opening it, I found an envelope sitting on top. Instructions for the kit contents? Except there was only a half-sheet of paper inside that simply read, "I'm disappointed, Linda. You failed your last Mission."

I frowned and showed it to Anita. "What's this?"

Driving, she spared the letter two glances before cursing and yanking us to the highway shoulder. We left tire treads as she braked us to a stop.

"Where did you find that?" she asked.

"In the kit, on top."

"Shoot," she cursed again, putting the van in park and standing from her seat. "Grab the disguises and get out. Now!"

Confused but trusting, I donned a ball cap and sunglasses and jumped out. Anita remained inside the van, doing a twice and twice-as-thorough sweep. I asked to help, but she only warned me to "Stay back!"

Eventually, she came out with a bunch of electronics including (but not limited to) a mini-fridge, oven, portable stovetop, and solar panels. Without any care of littering charges, she dumped them on the edge of the road.

"Let's hope that's enough," she muttered, then gestured for me to return to the van. "We need to go."

I followed her back inside, asking, "What was that all about?"

"He knows about this van. If he snuck in to plant that letter, he knew I'd find it because he knew I'd been injured. That means he saw me during our chase from the house. I thought I recognized him when I was injured. He was there, and he was here. I needed to make sure he hadn't planted anything else to track us."

I gulped down those worrisome implications. "We still need to dress that wound."

"Not yet. We need to put some distance between us and the discarded electronics. Next stop."

True to her word, she pulled off at a barren exit to finally let me address her shoulder wound, which wasn't as bad as I feared. I added the extra gallons of gas, and then we were off again until the next small town with little more than a gas station and fast-food restaurant. Anita filled the van and her spare tank while I went inside to pay with cash, using the disguises again to block my face from the cameras.

After another two hours, Anita pulled us off the road at some forgotten exit, drove an extra mile to hide away from the main highway, then turned off the van.

She let out a long breath and rolled her shoulders.

"Tired?" I asked. "Even if that shot was just a grazing, you lost blood and pushed your body with adrenaline for maybe an hour back there."

She nodded.

"Do you want me to drive?"

Her head went side-to-side this time. "Special Operatives work better at night. We'll be better off driving during the day and resting during the night like a typical delivery van."

"Does this mean I get to see the back?"

She twisted her back with a stretch, but I caught her slight blushing first.

"Well, I guess it's only fair since I've seen your home." She finished her stretch and unlocked the door to slide open the cargo area. "Welcome to my home, sweet home."

When she put it that way, my face grew warm too. Yes, she'd stayed at my childhood home, but a castle gave us plenty of space to ourselves. Her van of one-hundred-thirty square feet was a lot more intimate. She said she had multiple beds, right? Where did they fit?

Stepping through the door, I found myself in a gutted little kitchen with gaps where there'd once been a personal refrigerator, space for a portable stovetop, and oven. Remaining was a sink and only the necessary space to store kitchenware for one or two people. I wouldn't try to cook a festive feast with it, but it would have served all the basic purposes of a regular house kitchen.

One of the countertops extended as a table. It was currently secured against the wall with not one, but two folding chairs. Had she picked up the two chairs before asking me to join her?

Continuing down the aisle, floor to ceiling lockers lined my right as the bathroom bulged from the left. A sliding door revealed a camper toilet, narrow sink, and standing shower. There was even a portable laundry washing machine below the sink.

Beside the wall of storage was Anita's "bike." It was a black motorcycle. I'd seen them around Noir, but I never caught the allure when I had a convertible roadster. Also, I was 100% certain that my mom would grill me alive if I ever purchased a "death machine."

Imagining Anita on the bike, however…yeah, I could see the allure.

Speaking of allure, I turned to my left for the bedding. Where normal delivery vans had shelves, Anita had fitted a military-grade bunk bed. Yes, the mattresses were better than cots with over three feet of headspace, but…

"There are two?" I asked.

"Well, yeah. To keep you from getting any ideas," she said. That was about as effective as telling me not to think about elephants. Suddenly, I had all sorts of ideas—military beds, regardless.

"That wasn't—" I cut myself off before I said something else stupid. "This isn't something you could have arranged in the time we started traveling together. You said you had this van set up seven years ago? It's obviously customized. Why did you install bunk beds in your lonely getaway van?"

Her face grew solemn as she stared at the bottom bunk. "I once shared it with someone."

I reminded myself that they were bunk beds (not a large bed for sharing) to stomp down any jealousy. Prodding, I asked, "Was it the man who left the letter?"

She turned sharply on me. "I told you to forget about him."

"And I told you that I wasn't dismissing your past and won't condemn you for it."

"Even if it condemns you?" she retorted. "My past isn't something you need to 'solve' anymore. Some Cases are too big, too deep, and too corrupt to resolve. Please, Aeron. Drop it."

Curses, she was close to pleading. She must have seen the determination in my eyes as her bottom lip quivered and she muttered, "Shoot. You've never dropped anything, no matter how dangerous or powerful your opponent was. Not against Neil, or Baldi, or Keys, or Sponsor. But this is different. I can't protect you from him."

I took her hand with a hopeful smile. She knew me as well as I knew her.

"I'm in this van with you. We're literally in this together. I'm already involved. But I can't fight back until I know who I'm running from. Please trust me with the truth. What was he to you? A trainer? Father? Lover?"

I waited in painful silence for her eventual answer.

"Master."

"Alright." I stewed over the many definitions of that word. "Then you were his servant?"

There was another drawn-out silence before she relented with a sigh. "I was his apprentice. At least, I liked to think so. Back then. Remember how the Arrowhead guide explained that their agents have no family and live to serve the company's clients? Well, he was my company. Everything I did was for him."

"Oh." Calling him "her company" meant she'd been lethally loyal to him. What else did "everything" include? How had he tested her loyalty before giving her the Mission to upend Arrowhead?

Needing to know more, I asked, "What did you call him?"

"Stryker. That's his name," Anita whispered, almost with fear. "At least, that was the name he told me. But you need to promise me you won't ever tell anyone. Knowledge is power, and power is dangerous. I can guarantee you that the man who raised me has dozens of solid aliases, and he only gave me one. He taught me to have a dozen of my own and to give different names to different circles. That way, when one gets flagged, I'll know exactly which circle betrayed me—which circle to burn and eliminate." She emphasized her words with dead seriousness in her eyes.

She caught my arm, holding my attention. "If Stryker becomes flagged in the system, if you so much as say it in public, then he will know exactly who to blame. He will kill me. I can run and hide from Thrillers. I can't from *him*. I have no idea where he is, but given the fact that he knew I was injured and would use this van, I know he could find me anytime he wanted to."

I swallowed hard and mulled over her words. From her grip on my arm and seriousness in her expression, I knew one thing for sure: if we ever met Stryker, Anita wouldn't be able to beat him. Even if she had the physical capabilities, she had a mental block against him.

"Alright, fine," I said, putting my hands up in surrender even as my mind plotted how to learn more about the anonymous person. Anita wandered back to the kitchen to toss me an apple from my earlier purchases and to search her small pantry cupboard of canned fruit, vegetables, meats, and soups.

"Would you prefer chicken noodle or minestrone?"

"Chicken," I said. "You kept this place stocked?"

She shrugged as she opened two cans of chicken noodle soup. "What's the point of a getaway van if it can't help you get away?"

"Far, far away, apparently," I said, biting into the apple. I took advantage of her mobile lavatory as she turned the sink into a little firepit to cook our dinner. I had to get away from the impression of her working in the kitchen of this little home, as if this was our life now…our life together.

Curses, we'd barely confessed our love for each other, and now we cohabitated? In this tiny walk-in van of just over a hundred square feet? My bedchamber was larger than this.

But what were our options? We were on the run. We were fugitives, nomads, renegades. We fled toward Fantasy, but was it safe there for us? Would I see my family again? What would happen to the duchy?

Maybe the long car ride and lack of food in my stomach influenced the bile that rose through my throat. There was barely any space for me to kneel beside the toilet and regurgitate. This water closet took the "closet" part literally. No, my closet at Ruezdad was larger than this. When I managed to turn around and put my correct end to the toilet, my knees wedged against the wall.

Horror, I'd thought "roughing it" meant moving out of the castle for university and work in Shigaqua. I loved Anita, sure, but I had a hard time imagining a Happily Ever After like this. Maybe others could do it, but not me.

Curses, I was still spoiled by my inheritance. You could take the royal out of the castle, but you couldn't take the castle out of the royal.

The limited ventilation of the water closet didn't help my sour thoughts.

I cringed with embarrassment as I stepped back to the main area—hallway/kitchen/bedroom/dining room/garage. "Can we open the back door?"

"I don't advise it," Anita said, stirring the soup. Maybe I should have picked a flavor with a stronger aroma. "Doesn't your mom's book say something about not going into the woods at night?"

"Yes," I grumbled, "but I'm not going out into the woods, just opening the door." Technically, that still broke a Haunting survival rule, but we weren't in Horror, and I would go stir crazy if I remained cooped up in that little space.

Pulling the handle to slide up the back garage door, I sat on the floor bunk and dangled my legs over the back ledge. The air was fresh and chilly enough to wake my senses.

Anita joined me, with two large bowls of soup. I took one off her hands, and we sat on the edge together, staring into the dark woods as we ate. Not that I expected gourmet cooking from a can, but the broth had a slight metallic after-taste. I needed something else to distract my mind and found an easy subject.

"So…about Stryker—"

"Aeron, stop, please." She breathed heavily, struggling with an internal war. I took her hand for light encouragement. "I'm sorry; I don't want to keep secrets from you. I want to tell you, but…I'm scared. What if it makes you hate me as much as I hate myself?"

"I couldn't hate you," I whispered. "Trust me, and I'll know I can trust you." Regardless of what my father said.

She bit so hard on her lip that I feared she'd draw blood. She nodded and took a deep breath. She let it out slowly and began, "Stryker…trained me. He rescued me as a child and took me in." Was he a father-figure to her then? "He raised me, taught me everything to survive in the wilderness and to be a good hunter. He taught me the ways of society, how to mimic others, how to act for certain results from people."

She paused to sniffle. "He sent me on Missions to steal papers from politicians, to infiltrate gangs… and to kill the corruption. I thought I was making the world a better place." Her eyes began to glisten, and she blinked rapidly to clear them. "He enrolled me at Arrowhead and told me to learn as much as I could…to get close to people, but not to make friends. A week before the new year and graduation, he came to visit. It was my first time seeing him since enrolling. I'd missed him so badly. I wanted him to be proud of me."

She swallowed hard, and another tear escaped. "He asked me what I'd learned and whether I could finish the Mission. He ordered me to eliminate the director and anyone who would defend him… Essentially, he ordered me to kill everyone."

"Just like that?" I asked. "He asked, so you obeyed?"

Tears flowed freely down her cheeks now. "I didn't want to…but he said it was for my safety and for the good of the world. He said I'd understand when it was all over, but—I don't! Were they creating their own assassinations without clients? Were they plotting to overthrow a government? Were they building a secret army to take over another genre? I don't know, but I can't stand the thought that I murdered innocent people—people who called me friend!"

Fat tears rolled down her cheeks, and I took her in my arms, stroking her hair back with my hands. She choked down her sobs and sniffled for a few minutes before she continued, "Even still, I hardly remember it all. I just remember the numbness. I left the base covered in blood and scratches as it went up in flames. Stryker patched me up and congratulated me. He said he had one more Mission for me. Next thing I knew, I was screaming awake in the hospital with no memories at all."

"Anita," I whispered into her hair, "I'm so sorry you went through that. I'm sorry for asking you to relive the memories, but thank you for trusting me with the truth."

"I don't deserve your kindness, let alone your affection."

She did, and also Arrowhead's mercy. But her words gnawed at me. "Did you… Did you love Stryker?"

"As a daughter to a father." Thankfully, she didn't make me wait as long to answer since every breath of silence ached. "He taught me about romance, mostly about how to use it against others. But he never showed me mercy. I knew nothing of love…until you."

CHAPTER 13

After finishing dinner, I cleaned our dishes while Anita prepared for bed. The sink was a mess from Anita's firepit and barely large enough for a single plate. Without electricity, the water's temperature ranged between cold and frigid. I returned to the open back door to gain some space and cool my frustrations.

Here, I thought I'd acclimated to the life of a middle-class civilian by washing my own dishes these past ten years. Nope. I still had a long way to go.

I stared at the wide-open, dark, and mysterious forest, missing the familiar forests of Margen with their mythical creatures, fairies, and glowing foliage. I missed Sam and my parents, wondering if Arrowhead and/or Thriller agencies had contacted them. They didn't need my troubles on top of Grandfather's.

Anita stepped out of the bathroom, dressed in a black set of long pajamas. She shivered in the night air. "Burr. Somehow, it seems colder here than in the city."

She pulled out a tube of lip-balm and grazed it across her lips. Such a simple thing. It wasn't shiny or even colorful, but it drew my eyes to her soft lips.

Noticing my attention, she gave me a sad smile. "We need to close the door for the night. Sorry. You're not claustrophobic, are you?"

I didn't think I was, but the last few hours in this van made me doubt. "I should be fine once I'm asleep. Did you want the top or bottom bunk?"

"The top bunk is mine," she said matter-of-factly. Then Stryker had always slept on the bottom bunk. I didn't love the idea of sharing an imprint with that man, but it was better than sleeping on the metal floor.

I stretched my arms out and yawned. "I'll take the night watch."

She stared at me for a moment before it clicked. "Right. Well, *that's* handy."

"I know; it's kind of awesome." I smiled and slipped between the blankets. "But my spiritual friends might be the cause of the extra chill in the area. And I apologize in advance if they make too much noise or too many disturbances. It takes time for me to enter the Spirit Realm, so if you don't mind taking the first shift for two hours, I can take the rest."

"Only two hours? Sure, no problem."

As much as I wanted to stay awake and spy on Anita, I closed my eyes and began my sleep routine.

"Aeron?"

I debated whether or not to answer. Her small voice broke my sleep concentration, though the fact that Anita's voice was small concerned me.

"Yes?" I asked.

"Thanks for believing in me."

"Of course," I said. "It's what partners do."

She went quiet again, and I restarted my sleep routine.

"Aeron?"

"Yes?" I sighed.

"I love you."

I smirked back. Alright, that was worth the routine interruption. "It's about time. I love you, too."

"Good night, Aeron."

"Good night, Anita."

Lying directly below the woman I loved made it difficult to clear my mind for sleep. It didn't help that my spirit friends were already gathered around us, causing air drifts without direction, faucets to leak, and boards to creak.

With each disturbance, Anita remained invisibly still in her bed. Not even a creak of readjusting on her mattress or rustle of her blankets.

Before I knew it, I drifted as a spirit from my body. Floating in the middle of the room, I found Anita hunched against the wall with her eyes closed. I smiled at the thought that she'd dozed off. Agent B from Arrowhead sat beside her, analyzing her with no concern for personal space.

"I think she can sense me," Agent B said, poking her finger through Anita's ear.

Anita's eyes snapped open, completely alert and focused. Supernaturals, she was incredible.

"Agent B?" I asked. "Did you link yourself to Anita—er, Agent Moreno?"

"As a temporary assignment," she said. "I need to know who she really is."

"You and me both," I muttered. I knew who she could be, but was that enough?

Stakeouts were quite different in the afterlife. First of all, I didn't grow tired. Second, I could float around and follow people without alerting anyone of my presence. Third, I had supernatural friends to help me. Neil stayed by my body, ready to poke me awake if necessary. Daphne and Fredrick had gifts to transform into owls to scope the world naturally from above, and Trevor had the gift of presence, to sense people within a fifty-meter radius. There wasn't much left for me to do except talk among the spirits.

"If you're hanging around," I said to Agent B, "what are your gifts? I know you have the gift of multiplying yourself. What else?"

She sniffed and eyed me with a debating expression. Finally, "I can make myself visible among the living for a brief time."

I considered that and the ways it might help us against Thriller. More importantly, "Do we know what Arrowhead is planning?"

"You gave them the slip for now, but they'll eventually discover Agent Moreno's storage unit and find camera feeds of you two driving out of town with this van." The agent nodded with impressed approval of the rig. "Still, it wouldn't be hard to switch out the license plates, add some brand-name decals, and slip under the radar for a month or two."

"A month or two?" Far too much time to spend running with targets on our backs, yet not nearly enough time to clear Anita of her crimes. Curses, could I clear her? She'd confessed her guilt to me, but she'd acted under orders and would take everything back. Whose orders? Maybe if I could learn more about her commander, then I could pin the bulk of offenses on them instead.

How was I supposed to do that while on the run and without resources? Was this my new life? Dodging bullets, sneaking between alleys, and speeding out of town in an off-grid mobile home?

No, I needed to return home to Ruezdad and warn my family of Arrowhead's threats. I needed to be there for my family during Grandfather's passing. I needed to support my father and mother in their coronations. Either as their heir or simply as their son, I wanted to help them to take the next step.

Considering everything I knew about Arrowhead's resources versus Ruezdad's security, I had little doubt; my family and I would be safe in Ruezdad. Anita would need to take some extra precautions, but I imagined some scenarios where she could hide, escape, and fight off any spies who managed to sneak through the castle's security.

We spent the next day taking turns driving south through back roads. Anita estimated that Medical, Thriller, had fewer police running around than Legal, Thriller. Indeed, I spotted more hospitals and local care stops than police departments as we skirted around suburbs and small towns. While the scenery was quaint, I couldn't shake the prickling sensation that someone was watching us. I hoped it was just my spirit friends.

Each time we stopped for gas and fresh food, Anita warned me not to trust anyone.

"Keep your hat on and look down to hide your face from cameras."

I mentally cringed as instructions from my childhood teachers reprimanded me, "Keep your chin up. Face people directly. You are the Earl of Margen. Be proud of who you are, then no one can bring you down."

Anita must have seen the hesitancy on my face as she gave me a downward stare. "I know you can go undercover. Use your investigating skills to snoop around unnoticed. Pretend you're an average Joe who had a really hard day at work, and you're weighed down with heavy thoughts."

Alright, I could do that. That last part didn't require pretending.

I listened and obeyed as well as I could, worrying that someone would follow us or call in our location to the authorities. Every time I spotted a helicopter (hospital colors or not), I watched for operatives to jump down to apprehend us.

On our third day of driving, I could feel our destination nearing. The borders between Sci-Fi, Fantasy, Mystery, and Thriller were hazy at best, but the air grew lighter with each passing hour toward the Mysterious Mountain Range.

"What about now?" Anita asked for the third time in so many hours. She must have been bored as I drove. "Are we far enough into Fantasy that the traveling candle will work?"

"Traveling via candle near the borders is risky because the borders are constantly shifting. We were able to take it to the Urban airport because we'd started in Margen. Candles use more magic to ignite the journey than to end it. We need to be sure we're solidly within the bounds of magic before lighting the candle, or it might malfunction. And trust me, you do not want to be around magic when it malfunctions. When we see mythical creatures, you'll know it's safe to use."

Anita sighed, but turned her attention to the windows, as if she hoped to spot a mythical creature through the trees. At least the walk-in van would continue working as long as we were in Urban, Fantasy. It would sputter to a stop in Fairy, but we could ditch the shoebox on wheels and travel by candle long before then.

With a strong inhale, Anita asked, "Where should we go?"

I frowned. Was it not obvious? "Margen. I need to warn my family."

"You can warn your family without seeing them in person."

"We'll be safe in Ruezdad."

She frowned back at me. "We'll only endanger your family by going there."

"My family's already in danger, but if they know what's coming, they can prepare. I have full faith in my home and fam—"

"Aeron, we're fugitives. We don't have homes. We have safehouses and hideouts."

"Sure, and my safehouse is a castle on a hill in the middle of a city." I shared an ironic grin, but she didn't smile back.

I tried lightening the mood by turning on the radio. Being near the borders, we had a wide variety of music and talk shows, but most of it was fuzzy with static.

An hour later, I needed to pull over to relieve myself. It took some convincing, but Anita let me walk around the outside of the van to stretch my legs and breathe.

"Agent Renolds?" I asked the open air. "If you're here, please take Neil to my home in Eimad of Margen. He's familiar with the place. Neil, I need you to contact my father. Warn him that Arrowhead is going to investigate them and let them know that I'm on my way home. You can give them this location, and they'll be able to map my route home. I hope to come by candle as soon as—"

I cut off as a faint light drifted between the trees. When the light moved like a swarm, I smiled.

"Anita?" I called back into the van. "You need to see this."

She was at the door before I even finished speaking. "What is it? Do we need to leave?"

"No, no. Come here," I said, reaching for her to join me outside. Confused and weary, she let me wrap my arm around her. I pointed at the glow that grew brighter between the trees. "Look."

Anita narrowed her eyes, then gasped as the first batch of lights flew into sight.

"Are those lightning bugs?"

"What? Bugs of lightning? That sounds scary."

"No." She frowned, too concerned to understand my tease. "Like fireflies."

"Flies of fire sound no less frightening."

A yellow-orange light zipped up to me, while a murky brown light bounced in the air to Anita.

"They're emotion fairies," I said. Anita flinched back from the tiny brown humanoid before her face. "Careful, don't spook them."

"Fairies?" she asked, her voice breathy with wonder. She slowly lifted a hand to the fairy as it changed to a light pink and blue.

"They're originally from Faenor, Fairy," I explained. "But their influence and abilities have been spreading into other kingdoms lately."

"Why are they called emotion fairies?"

"They feed off the emotions of others," I explained. "Don't worry, it's commensal. We aren't affected. But they prefer positive emotions over negative, don't you?" I asked a bright yellow fairy that zipped by. He zipped by again to nod in agreement.

The fairies swarmed in a slow circle around us, one or two coming closer for quick inspections. I analyzed the fairies that approached Anita. They changed color as they absorbed her feelings. The murky brown fairy that represented Anita's confusion was replaced with the soft pink and blue of wonder. My own yellow-orange color of delight shifted to a thoughtful soft orange.

"There are so many colors," Anita said, her mouth almost as wide as her eyes. "The way they change is magical."

I grinned. "Keep complimenting them. They like it."

"They're…mesmerizing and beautiful."

The fairies closed in a little, flattered by her honest awe of them. Their closeness encouraged me to tighten my arm around Anita. Her multicolored eyes changed shades with each rotation of the fairies. The colors sparkled around her, adding the soft yellow of pure joy to her soft pinks and blues. She glowed like a kid on their birthday.

Some of my fairies shaded to a deep pink. Curses, even the fairies could tell that I was enamored with Anita.

Her kaleidoscope eyes met mine, and she grinned. A true grin of pure joy with none of her former stoicism. "I never knew the world could be so beautiful. Thanks for sharing this with me, Aeron."

Her fairies morphed into shy pink, bold purple, and…deep pink. My heart beat wildly with excitement and courage. Our gazes locked and drew us in. I wanted to be colorblind as the fairies burst with color and light. I decided to close my eyes instead.

A bear roared.

My eyes snapped open in time to catch the fairies flinching into a shocked blue. They scattered like a firework explosion. A single grey fairy of dissatisfaction fluttered over Anita as I followed the sound of the bear call.

Wandering between the trees, a bear walked on its hind legs, wearing a martial arts Gi.

"Master Bahr?" I asked. What was he doing out there? The sentient bear raised his paw to his mouth to call again. He called my name. He was part of a search party looking for me.

"Thank the Supernaturals, we're saved. Come on, they'll protect us back to Margen." I started forward and waved for

Anita to join me. Instead, she remained and hugged her own arms. That wasn't encouraging. "Aren't you coming?"

"Aeron, I can't go back to your home. Thriller will know to look for me there. Even if you hide me away for the rest of my life, they'll hound you and your parents…and Sam. Oh, they'll either hate her or want to recruit her."

I cringed. "Who's to say that won't happen anyway? You can't protect us by running away, but I can protect you in Margen."

She shook her head. "I can leave clues to make them chase me and leave your family alone."

"What are you saying?" I asked, nervous about her answer. "I thought you wanted to be together?"

"I do," she said, pleading with me to understand. "I don't want to leave you, but I can't go to Margen. Please, don't you see? Your family will be safer if you stay away too. We can't go back to Margen."

"We?" My nerves grew. "Anita, my family needs me."

With a small puff of determination, she met my eyes. "You said our pasts don't need to define us. We can choose who we want to be. Did you actually mean that?"

"Anita—"

"Come with me, Aeron. We'll go anywhere you want. As long as we're together, I don't care. We'll *be* anyone we want."

"Anyone?" I asked. "Anywhere?"

"Yes." She grasped my arm with desperate hope. The pleading in her eyes said that she saw no alternative for a future together. But I had to believe we had a chance.

"What about a son of a duke in Margen, Fantasy?"

Her face fell. "I thought you didn't want to be your dad's heir?"

"I…it's not my dream job, but running away isn't the answer. We'll be safe in Ruezdad, and as Margen's Earl, I'll have the influence and resources to fight back. I was raised, trained, and schooled for politics like this."

She stepped back, lips trembling and eyes glistening. Curses, I'd made her cry.

"Aeron…please. Come with me. I don't want to leave you. I don't know who I'll become without you."

"Then stay with me!" I said. "You are who you choose to be—you always have been! You have the freedom to choose. I don't. Don't you see? Everything's been ripped away from me. All the choices I made for myself—living in Mystery, being an investigator—"

"Loving me?" she added.

"Yes," I whispered. "Yes, I chose to fall in love with you."

"A choice you couldn't make as a future duke. They'll rip me away from you too. Because I'm not royal, or noble, or even a proper citizen of any land. I'm a renegade labeled as a terrorist. That's why the only way for us to be together is to run."

I hated how right she was. Bringing her into Fairy as a refugee already added insult to injury toward Thriller's hunt for her head. But I couldn't completely abandon my parents, my sister, Master Bahr, the Beckers…everyone. Maybe if I convinced Anita to stay, I could figure out the rest later.

The next shout from Master Bahr came closer, and the whirring of helicopter blades grew from the distance. That wouldn't be my Fantasy friends, but it had a searchlight… Thriller?

Anita also noticed the helicopter and started toward the van. I grabbed her wrist to keep her with me. "Wait—"

"We don't have time to argue," she said.

"Anita, I forgave you for the past you didn't choose. Can you forgive me for the future I can't choose? We're adults with rare skills and abilities who serve justice. So let me do my job to serve you and bring justice."

A single sob broke from her mouth before she lunged for me, grabbing me by my lapels and smashing my lips with hers.

I wanted to hold her there with me forever. I wanted to kiss her with the sweet passion of our previous kisses, but the emotions were wrong. This wasn't a kiss of acceptance and oneness. This was a kiss of frustration, of begging for the sensation of oneness and rightness, but instead feeling pushed away.

My answer hadn't been what she wanted, but I didn't know how to make it right. What had she expected? That we'd run off to some green hill in Childrens and live off the land? We couldn't live Happily Ever After out of go-bags and always looking over our shoulders.

She released me and squeezed her eyes shut. "Justice will have me killed. My only hope for mercy is to run away."

"Anita—"

"I'm sorry, Aeron." She grabbed a pack from her van and pulled out my slightly used traveling candle. "If only your enduring optimism wasn't one of the reasons I love you."

"Anita—wait!"

She struck the wick, and the area flashed white. The light signaled to the searching group, and they found me within a minute. I didn't bother meeting them halfway. I couldn't move. Master Bahr reached me and wrapped his warm paws around my shoulders. I still felt cold inside. As the light had faded, so had my hope. Anita was gone again.

CHAPTER 14

Stupid! Stupid cursed bullbegger!

The more often I reviewed the events and conversation with Anita in the borderland woods that night, the more I cursed myself. I'd shown her mythical creatures to confirm our location in Fantasy, dumped a load of passion on her, then gone cold into duty-mode.

Stupid, idiot, dolt!

Still, I smiled at the memory of her last words to me: "I love you."

She loved me too. She'd kissed me back. She wanted me to join her in hiding.

Hiding. I grimaced at the thought. If her only hope was to run, then it was all the better that my recognizable face didn't accompany her. I was famous in Fantasy, Horror, and Mystery. She was Novel's Most Wanted. What place could she have with a marquis? What kind of future could we have? All the better for me to remain and search for a way to clear her name. Even if she didn't see the possibility of making peace with Arrowhead, I had to try.

My grandfather's health was like a rock tower; steady, balanced, and stable enough to last a few weeks, but one bad blow would knock him over. I needed to be ready for that blow.

With a heavy heart, I realized my next step was to officially close the Visionary Investigations Agency. Better to rip off the bandage quickly while my grandfather was in stasis.

"You're leaving already?" my mom asked the next morning at breakfast.

My father shared her concerned expression. "You just got back. And you have yet to report on your visit to Thriller. All we know is 'Beware of Arrowhead,' from Neil's message."

My mom shuddered at the mention of my poltergeist friend. I thought about sharing the whole story about the tour of Arrowhead, discovering Anita's past, and running from special operatives, but I didn't want to sour my parents' opinion of Anita. They'd never let me bring her to Ruezdad again if they knew about her past.

Keeping it to the basics, I explained, "My partner remembered her past as a former special operative and…she's ashamed of the person she was, but Thriller wants to condemn her for it. Possibly me too because of my connection with her. I'll explain everything once I have more information. In the meantime, just keep Ruezdad fortified from strangers—especially from Thrillers, and don't believe anything they say about Agent Moreno. That's not who she is. The woman you met—Anita—is her true self. I just need to finalize some business with my PI agency. I'll return before the week is over."

I wished to tell them more, but my ominous warning would make my mom prepare for anything and everything.

My father gave me a hard stare as if to read between my blurry lines, but relented with a grim nod. "Do what you need to do."

"And return as soon as you're available," my mom added.

"No promises to be right back," I said, quote-mashing her brother's Haunting Survival Book. My sister pouted and hugged me with all the strength of her thin arms, then the duke didn't wake when I held his hand and said goodbye.

With a verbal slap on my wrist for losing my last candle, our royal magicians reluctantly bestowed me a new one with demanding stares, reminding me of their rarity and price. A quick match sent me back to the border of Fantasy and Mystery with my Noir roadster. I lived for every second during my drive, knowing this would be my last time in the vehicle. I'd need to sell it to a collector to ensure its proper care.

Before I left the Mysterious Mountains, though, I added a stop in my route. Truth Locke Johnson currently lived in the area, caring for her ailing mother.

As it was my first time traveling to Truth's current residence with her parents, I was grateful to have specific navigation instructions. One never knew what to expect in the Mysterious Mountains. Much to the annoyance of those behind me, I slowed around corners and around the estimated location of the trail.

They probably blamed my old-fashioned car, thinking I didn't know how to take advantage of my roadster's high speeds. Honestly, I was a little nervous to speed beyond the legal limits after the car chases in Thriller.

I drove especially carefully across an old wooden bridge to a peculiar lot. Gardens of fungi, herbs, and crystals edged the rising hill up to a house that screamed of Hauntings. I blinked up at the house with its black shingle walls, sharp-angled roof, narrow windows, and colorful smoke rising from its chimney.

I checked the address three times to confirm my location. Thankfully, the best confirmation walked out to the porch wearing a colorful dress of kaleidoscope patterns, bulky jewelry, and a big grin.

"Aeron?" Truth called to me.

I turned off my engine and walked over to meet her halfway up the hill. She reached to take my hand for a shake, but I wasn't about to fall for that trap again. Besides, "We know each other better than a handshake." I wrapped my arms around my retired boss for a hug.

She laughed. "What brings you out here? Do you need my help with a Case?"

"Not exactly," I said. "I thought you should be updated on Ani—Nita's situation."

Truth's eyes went as big as saucers. "Oh? Where is she? Oh…"

With Truth's ability to see people's characters and possible futures, she probably already knew half of it all. I asked, "Can we talk inside?"

"Sure, as long as you don't behead my mama or papa."

I frowned, vaguely recalling her description of her parents. Her adopted papa was a vampire, and her mama had dog-like tendencies.

"They're, er, tame, right?"

Truth laughed and led me up the hill to the house. "They won't bite."

"I'm holding you to that," I said. "But I've met enough tame vampires and werewolves in Fantasy to put a little trust in you. Is Micro home?" I asked, referring to her husband, Michael.

"He's volunteering at our local library but should be home in an hour or so. My mama is in her room upstairs. Papa's in the kitchen, preparing lunch. Will you eat with us?"

"As long as it doesn't involve blood," I half teased.

She scoffed. "No blood. My papa's the type of vampire breed who can keep his humanity with a regular overdose of garlic."

Indeed, the moment we stepped into the house, the scent of garlic bombarded my nostrils. Hey, if it dulled the teeth, I'd tolerate it.

Ricky Van Pier turned out to be a real gentleman and every ideal of a generous father. He served us spaghetti (with extra garlic in the sauce), cracked dad jokes (especially about his curse), and seemed genuinely proud and grateful for his adopted daughter.

"Truth and Micro have been lifesavers around here. Shasta," he said, speaking of his wife, "had the energy of a poodle pup until this last year. She could keep this old place and this old man—" he gestured to himself "—from becoming a bloody mess."

Truth gave him a sad smile. "It's been hard to see her slowly wither, but…that's life."

He nodded. "This is the life I chose. I could have avoided this pain of losing Shasta, enjoyed supernatural strength and immortality, but even if I could go back, I wouldn't trade these past years together for anything. If you'll excuse me, I need to take this plate up to Shasta and let you two catch up. Holler if you need anything."

Truth flashed him a quick departing smile before she turned to me. "Speaking of life choices, tell me about Nita. All I know is you two went to Arrowhead, then I got a call saying to 'call this number if she tries to contact' me. What happened?"

"They called you? What else did they say?"

She waved her hand without a care. "Some threats about them knowing if I withhold information from them, which made me say, 'If you know I know something, then you already know, and don't need me.' That put them in a stupor long enough for me to hang up. So, come on. Answer my question."

I sighed and told her. Everything. About the facility tour, the memorial wall of plaques, Anita's moment of remembering, and her escape.

"She fled?" Truth asked.

"They called her a traitor named Agent Linda Moreno. Half of the plaques on the wall were because of her. They were out for blood."

Truth had listened quietly to my recounting, but at this point, she picked up her knitting needles. She usually knitted when pondering deeply about a tough Case.

"Do you want me to keep going, or do you need to think?"

"If there's more, then keep going."

"They followed me after I left the facility, but I managed to lose them before booking a vacation home that night and ditching the VIP sports-car. That poor, beautiful luxury. But I wanted Anita to feel safe to reach out to me. And she did. She found me at the house, and, er, then we ran together until we reached Fantasy. Then, she took my candle to teleport away, leaving me to be found by my guard and transported back to Margen."

Truth narrowed her eyes at me. "You're not telling me everything." I struggled to keep the blood from my cheeks. She must have noticed as a smile grew on her lips. She accused, "You kissed her, didn't you."

"She started it," I defended.

"Finally!" Micro shouted from the other room.

Truth laughed in her husband's direction. "I wondered how long you'd spy on us. About fourteen minutes? Come in, Micro. The game is up."

Truth's husband entered the room. His grin was the widest feature on his lean figure. His narrow-frame glasses didn't help the image of the man looking like a living incarnation of graphing paper.

"All I'm gonna say," he said, plopping down beside Truth, "is that it's about time."

I lost the fight against the blood rising to my face.

Truth smiled, but it was the same sad smile as before. She knitted faster. "You two are an odd couple."

"Said the kettle to the teapot," I returned.

"What do you mean? Micro and I are a perfect couple." She and Micro grinned cheerily at each other.

"You're a Gypsy PI raised by a fake vampire and fake were-wolf." Turning on Micro, I added, "And you're a vanilla human, record-keeping nerd. All compl-i-mentary character-istics, but not exactly compl-e-mentary."

"And you're a future duke," Truth rebounded, "and Nita's a supposed murderer. Obviously, opposites attract. We help balance each other and encourage one another to learn more while supporting their interests." She shared another adorably gag-worthy smile with her husband. Her smile dampened as she returned her focus to her knitting. "For you and Nita, your opposites are both good and bad."

"What do you mean?" I asked.

"How many times did I warn you not to get romantic with Nita?"

"Enough that I lost count."

With a long exhale, she set aside her knitting. "She's chosen the harder path. I'm proud of her for it, but…it's going to be rough for her. Especially since you've chosen your wider path."

I squirmed and rubbed my hands together, remembering the times Truth had read my past, present, and possible futures through my palm. "You knew this would happen? That's why you warned us not to fall in love? You knew Anita would become a fugitive, and I'd need to step up as my father's heir, making us incompatible?"

"I saw in Nita's palms a dark and deadly past of betrayal. I didn't know the specifics, but I kept an eye on her, first for the security of others, then for my own curiosity as she became a new person without her past. Your future, yes, has a high probability of you returning to Margen to fulfill your birthright, because, despite your qualms about it, you will be a good duke."

I blinked. Truth—my former boss and a woman I trusted to know me better than I knew myself—believed I'd be a good duke. There was something oddly comforting and resolving in that.

She continued, "Nita's future, however, was evenly split between returning to the person she once was or choosing to continue as the person she became. I can't say whether it's from our influence or simply from time passing, but the longer her amnesia lasted, the more likely she would choose the second option." She swallowed. "I almost didn't want her to regain her memories, but I knew Special Ops would find her eventually, and she needed her full memories to survive their attacks."

"You knew they'd attack? What do you know about them?"

Even as I spoke, a woman's hoarse voice barked from upstairs. "Truth? I smell a lot of visitors outside."

Without questioning her mother's odd dog-like instincts, Truth pulled her husband to the floor. "Get down! Papa!"

"I know!" he called back from the kitchen. If he moved, he was deadly silent about it. Micro, Truth, and I hunkered on the living room floor, waiting for the attack. I drew my Colt Detective Special and rested my other hand on my side emergency holster, ready for anything.

Except the doorbell.

I frowned at Truth and Micro. Crawling to the main entryway, I spotted a man's silhouette standing at the front door. He rang the doorbell again.

"Truth Locke Johnson?" he shouted from outside. "We know you're in there. We just want to talk. We recognize Earl Aeron Fromm's vehicle here and would like to speak with him too."

Truth cursed with a string of Latin as Micro scoffed. "I could give him a four and one-thirty-two."

I had no idea what he meant by that, but Truth shook her head. She shouted toward the doorway, "Arrowhead is a company of liars and spies. How can I trust you to talk civilly when you have us surrounded?"

"Shasta Van Pier can sniff us out, right?" Quieter, the man outside muttered, "Men, back down. Your presence has been noted." Calling through the door, he said, "I will have my men retreat. Now, Truth Johnson and Earl Fromm. By the law you have both sworn to uphold, it is required of you to turn over any and all information you have about your former partner, Agent Linda Moreno—or as you once called her, Nita Incog."

I shouted back, "I already told you everything I know. She's a changed woman. She regrets her past and chooses not to kill anymore."

"You're a fool for believing that, Earl Fromm. She has played others for far longer than she played you. She's dangerous and must face the consequences for her crimes."

"Mr. Arrowhead," Truth said, "I swear on my reputation as a private investigator that the woman you're looking for hasn't visited me or contacted me."

"Will you swear on that same reputation to inform us of future contact?"

"Only if you'll shake hands on it."

I blinked at Truth. Bold move. She'd learn his personality, loyalties, and lifestyle in trade for no contact with Anita.

The man behind the door stood silently in thought. Truth made no secret about her ability. If he'd done any research at all, he'd have known the risks of shaking hands with her.

"I'd have a written contract."

"No deal," Truth said. "I'll only do a handshake agreement."

"That's unfortunate," he said. "Speaking of reputations, the young Earl's is in jeopardy. As the one who escorted Agent Moreno into a private facility, he may be viewed as a co-conspirator. Not to mention, he harbored her within his own one-bedroom rental house, then traveled with her in a van for three days. Such cohabitation is frowned upon among Fantasy royalty, isn't it?"

Truth raised an eyebrow at me. Curses, I needed to warn my parents about that condemning gossip. I snarled at the door, "If you know about the van, then you know it had bunk beds. All of your public reports are lies that withhold the full truth."

"I don't think you understand your situation here—"

"Better than you do," Truth called back. "You dropped legalese, but your agency views itself as above the law. So, speaking above the law, do you know how many or what kinds of fungi and crystals you passed to reach that doorstep? Do you know how many are poisonous or explosive? Within the law, you're trespassing on my parents' property. I've told you the truth, the whole truth, and nothing but the truth, so unless you want me to start making up stories, I have nothing left to say to you. If you cause any undue harassment, please remember my friends in high places, including but not limited to the young earl currently in my house. And while my papa may be civilized, good luck dealing with his buddies of the court."

"Then," the Arrowhead agent said, "it seems that we're at an impasse. We can't come into Fantasy with guns blazing, and you can't use magic in Thriller."

I growled. "You underestimate our abilities."

"Oh, we did our research before inviting you to our facility. We know all about your family's gifts. You're still no match for us."

I flashed a smile. "We'll see."

"I suppose we will."

The man didn't wait for more before pivoting and marching away.

I called up the staircase, "Mrs. Van Pier, are they gone?"

"I smell…they're leaving. It's a little hard to tell. Their sweaty stench is the kind that lingers."

I cringed but gave a victorious fist bump to Truth. "Good job. I think they'll leave you alone until you give them a reason not to."

She nodded seriously. "They'd better. But now you have all the more reason to be careful. I can warn Nita—or Anita—not to contact me, but she needs a friend, Aeron. More now than ever. Promise me you won't give up on her?"

"I promise." Despite my Uncle Oz's warnings never to make promises, I didn't even hesitate.

"Shake on it?"

I laughed but took her hand. I didn't have any secrets from my former trainer and working partner.

Her hand paused as her distant gaze went wide and her cheeks reddened. "Oh, um, yeah. So that's how you parted with Anita?"

I snapped my hand back. "How far back did you go?"

"Far enough. But I think it's time you headed to Shigaqua. You have a lot to do before returning to Margen in time for your grandpapa's passing."

My gut clenched with worry. "Do you know how much time he has left?"

"I only sensed him through your own touch, but it doesn't look good. Go."

CHAPTER 15

I didn't wait for a second urging. I ran to my car and gunned for the road.

Almost immediately, a nondescript black sedan pulled in behind me and kept pace.

"Nuh-uh," I said, staying the course. "No way you're egging me into a car chase this time. Even if I plan to sell it, I'm not trashing my own car. My grandfather gave me this car, and he's on his deathbed."

If they wanted to tail me, I would make it the most boring job ever. I slowed my speed well below the road limit. Turning on my hazard lights, I slowed even more to a painful crawl on the highway. "Let's test their patience."

They followed me, turning on their own hazards as cars blared horns to weave around them. I turned on my radio and sang along with the jazz bands. Blues songs were annoyingly relatable, so I skipped channels as they became clearer and I neared Noir's border.

Checking the car model of my tail, I recognized it as one that would function within the older technology boundaries of

Noir. The oldies radio station clicked into clarity as I officially left Cozy. I smirked, knowing that within the retro state of Noir, no other cars could beat my LXK120.

"How about one last run?"

I patted the dashboard of my car, turned off my hazards, and then slammed down on the gas. This baby could go from zero to sixty in ten seconds, but I hadn't started at zero. It had been a long time since I'd tested the manufacturer's claim of its top speed at a hundred-twenty miles per hour. I suddenly wished I'd pulled down the convertible hood as my engine roared. I'd been too afraid of guns and bullets, but those fears became dust as I quickly lost sight of my tail.

Not that it mattered. He wouldn't be lost for long. My car had a custom paint job and was far too recognizable. Also, I didn't have a getaway car or safehouse. They'd find me again at my house, office, or my other favorite haunts. Still, it felt good to lose the tail and push my car to its limits one last time.

I made it to Shigaqua in record time. Considering my many errands and tasks to complete, I went first to the Visionary Investigations Agency.

The bakery on the main floor left a lingering scent of pastries, encouraging me to inhale deeply as I stepped through the door. The small office smelled like memories of naps on the leather couch, early mornings with cheap tea, and of Anita and Truth as they wore the same blend of herbal perfume.

Even though the double-room office was smaller than my bedchamber in Ruezdad, it felt large compared to the walk-in van I'd shared with Anita. It was especially large as I stood there, utterly alone.

I needed to make some phone calls and file far too much paperwork to officially close the business. I found a note in Neil's handwriting by the landline telephone. It simply said, "Anita" over a list of numbers. A phone number? It was long enough to be a cellphone number. Did I recognize that area code in Cozy?

"Neil," I said, supposing he was nearby. "You planted a phone on her? How did you find her? Where is she?"

A pen on the desk floated over to a notepad. Neil slowly scribbled, "Agent B."

From Arrowhead! Of course, she'd linked herself to Anita! "Where is she?"

Neil simply answered with a question mark. He didn't know. Even if Agent B had linked herself to Anita, if Anita traveled by candle, Agent B might be able to follow, but sending word back would take time.

I took a deep breath and hoped Anita was still in a land that allowed the technology of cellphones. Only one way to find out.

I dialed the number. Typical of Anita, she answered on the second ring.

"Who is this?"

"Don't hang up," I said as hello.

"Aeron? How did you—did you plant this on me?"

"In a sense."

"Did you just claim 'innocence?' Because I'm not buying it."

"No—I mean—" I flustered as my plans crumbled. "Where are you?"

"Can't say," she said. "They might be monitoring. I'm hanging up before I'm tracked."

"No—wait—"

"Aeron, don't follow me."

"What? Why not?"

"Because I don't deserve to be happy, especially with you."

"That's a terrible lie. Besides, don't I deserve to be happy?"

"More than anyone," she sighed. "But you've deluded yourself. I can't be anything more than a traitorous spy, and you can't be anything less than a future duke."

"Anita—"

"I love you, Aeron, but this is goodbye."

"Anita!"

My phone deadlined.

I stared at it for a frustrating second. When she didn't call back, I did. It went straight to voicemail. Cursed woman. I was trying to help! Growling, I hung up and dialed another number.

"Ross," I said, "I need you to track a phone. It's probably off now, but it was activated only a minute ago."

"Oh, hi, Ross," my friend in the Shigaqua Police Department jested. "It's been days since I've talked with you and loaded a bunch of Cases on you because of some 'family emergency.' I could call and demand a favor, or I could ask how you're doing first?"

"Ross, there's no time! I'm trying to find Anita!"

"Oh, it's A-nita now? Don't nicknames typically shorten a person's name?"

"Ross!"

"Fine, fine, Digger," he said, using his personal nickname for me (which was longer than Spade). "Send me the phone number, and I'll see what I can do."

"Can I send it to you in an encryption? Anita seemed worried that my phone was tapped."

The other end was silent.

"Ross?"

"Yeah, um…maybe we should meet somewhere? Maybe that place where you and I played chess? You were really at your peak there."

"Sssure," I slurred. I'd never played chess with Ross. Was there a code in there to throw off listeners? I was at my peak… was it on a peak? A game of chess… Ah! "Can you be there in half an hour?" I asked. The sooner we met, the less time spies would have to set up.

"Yeah, see ya there."

I took the scenic route with multiple turns and quick straight-ways to Chesapeake Beach. Ross waited for me on a dock bench. He wore his usual fedora to hide his greying hair, and his suit coat hung loosely on his lean figure. I grabbed the Shigaqua Times from a nearby stand and sat behind him, facing the other direction.

"Were you followed?" he asked.

I flipped open the newspaper to hide my lips from any spies and pretended to work on the crossword puzzle. "I took precautions."

"Good," he said, "because you can't trust anyone, even me."

"Huh?"

"The Special Ops recruited me. They knew you'd find Nita first and knew you'd ask me for help. So, they asked me to keep tabs on your findings and report to them."

"Ross…" I didn't know what to say. I felt betrayed and honored at the same time. Yes, he was helping my antagonists to spy on me, but at least he was honest with me about it. "What did you tell them?"

"Nothing they couldn't have figured out on their own, eventually. But be careful, Digger. If Nita had been on that phone call for two more seconds, they could have tracked her. She's safe as long as she's lost. And you're safe as long as you don't go looking for her."

I sighed. "Easier said than done. She came to me."

"She—what?"

"They didn't tell you? She was waiting for me at my Thriller vacation rental. Operatives attacked us. We traveled to the edge of Fantasy, then things became complicated, and she ran away."

"You mean you saw her? Did she attack you?"

"No! She—" My cheeks heated to think of what she did—what *we* did; instead. I wished for the time to relive those kisses. "She asked me to run away with her, but I can't. I can't have my family at war with Thriller."

Ross cursed under his breath. "What difference does it make?"

"What?"

"Why do you think they assigned me to watch you? They know you're involved with her, Digger. Even now, they're probably watching you, listening to this conversation. You might not be on the run with her, but they'll be watching your every move, waiting for you to reach out to her and lead them to her."

"Aren't you supposed to be the one watching me?" I asked. "Why are you telling me this?"

"Because who's to say they aren't watching me too? I'm going to do my job and report your activities, but if I don't catch you doing anything suspicious, then what can I report? Just be careful, okay?"

"Alright," I said.

"I can't offer you resources, but I'll try to pass on any information I hear."

"Sure. As long as I find her before they do."

We sat in silence for a moment, each too busy with our own thoughts.

"So," Ross said, "she asked you to run away with her? That's as good as an elopement, ain't it?"

I blushed and scoffed. "It was the only way she could see us being together. My spirits managed to slip a phone into her pocket. When I called, she asked me to stop searching for her."

Ross grunted. "Probably because she knew you'd lead the Thriller agents to her? Did she say anything about her past?"

"Yeah, Ross, she's afraid of the person she once was. She hates what she did. If she could redo it, she would."

"Repentant, huh? How do you know she's honest?"

"I know," I said. "She hid truths from us—whether in ignorance or on purpose—but I don't think she ever lied to us. Also, she had a master. I'm willing to bet that everything she did—every death at her hands—was by his orders. I don't have the first clue of who he is, but he's the one who should serve justice for the Arrowhead massacre."

"No clues at all to his identity?" Ross asked.

I debated whether to give him Stryker's name, but Anita's warnings made me hesitate. Besides, it was probably an alias, anyway.

"All I know," I said, "is he was in Thriller during the attack at my vacation rental. He has sniper skills and taught Anita everything she knows. Poking into him might make us targets, so any research will need to be off the books and taken with precaution. I won't blame you for stepping out of this Case."

Ross leaned back to drape his arm across the back of the bench. He tapped his finger near my shoulder in a strange pattern. Was that Morse code?

"Sorry, Digger," he said. "They're watching me. You're on your own this time."

Meanwhile, his finger tapped, "I-M I-N."

I inhaled deeply, grateful for the support.

"I understand," I said. "Thanks anyway. Maybe you could help me with this crossword instead?" I twisted in my seat to show him my newspaper and note that said, "Stryker (Anita's master) wanted her to eliminate Arrowhead's director and any supporters. Why? What was Arrowhead doing or planning three years ago to make Stryker orchestrate a revolution on Dec. 31st? Finding Stryker's goals and motivation may help."

Ross nodded thoughtfully. "I see where you got confused. The answer for seven down ain't *sensitive*. It's *tentative*. That gives you the T for two across, in *opportunity*, right?"

"Ah, thanks." I twisted back around. If I understood correctly, he could tentatively get a look at Arrowhead's sensitive historical files, if he found the opportunity. Such research shouldn't be enough to raise flags and suspicion. It would only scratch the surface of Stryker's schemes, but it could give us a lead. It was a start.

CHAPTER 16

Back at the Visionary Investigations office, I took a late afternoon nap to reconnect with the local spirits. As much as I would miss my own house with my own kitchen, I was also going to miss that office and couch. Unlike my childhood home of multiple generations or my rented house in the suburbs, this building was entirely my own. I'd purchased the condemned lot of Margaret's old house, then—with her permission and supervision—demolished it to build the commercial kitchen on the ground level with stairs leading up to two offices (including Visionary Investigations), then a condo on the third floor. I'd gifted the penthouse to Truth and Micro as their wedding present. Despite their frequent visits to Truth's parents, they loved that home and this windy city.

An hour before dinnertime, my spirit rose from my sleeping body. My usual Mystery friends greeted me, including Neil Martin, Margaret Norris, and Sherlock Holmes.

"Welcome," Sherlock Holmes said. "The poltergeist has informed us about the incidents in Thriller. Personally, I'm more curious about the incidents in Fantasy. Does your grandpa's failing health mean you're leaving Mystery?"

I released an unnecessary exhale. "Yes. Anita and I have disbanded Visionary Investigations."

For some reason, Margaret turned her face away as I spoke. Did she take that to mean that I was abandoning her?

I finished with, "It's time for me to hang up my trench coat."

"And pick up your glitterati Fantasy cloak," Neil said with a smirk. At least I wouldn't be saying goodbye to him.

I appreciated his tease with a smile, then turned sadly to the others in the room. "Thank you, everyone, for your help, efforts, and tireless work—"

"I believe the words you're trying to say," Sherlock said, "are 'You're welcome.' You gave us a voice. For decades, we struggled to use our gifts in ways that appropriately influenced the living without breaking the laws of mortality. With you, murders were solved, the lost were found, and Cases were closed."

My cheek felt wet. A glance at my sleeping body confirmed my tears. "Thank you."

"Nah-ah," Sherlock chided. "You still haven't said the correct words."

I chuckled. "You're welcome. I'll visit as often as I can and gladly make your voices heard again."

Unable to clap, many of the spirits hummed with pleasure. When Neil hummed, his voice reverberated with a sound heard by the living.

Everyone seemed satisfied and pleased...except Margaret. I could guess why.

I floated over to her. "Margaret? Are you alright?"

She turned to me, bewildered. "Alright? You spend three short years here, then suddenly, you say goodbye?"

"We did a lot in those three years. Do you regret them?"

"No, but…" She sniffled. "Is that all we were to you? A fleeting hobby to pass the time until you were called home?"

I eyed her. "Of course not. This was how I chose to live, and I'd continue to choose to live as an investigator, but after Truth retired, then my grandfather's declining health, and Anita's memories—"

"Ah, there it is. The real reason you're no longer keeping the agency."

I frowned. Her sadness had turned bitter at my mention of Anita. "Are you…jealous?"

"Hah!" she laughed humorlessly. "Me? Jealous of the time you spent with a fugitive? Of the dedication you give to clearing the name of a traitor? Of your stubborn desire for a woman who denied you for three years and rejects you even now? What do you think?"

I cringed at the truth of her words. "What do you want me to say? Is there anything I can say, anything I can do to help you understand?"

"At least say sorry!" She rushed up to me in one quick swoop.

I rocked back in surprise, then floated a step closer. "I'm sorry."

She froze as if her breath caught, but she didn't need to breathe. Her eyes drifted down to my lips, and her own trembled, full of desire and disappointment. She turned away. "No, you're right. There is nothing you can do, which means the fault is with me."

"Margaret—"

"I'm the one who's dead. You could never feel me, embrace me…kiss me as you did with her. Thank you for allowing me to help you with your Cases, but you should go."

I nodded. "I'll find someone else with a gift of awareness to help me find Anita."

That caught her attention, and I mentally cringed, realizing I'd accidentally manipulated her again.

She folded her arms and stared at me. "The gift of awareness is not a golden gun to solve your problems. When you asked me to search for Sponsor's number one man, you gave me his name, and I had a good guess that he was within the vicinity of Shigaqua. Even still, I could not tell you which of the three men I found was linked to Sponsor—which, as it turned out, none of them were, because the name you gave me was an alias. To locate anyone, spirits need to know the person's general whereabouts and their true name. Nita Incog is an alias. No spirit could find her with that false identification."

I grumbled about the limitations. "Her real name is Agent Linda Moreno." But she was last seen around the Urban border, near Medical, Thriller, before traveling by candle. She must have teleported within Fantasy, but that was days ago. She could be anywhere by now.

Margaret closed her eyes. She remained that way long enough to make me worry.

Finally, her eyes blinked open. "There is no one in Shigaqua by the name of Linda Moreno. I can search beyond the city limits, but it would require more time."

I sighed with gratitude and resolve. "Thanks. I hadn't meant to ask you to search for her, but I appreciate your help. You're a good woman who deserves better."

The lovely spirit turned her face away and bit her bottom lip. "I always admired you from afar. Nothing has changed. Though any search assumes that her real name is truthfully Linda Moreno. If she entered the operations agency with the intent to betray them, then it is highly likely that Linda Moreno is simply another alias."

Curses, she was probably right.

"Thank you, Margaret," I said. "You really are a sweet killer-diller with dame moxie."

She shied her face away again, and I turned to the next order of business. The room was filling with Mystery legends, coming to bid me farewell. Neil nodded back at Margaret.

"That was a waste of her gifts. Anita could be anywhere. The only way we found her after she left Arrowhead was because she came to us. We need time to spread the word that we're looking for her, and you know how we can get distracted when we're not focused on our links. Be patient."

I groaned and felt my physical body clench my fists. I hated when "patience" was the answer. "What am I supposed to do? Without Anita, the agency is completely dissolved. I can't go back to living like nothing changed and solve Cases by myself, especially with my grandfather on the brink of death and putting me closer in line for the duchy."

Neil folded his arms and raised an eyebrow at me. "It sounds like you know exactly what you're supposed to do; you just don't like it."

I grumbled. "Sure, I'm supposed to return to Ruezdad, forget Anita, and forget my career as a private investigator." My chest tightened at the thought of leaving this all to memories.

John Watson frowned at me. "Why does your face say that all signs point to doom? Aeron, do you know why I'm linked to my family, not to Cases as Sherlock is?"

"Because you actually have descendants to fawn over?"

"Yes, I suppose that helps, but that was one of the big differences between Sherlock and me, one of the reasons we made such a good team by balancing each other. Sherlock gave his life to his Cases. I gave mine to creating legacies. I had my family, and I wrote about Sherlock's Cases to give him one too. Aeron, you have already created a legacy for yourself as one of the best paranormal investigators of Noir, but what of the legacy of your family? If you close your eyes right now and imagine the people you love the most in this world, who will you see?"

I thought about that. I saw Anita, Sam, my mom and father, and even Neil in the background.

"Now," James said, "who among those people needs you most?"

"Anita," I said, "but I can't do anything to help her—she won't let me help her."

James nodded slowly. "Then who needs you now?"

My parents. My father was about to lose his father. Even if I didn't have the best relationship with Marquis Theodor Fromm, his pain would cause me pain. We'd need each other's support through the grief.

I swallowed. "I don't know if I'm ready to be a marquis."

James smiled kindly. "You're already the Duke of the Dead. You have served us well in Mystery. It's time that you served your family."

After waking, I grabbed dinner at a local Mystery restaurant and then headed home. I called my realtor to end my rental contract at the end of the month, then posted a For Sale ad for my beloved car on a corkboard in a bar frequented by car enthusiasts. I had a few offers before the day ended, letting me scout the potential buyers as a spirit. With a heavy heart, I sold my car to a well-off car salesman in the morning. I had a hard time finding a taxi to take me back home because of the color of my skin. Racism was one thing I was glad to leave behind in Noir.

Throughout the day, Neil left me little notes about people watching me. Special Operatives, no doubt. It didn't matter. I didn't do anything incriminating. Just making a big show about packing away my life and settling all scores in Mystery. I didn't bother visiting the police department to say goodbye. Detective Ross was my best friend there, and I expected to stay in contact with him between our searches for Anita and her master. Maybe I was supposed to cut ties with him while operatives watched over his shoulder, but…when my friends were limited, I wanted to keep them close.

With most of my home assets packed or sorted, I went to the office to start the process of closing shop on the third day. I'd just hung up with Nancy Peters at Shigaqua's Personnel Records Center when my phone rang on its hook.

I answered, "This is PI Spade of—right, we're closed, but I can recommend you to another agency depending on your needs."

"Aeron?" my mom said. "Are you coming back home soon?"

"Oh, hey, Mom. Yes, I'm just sorting some final details."

"Can you hurry home? Konrad's health took a turn for the worse, and the healers haven't found a solution."

Icy worry encased my heart. I could probably ask Truth to finish closing Visionary Investigations. She could call me via my glow ball communicator in Ruezdad if she had any issues. My own issue was my sudden lack of a car. I couldn't drive down to Middle Novel anymore.

"I can catch the next flight to Urban," I said. "Can someone meet me there with a transportation spell or candle?"

"I can have it arranged in the next hour."

"It's a three-hour flight, so the soonest I can make it is five hours with the international flight."

She sighed. "That will have to do. With the way things look right now, I can only hope that he'll hold on long enough."

I swallowed back my emotions. "Hey, I'll see him again, even if it's on the other side."

She breathed a soft laugh. "I suppose. See you soon. Travel safely with my love."

"Thanks, Mom. I love you."

I didn't bother hanging up properly as I tapped the receiver to start a new call to the airport. Luckily, they had a flight going out that afternoon. I checked my pocket watch to confirm my two hours to clear out of Mystery and drive—no, take a cab—to the airport.

After several more phone calls to alert my mom of my ETA and to delegate the rest of my work, I headed home via the elevated rails (missing my car), to pack up my limited possessions. The place was still a mess, but I could hire a cleaning crew before my official check out at the end of the month.

It was only my second time going through the airport, so I didn't have a lot of experience to compare, but the airport security seemed more…wary of me. Had Thriller put a BOLO on me? They checked some paperwork and called over their supervisors before letting me through.

The wait to board was agonizing as Neil kept a running tally of how many agents he spotted spying on me. At least one of us was having fun.

It came as no surprise when I found my first-class window seat and a muscled man took the aisle seat beside me. He lounged, spreading his legs out, effectively blocking me in. He even pulled down the food tray the moment it was allowed just to prop up his paranormal Mystery book. We were on a plane with nowhere else to go. Did he think I'd ask for a bathroom break to sneak for a parachute and jump from an emergency exit to meet Anita?

I entertained myself for the first hour with more absurd ideas of escape that only Anita could probably pull off.

The plane shook with turbulence, and I gripped my armrest, hearing an unfamiliar "clink" as my fingers wrapped around the metal end.

What the Horror? There was a ring on my right hand's middle finger. It was golden and huge, like a championship ring. The center stone was a one-centimeter oval cut of a blue-gray gem that reflected better than mirrors.

Hold on, I knew this ring… Oh, Horror.

That was no random stone. It was a fortudo gem from the Faenor mines, strong as dragon scales. The last time I'd seen this ring was on my father's hand. It signified the next heir of the Margen Duchy, transferable by magic.

Cursed condemnations of Horror and bullbeggers.

I spent the rest of the flight mentally cursing and panicking. The potential operative next to me offered a barf bag and calming music. As if it was the flight that terrified me. No, the flight would be over in a matter of minutes. What terrified me was the rest of my life.

My mind was in a daze as we landed and I exited the terminal. I didn't even notice whether the potential operative followed or kept watch of me. I was relieved to find my father waiting at the exit with his three-inch fairy guard, Captain Greenblade. With the ring as my only source of information, there was the possibility that my father had somehow been killed. The ring could only be removed by the wearer or by death, meaning someone had died, and (given the options) I was glad it was my grandfather who was ready for that next great adventure.

My father was the same man as the last time I saw him only four days ago, but he looked the part of a duke. He was probably the only one ready for the transition, yet his eyes were dark with circles and red from tears. He stepped forward to wrap his arms around me.

Before I could consider the unique and tender moment, my father whispered in my ear, "We need to return to Ruezdad. Our auras are dark here."

I leaned back, surprised. "What endangers us?"

Rather than answer me, Father beckoned to his guard. "We can talk at home. The candle?"

The fairy slipped out a traveling candle as if from thin air. The new duke's eyes went wide. "Captain! Hurry! *Igni—*"

The magic spell to light the candle wick died on his lips as he twitched. His eyes rolled to the back of his head, and his body went limp. I tightened my embrace to keep him steady when something pinched my neck. Captain Greenblade fluttered around, waving crazily for medical aid. He moved so quickly, I barely saw him…Or…no, my vision was going blurry.

My knees hit the floor with just enough pain to alert my senses of how weak I felt. My father slumped out of my arms. Was that a feather in his neck? How was the floor rushing up to meet me?

The little captain grabbed the feather in my father's neck and began to pull against it, but people in black attire—including my flight seat neighbor—rushed in around us. The fairy used his camouflage ability to disappear as someone swiped for him. My vision went dark as multiple memories of my childhood played déjà vu. I remembered people grabbing me, kidnapping me, locking me away, and then sacrificing me for the sake of capturing power.

A deep, instinctual dread warned me that this time, my captors had a similar agenda to sacrifice me for the sake of capturing Anita.

CHAPTER 17

I woke to the sound of someone urgently shaking my shoulder and whispering my name.

As soon as I twitched awake, my father swore with gratitude to the gods.

I breathed deeply to assure him of my life but lay still and kept my eyes closed.

"Aeron, wake up. I believe we were abducted and taken to Thriller since my magic refuses to function. I met you at the Urban airport hoping to ask you for the details of what happened in Thriller. Ever since your trip there, agents from Thriller and Mystery have been spotted throughout the duchy and even Faenor. Before returning to Mystery, you had warned us that this might happen, though left out the exact reasoning. Now that they have abducted us, I need to know everything. Aeron? Are you listening?"

"Shhh," I said with my eyes still closed. "I'm trying to remember my dream."

"Your dream? You visited the spirit realm?"

"I was left unconscious long enough. I remember following our bodies in a black utility van through a city that reminded me of Londinium. They brought us to an abandoned veterinary clinic with a basement for surgeries."

"Fantastic," Father muttered. "Our auras are currently a middle-shade. While we may not be in imminent danger, we are far from safe. Do you think they want a ransom?"

"More likely, they want information." Unfortunately. A ransom could be easily resolved with money. Information, however, came with torture.

I blinked hard and sat up. A single caged bulb lit our little prison from overhead. Stretching my fingertips across to touch both sides, I measured our cell at 10x6 feet. We sat on thin mats glued to the floor in a concrete room with no windows showing outside, but a floor-to-ceiling mirror covered the wall beside the full-metal door leading to the next room. It was of a higher and thicker quality than those I saw in Mystery, but I still recognized the two-way mirror. They could see us, but we couldn't see them. This was confirmed by two cameras in opposite corners.

I stretched my muscles after the poor sleep. There had been more details from my dream that I couldn't remember. Unfortunately, I didn't have my pen and notepad for Neil to write notes for me.

Unsure if our captors were currently listening, I whispered to my father, "I don't think anyone besides the dead knows where we are. Captain Greenblade used his camouflaging ability to stay with us until we reached the border of Fantasy, then he was forced to fly back or be captured."

"Good man," Father whispered back. "He would have gone back to Fairy to alert others of our situation. Aeron, what happened at that Thriller facility to cause this abduction? Even our Mystery friends have warned us of their agencies sending

178

spies and investigators to Margen. You told us that your partner remembered a condemning past, though—from my understanding—all that Arrowhead seeks is justice. Why do they assume we stand in their way?"

"Because they want to kill her," I growled, "but she's not the person they think she is. They've shot at me too, with intentions of pinning my death on Anita. They've announced my connection with her over public broadcasts and have threatened to slander my name because I refuse to cooperate with them."

My father blinked, confused. "Please explain. Why would they want to kill a combat specialist who worked with private investigators to solve crime, and why would they spy on our home and abduct us because of your connection to her? Who is she to warrant such a response from both Thriller and Mystery?"

"She was, er, utilized to carry out a mass attack before her amnesia. But she's a changed woman who hates what she did. She's currently a refugee in Fantasy…somewhere…I think."

"A refugee?" My father stared, and his eyes became demanding. "From Thriller and Mystery? Aeron, I think you mean 'fugitive.' Your investigation partner is hiding from the states that have their fingers in the most pots. Mystery has jurisdiction everywhere except Horror and Sci-Fi, and Thriller's espionage takes care of the rest. Your connection to her has jeopardized the safety and balance of the entire duchy. I suggest severing your ties to her for your own benefit and that of the people of Margen."

I mentally planted my feet and ground my teeth. "Father, I love her."

Instead of showing surprise, my father moaned and slid his fingers up to his temples. "Aeron, forgive me for my lack of enthusiasm. I lost track of how many times you have confessed feelings for a woman."

I cringed. "It's different this time."

"Yes, it is. This time, you are the Marquis of Margen—" he gestured to his old ring on my finger "—and she is a renegade fugitive. Do yourself and the entire duchy a favor and leave her."

"Father—"

"Please, Aeron. You are still young with a promising future. I too thought I knew love at your age and even proposed marriage. Thankfully, her true character was revealed before I forged a bond with her, and I later met your mother. It seems that you were given the same grace to learn Nita's true character before it became too late."

I already knew her true character, and it wasn't what Thriller claimed. I remained firm, determined to keep my position and convince him, but recognized Nita wasn't the root of our disagreement.

"Who would be your heir if I abdicated?"

Father sighed with a groan. "Aeron, please. Now is not the time for—"

"Who, Father?"

He eyed me with a pained expression of grief mixed with disappointment. I turned away, unable to face him. "Hypothetically," I mumbled.

"I have limited options," he said. "Samantha would be the obvious answer, though I fear that the duchy would cage her. Despite Pansy's encouragement for Samantha to explore her options, your sister seems content with her marriage arrangement to Prince Thunderhelm that would elevate her to Queen of Erebor. Another problem comes with the people's slowly dying prejudice that women should not lead. Its death is not quick enough. Even when my aunt, Queen Alóvera, ruled, there were too many who wanted her younger brother—your grandfather—to take the throne. If Samantha were to be duchess, she would need to marry quickly to have a duke by her side." Father grimaced. "I could bestow Margen on your Aunt Godiva, except she is already settled in Sword and Sorcery with her husband's duchy. The next option would be Dunstan, though…there are reasons he serves as Lord of Divinity, far away from Vluz and the town he accidentally destroyed."

"Limited options," I muttered, failing to banish memories of my dream of Sam unhappily taking my place as heir, of her slowly fading into silence and darkness as her blurry-faced husband took over. "What am I supposed to do? I don't know how to be a marquis."

Father sighed again, but this time he sounded more tired than disappointed. "I said before: you know more than you think."

I grumbled again to disagree without actually saying so.

"Yes," he said, accepting my grumble, "you abandoned the people to serve those in Mystery. Except your experiences of working among the people, serving beside law enforcers of Mystery, and of ensuring justice for individuals and the community—these experiences will build your credibility, the people's trust in you, and your capabilities as you apply them and continue doing those same duties for Margen. I believe you will make a wonderful duke, one whom the people can be proud to call their own."

Really? "Would you be proud of me?"

His pained expression returned, but this time his disappointment seemed introspective. "Aeron, I am proud of you. Your mother and I are both proud of you. Pansy even has the Shigaqua Times newspaper delivered to Ruezdad to cut out articles mentioning you and your team. No matter your location—in Noir or Margen—you help people and do a bull-begging good job at it."

I almost smiled at his casual slip of Margen's harshest curse in regard to my work. His confidence in me lightened my heart, almost enough to ignore the breaks and leaks from Anita's departure.

"I need to help Anita."

"Your investigation partner? You can, and you may. Though I suggest you do so as a *friend* from Margen. You can help her all the more with your influence as marquis."

I swallowed that truth with a hard gulp. I couldn't be with Anita as a future duke, but I could help her better. I could accept my place as my father's heir…for Anita's sake.

I steadied my breath and readied my words to declare my love for Anita—to proclaim her true character as honorable—but our cell door opened. An ambiguous person layered in black stepped inside. They wore the same face-covering mask and glasses as the agents during my tour. This one was an inch or two shorter than myself, but I wasn't willing to bet on myself in a fight against them.

Father stood tall and demanded, "Who are you? Where have you brought us, and for what purpose?"

"We'll be the ones asking the questions," they said with a voice modifier. "Sounds like you're finally ready to talk. Which of you would like to go first?"

When neither of us volunteered, they tsked. "Since there are two of you, here's our offer: one of you will stay here, unrestrained, and simply tell us what we want to know. The other one will go to the next room for…persuasion." The floor-to-ceiling mirror shifted and became a window, letting us see a surgery room beyond, including a second agent clad in black and a gurney with restraints. Lovely.

They continued, "As long as the one here refuses to talk, the one in the next room will be…punished. If you give us what we want, then you may both go home without harm. Honestly, we don't want to hurt you. We should be on the same side as we have an international security threat on the loose."

My insides squirmed with the thought of Thriller's methods of "persuading" and "punishing."

"Interview my father," I said, volunteering to be the punished one.

My father's eyes shot to mine. "Aeron, no! Let me…" He paused as his eyes analyzed the space around me—my aura. I doubted he'd stay quiet to protect Anita over me, but he didn't have as much information about her. Also, I was younger, stronger, and more resilient to pain. Hopefully.

Turning back to our imprisoner, Father squared his jaw. "Yes, I will talk."

I cringed but trusted my father to make the safest decision for both of us.

The second agent entered our cell. How would they punish/torture me? They'd need to catch me first.

I'd trained under my mom and one of Margen's greatest self-defense masters since I could walk, then learned newer methods of combat during my university years in Procedural. Over the years as a private investigator, I'd kept up my health, strength, and flexibility.

And I never stood a chance.

I'd never challenged Anita to a sparring match, even in practice, knowing she'd kick my butt. This agent was no different. Every step I made to dodge or escape, they countered and changed tactics faster than I could react. They restrained me, pinned me with my stomach on the floor, then—pain.

I wasn't even sure what they did. All I knew was the piercing sting originated on the back of my neck. My father shouted for me and answers, but I couldn't hear his words beyond my screams.

By the time the pain finally waned, my captor had hoisted me onto the gurney in the other room, trapping my ankles, wrists, neck, and torso in metal clamps. My captor growled low over my ear. "Your father isn't the only one who can talk. Tell us where to find Agent Moreno."

"Go to Horror!" I spat.

"Is she in Horror?"

"I don't know, maybe. I don't know where she is." The truth of my own words sank in and morphed my pain from anger into despair. Curses, it was true. I could tell them everything, and it wouldn't matter, because I honestly didn't have a clue where Anita was.

"I don't know where she is!" I shouted. "I wish I did. I know you heard me earlier. I love her. But she left me. She doesn't want me to even contact her. She's hiding from me too. Don't you understand?" I cried. "If I knew where she was, I'd be with her!"

The agent grunted and picked up a surgical tool for analysis. The cell door opened as my father's interviewer motioned over the other agent. Somewhere between my heavy breaths and tears, I caught their low words.

"Did you get anything from the younger one?"

"Only pathetic desperation. He says he doesn't know where she is."

My father's interviewer grunted with disappointment. "The detectors say they're telling the truth. They really don't know where she is."

My interviewer released a long and slow breath. "Fine. Release the new duke but keep a detail on him. He can still lead us to her if he managed to fool the equipment."

"And the younger one?"

The agent walked up to me and stared from behind their mask and tinted glasses. "You love that traitor?"

"Yes," I said.

"Then you believe that no torture or means of coercion would persuade you to tell us where she is? I can keep you barely alive for years. I can torture you in too many ways for you ever to become accustomed to the pain. Would you like some examples? I can start by torching you inch by inch. Then, I can remove pieces of you that aren't…necessary, starting with toenails, then toes, then fingernails, then each knuckle until your hands are knubs. We can remove organs and—" they glanced down "—other parts. Of course, you'll be awake for all of it. Is that what you want? Is that backstabbing girl worth that much pain when she obviously abandoned you?"

With each description and method of torture, my insides squirmed, involuntarily imagining the agony that would come. Would they torture me even if I had nothing to tell them? I gritted my teeth and let my squirming show as anger. "I can't tell you what I don't know, but even if I did know, I wouldn't tell you."

"I see." They nodded. "Then he's stupidly in love with her. Very well. Tell me, Lord Fromm, do you know the tale of <u>The Man Without a Heart</u>?"

I gulped, recognizing the folktale.

"I expect you do," they said. "It's from your homeland after all. About a man who had his heart removed in order to live a life of fortune and misery. There are variants with giants and ogres who keep their hearts in eggs or boxes. I've always found Fairy's tales to be a little…unbelievable. Should we test to see if it works? Can a man who's so in love and so heartbroken live without his heart?"

They pulled over a tray of surgical tools and picked up a scalpel. As if it knew they spoke of it, my heart pounded from the attention.

They continued, "Because if you're truly in love as deeply as you say you are, we may torture you endlessly and fruitlessly. However, we won't need you to talk if we have your heart in a box. A heart that will never stray. A heart that will lead us…right to her."

Oh, curses. Would my Fairy-native heart work like a compass, pointing to the one I loved? I figured it was a fifty-fifty chance—it either would or it wouldn't. My only hope was to die in their attempt to remove my heart.

The fabric mask covering my captor's mouth pushed up with their smile. "We'll let you think about that."

They turned away, but the other agent whined, "Can't we play with him a little longer? I want him to be haunted by this moment so he knows better next time."

A chill shivered through me with ideas of how they'd "play" with me. Yet, the chill itself was an odd reminder of my friends on the other side.

What a strange time and way to feel comfort.

I murmured a thought aloud.

"What was that?" my torturer returned to my side.

I repeated myself.

"Speak up, boy."

"You don't haunt the Haunted," I said, each word building my strength. "The Haunted haunts you."

My torturer hesitated just enough to show their doubt. "We'll see about that."

"Yes," I muttered. "We will. You've abducted and threatened the Fairy King's cousin and his heir. Grovel for mercy before we become enemies."

The agent bent down to hiss in my ear. "You made us enemies the moment you brought that *thing* back here."

"Your words, not mine," I said.

Then, the lights went out.

CHAPTER 18

My torturer swore, and my mind began to panic for a new reason. Darkness swallowed me like the Valley of the Shadow of Death. Like the time I'd been killed. No, I'd practiced for this. I forced back the memories from my childhood and focused on the present. The present where I was abducted—again. Where I was restrained and immobilized—again. Where I was at the mercy of hateful enemies of my family—again. Where I was in the dark—again.

This wasn't helping.

A door opened from across the room, but no light flooded inside as the next room was also pitch black. A new agent's voice rasped through the dark. "J. T. We have company."

"That traitorous monster?"

"Hopefully. We've set traps in case the rumors are true about her concern for the guy, but I don't think this is her work. My night-vision goggles aren't working."

"Neither are mine. We didn't lose power, just light."

Footsteps whispered away, but one of them cursed as they bumped into something in the dark. The door slammed shut, leaving my father trapped in the cell and me on the gurney. The silence turned my thoughts into screams by comparison.

Had Anita come to rescue me? But they'd set traps for her. I couldn't let her come for me, but my pathetic desperation begged for a hero. The voices from my past echoed through my brain, "It's never just a power-outage."

"S-stop," I muttered, closing my eyes and trying to focus on my other senses. I smelled sterilization, almost like my mom's medical lab/drawing room. I heard my father's muffled calls for me from the other room and my own breathing that came far too fast.

"Deep breaths," I told myself, but the pain in my neck and around my wrists and ankles kept me from relaxing. "Breathe in… Breathe out…" I coughed with the need for more air. How long would this power-outage last? It was extremely unfair that leaving me alone in a dark room had a stronger effect on me than the threat of torture.

A hand wrapped around mine.

"Who's there? Father?"

A soft, creepy, yet familiar chuckle wafted into my ear.

"Neil?" My relief was almost as surprising as his touch. My mom would never understand the relief I felt at discovering a poltergeist beside me in that dark room. "Did you see how they set in the metal restraints? Is there a button, switch, or crank?" The metal clamps popped open around my body, releasing me. My breathing still ran in panic-mode, but at least I could move and sit up. "You're a lifesaver. And, er, could you keep reassuring me with your presence by holding onto me?"

His hand went to my neck.

"Don't be weird about it," I scolded and waved my hand around as if to slap him. His hand moved to my shoulder, and

I thanked him. Careful in the dark and not wanting to make too much noise, I lowered myself to the floor. My quick breathing made my body shake as I considered how to wander in the darkness toward real freedom.

With Neil's gentle nudging, I found my way to the cell door. I opened it to the sound of my father cursing.

"Father?"

"Aeron? Are you alright? Is that Neil with you?"

"Yes, Neil helped me. How are our auras?"

"Light enough that I can see you both in this darkness." He proved it by meeting me at the doorway. "Though far too dark for my preferences. We need to escape this place."

"We need to hurry in case they come back."

My father scoffed with a little laugh. "If they come back, that would be a surprise. This is no mere power-outage. This is Dunstan's work."

"Uncle Dunstan's here?" On one hand, it meant our rescue team had arrived. On the other hand, it meant that a simple light switch or stepping outside wouldn't dispel the darkness. I measured my too-fast and too-heavy breathing and felt for Neil's hand on my shoulder.

Another hand rested on my other shoulder as my father spoke, "May I assure you; your aura is lighter than it was while those agents were present. Dunstan probably brought friends. We should hurry to help them."

"Agreed," I said. "Neil? Can you lead us out?"

His hand on my shoulder nudged me toward my left.

"Thanks. Father, follow us."

"Right. I count my blessings that I came to fetch you at the airport instead of your mother. Pansy would never follow the lead of a poltergeist through the dark."

Another agreement, though I expected my mom would know a little more than my father about how to take down a

Thriller agent. Even with Neil's directions, we bumped against corners and edges, fumbling our way from the room and into another void of space. He turned us, bumping me directly into a staircase going up.

"Is this the way out?" I asked.

Neil simply responded with a moan. Father said from behind me, "His gestures upward would imply so."

I fumbled for the stair railing and carefully crept upwards until my outstretched hand bumped into another door. It was locked with a keypad.

"Curse this magic-negating land," Father muttered. "I cannot use my magic to unlock the door."

"Neil?" I asked. "Did you or any nearby ghosts see the lock combination?"

"Even if they did," Father asked, "how would they tell you?"

"Neil can punch in the code…with effort. Just give him time."

Father scoffed with a little laugh. "I cannot wait to tell your mother how we were saved by a poltergeist."

I joined in with my own chuckle. "It's not my first time."

The door clicked with release, and I whispered a thanks to Neil. Again.

"Hold on," my father whispered. "I should go first to see if anyone is standing guard."

I answered by stepping aside and placing my hand on his shoulder to lead him forward. Leaning through the doorway, he placed two fingers on my hand and then shifted to point ahead. Two guards ahead?

I could faintly pick out their murmuring across the dark space. There were also echoes of gunfire from somewhere above.

With Uncle Dunstan's blackout ability to absorb light, we could have been entering a greenhouse and wouldn't have seen the difference. There was no breeze or sounds of wildlife, leading me to believe we were still indoors.

Neil's hand on my shoulder urged me to the side. Did he see our way out? I followed his lead, and my father followed our auras into another room. I held tightly to the door handle to silently slide the latch back, opening the door and then carefully closing it behind us.

"No agents in sight," my father whispered, but still seemed far too loud for my comfort.

The sound of wood sliding froze me. If there were no agents, who made that noise?

Father said, "Neil seems to be looking for something. He's making the motions of opening the drawers and pointing."

"Can you lead me to him?"

Father took the lead this time to slowly maneuver us across the room to where Neil was floating. His hand patted blindly in the dark. "This is a gun. Here." Untrained with the weapon, he handed it to me.

In the dark, I recognized the weight, shape, and material of the gun model. "This is my Colt Detective Special. This drawer must be where they stored our personal effects. Good job, Neil, for leading us to them."

Light returned with a blast, and so did my normal breathing. We stood in a simple room designed for storage that currently worked as an office and bedroom with military bunk beds, a computer desk, and several wooden drawers and filing cabinets. I found the rest of my Haunting emergency holster and effects in the drawer and quickly strapped it around myself.

Father, however, looked worried. "If Dunstan cancelled his blackout, he may be in trouble. Make haste. No, there are two guards back the way we came. The window? No, too dangerous…" His focus bounced between us and our sur-roundings, analyzing our auras and the safety of our plans.

I searched for an exit but found only the door we came through, a closet, and a small dirty window that had probably never been opened. Even with my gun and my shooting skills, I'd be lucky to catch one agent by surprise. Two would require a miracle. Could I separate them?

"Neil," I whispered, "could you create a distraction to make them check the basement?"

Father frowned. "That would alert them to our escape."

"Yes, but it'll give us a chance to sneak out and hopefully join up with Uncle Dunstan and whatever backup he brought."

Father studied my aura. He didn't outright reject the idea, meaning it wasn't a guaranteed failure, but his hesitancy gave me a clue to the dangers of the plan. There wasn't time to properly plan as gunfire continued to bark regularly from the floors above. Father turned to an empty spot beside the door and gave a nod. "Do it."

I smirked. Sometimes, my father's ability to see Neil's aura and location made me jealous. We stood by the door, waiting for the sounds of Neil's screaming distraction, then footsteps hurrying by and down the stairs. Had that been one or two sets of feet? Either way, it meant there were fewer agents in front of us.

I stood at the door, ready with my gun aimed ahead, as my father silently counted down from three and opened the door.

One agent stood directly at the top of the hallway, staring directly at me. He didn't have his gun up already, which let me shoot first. Barely.

My shot threw him off balance, shifting his bullet into the wall instead.

"Aeron!" Father cried.

"I'm fine," I said, "but the two shots will tell the agent below that we're upstairs and armed."

"We could lock the stairwell door from our side except that I expect that the agent below knows the key code to unlock it."

Probably. Grabbing the desk chair from our current room, I wedged it under the door handle to the basement stairs, effectively locking out the agent below.

"Good thinking. We must go," Father said.

We made our way down the narrow hallway as quietly—yet quickly—as possible, following the green EXIT signs. They led us to a stairwell and a set of elevators that I'd never trust even if we weren't in an abandoned building and I hadn't been raised by a Horror. Wondering where we were, I took a moment to scan the list of seven floors and services, including the basement vet clinic (The K9 Unit), a scratched-out hair salon (Business in the Front), an insurance agency (Bourne and Sons), and other businesses. Floors five and six weren't listed, which made me far too curious.

"There's a parking garage below us," I said. "I bet we can find and grab transportation from there."

"You want to steal a vehicle?"

I deadpanned my father. "They wanted to torture us. Laws won't condemn us for fleeing for our lives."

The future duke grumbled. "I never learned to drive automobiles."

Right, he only knew how to drive unicorns and pumpkin-turned stagecoaches. "You can leave that part to me."

Carefully opening the door to the stairwell, the gunshots from above became louder, echoing through the cemented well.

Too close for comfort, a conversation between mutated voices bounced down to us. "Did you get her?"

"I can't tell. She moves too fast."

Father's eyes went wide. "Pansy."

Oh, curses. They were shooting at my mom.

Of course, that had to be the moment that my uncle Dunstan decided to shroud the building with his ability again.

Darkness. My parents and uncle fought to rescue me… again. I remembered the bark of gunshots as my mom had fired on a whole pack of werewolves. The Valley of the Shadow of Death was sucking away my life again.

Stop! Stop it!

"F-Father? Neil?" I stuttered, needing their support. I needed to ground myself.

Reaching for where I remembered seeing the wall, I found its cold reassurance. A chilled hand slid over my shoulder again. Neil. His touch gave me the courage to move forward. I followed the wall into the stairwell and started downward to the parking garage. Father could see my aura and follow me, but before I could worry about going too far without him, the lights returned.

My father was nowhere to be seen.

"Father? Father," I whisper-shouted. No response. "Father? Theo?"

Curses, where had he gone? "Neil? If you can find my father, go to him. Keep him safe for me."

He responded with an unhappy chuckle. He'd obey me, but he didn't like it. Too bad. I had a gun, but my father was defenseless without his magic. His ability only warned him of dangers; it didn't protect him from them.

More gunshots from above. Right. Our goal had been to find Dunstan. Maybe if I found my uncle and his backup—including my mom—I'd find my father too.

Following the sound of gunshots, I made my way up the stairwell. The next floor was likewise abandoned, with an open floor plan leading to several offices around the edges.

I barely had the presence of mind to register myself as an open target before the gunshots began.

I didn't bother trying to shoot back. I dashed, dodged, and scampered. I made a mess of noises as I ducked back into the stairwell and up the stairs despite my uncle's survival book that said, "Never run upstairs to escape." There was an addendum to that rule, specific to Thriller, but I didn't expect a helicopter waiting for me on the roof. Winded from running up six flights of stairs, I reached the top of the stairwell to find the rooftop access locked. Just my luck. I stopped to crouch with a spin, aiming my gun back the way I came. Half a second later, a pursuer ran into view.

I fired a moment too late. They managed to duck behind a doorway before my bullet hit them.

Still, I had them pinned with my gun aimed at their one exit.

"Surrender," I shouted. "If you come out shooting, I'll shoot first. It's your move."

Nothing happened for three pounding heartbeats. Then—

The lights switched off with a click. Unlike Dunstan's pitch-black ability, light still filtered in from the connected rooms, but I lost my enemy's position.

Curses. "Good move," I muttered.

Not only was I left blind to their escape or shooting, but the fears of my past threatened to grip me, hold me, and paralyze me.

No, I could still see shadows. This wasn't the abysmal darkness of my uncle's ability or the Shadow of Death.

I rubbed my thumb against the metal of my gun, warmed by my sweating hands and recently fired muzzle. I tried to ground myself by focusing on my other senses of smell and hearing, but I was in a black void.

Good move, indeed.

Another voice spoke nearby. "Wrong move."

Before I could register the new speaker, painful groans followed a sickening sound of fabric and flesh being pierced and sliced.

The lights returned, and I found my uncle Dunstan, the Night Shade, at the switches. He wore his usual black adventuring tunic and cloak with its hood covering his dark hair. He and his signature copper short sword with its jeweled handguard were covered in blood.

CHAPTER 19

My uncle's emerald eyes squinted at me with mirth. "Oh, good. I half expected to find you crumpled on the ground, like this guy." He indicated the agent by nudging them with his foot. The agent struggled for breath and their weapons.

I frowned. "Crumpled from wounds or from my fear?"

"Either." He shrugged. "Glad to see your improvement on both accounts. What are we to do with them?" he asked, gesturing again to the injured agent. "I wasn't trying to kill them, but…it's hard to know exactly what I'm hitting in the dark. They need immediate medical attention."

"Agreed," I said. "Who else did you bring?"

"Your mom."

"That's it?"

He gave me another smirk. "Did I need to bring anyone else? Cousin Alun helped to teleport us over, but he's a bit busy with the Sci-fi-Western Boundary War. Besides, your parents and I rescued your sorry butt in Horror with no other help. I figured Thriller would be similar."

"You're fighting trained humans with advanced weapons instead of monsters with claws. Also, Horror gave you access to remnants of magic."

He grunted. "I was never any good at magic. Where did Theo go?"

"We were separated on the floor below. I thought he went looking for you or my mom."

My uncle cursed under his breath and then raised a small device for my inspection. "Alun also gave us this thing to plug into a computer somewhere and a phone number to call if we had any questions. Do you know what this is?"

"It's a thumb drive," I said, taking the device. "I used these during my university days in Procedural. Did he say what's on it?"

Dunstan shrugged. "Something to make Thriller hesitate before acting against one of us again."

That sounded like a good plan to me. "Did you see any computers in the areas you've cleared?"

My uncle gestured across the stairwell. "I cleared the top two floors, but no computers. Your mom should be on the floor below. I guess we need to find Theo before blowing this balloon stand. Will you be alright if I blacken our immediate area?"

I gulped, but nodded. He instructed me to take his shoulder and then absorbed all light within his reach. We could see the lighted areas beyond, but anyone looking at us would only see darkness. Reaching the landing two floors below, the door was absorbed by Dunstan's black hole as we headed for it.

"Neil," I whispered. "Can you scout ahead and distract the agents before we meet them? Have fun with them."

Neil chuckled darkly, making Dunstan's shoulder shiver beneath my hand. "By the gods, is this how you worked in Noir? What will he do?"

A yelp and gunshots answered. I smirked. "He probably gave them wet willies."

My uncle coughed back an approving laugh and then opened the door quietly. It was already shrouded in darkness on both sides, cloaking our entrance, but spotlighting the agent in the room. We entered an abandoned video-rental shop, judging by the looks of the shelves and remaining wall posters.

Dunstan's shoulder slipped away from my hand as he raced forward, absorbing all light from the room. The agent fired wildly into the dark. The bullets stuttered to a stop, replaced with screams. Light returned, revealing my uncle standing over the wounded agent.

Confirming the agent was down for the count, Dunstan spared me a concerned look. "Are you holding up despite the darkness?"

I coughed, partly gasping for air. The darkness had been brief enough, but the sight that greeted me after had threatened my composure. My teasing, mirthful, light-hearted uncle had severed and cauterized the agent's hands with his heated blade.

He wandered around the agent without concern and pointed at a dusty device with a large screen. "Is this a computer?"

"It's a TV," I said, not trusting my throat to expel only words.

He shrugged and walked back, grabbing my hand to place it on his shoulder as he passed me. "Next."

Right, don't mind me, your speechless and mortified nephew. He blackened the area around our bodies again and paused before entering the next room. "We made a pretty good team back there. Can your ghost friends help again?"

"I, er…"

A muttered curse and a woman's shout erupted from the other side of the door. Apparently, Neil hadn't waited for my permission this time. Dunstan took the cue for his entrance, but this time, there were two agents, and they were ready for us with guns aimed at the door. I ducked behind the doorway as bullets fired blindly into Dunstan's shadows. A slice and groan slipped between the sounds of barking guns. A grunt followed, then a sharp gasp that morphed into a high-pitched scream. Light returned, and I debated whether to check the damage.

"Aeron?" my uncle asked. "I think we found a computer."

I slipped into the room, finding two agents on the floor. One had taken multiple shots to the head and chest. Had Dunstan used them as a shield? The female screamed in jerking gasps from the pain of losing her right hand. To her credit, she still fumbled for a knife at her thigh with her left hand.

"Dunstan!" I shouted, drawing my own weapon and firing at the easiest target; her chest.

Her screams hiccupped, and she jerked from the impact. Her breath caught in her throat as her eyes slowly slid to mine, and blood soaked through her clothes. Forgetting the knife, her trembling hand went to her chest. Then it fell limp.

Curses… I dropped to my knees at her side. I'd killed her. I felt as if a piece of my soul departed with her.

"Aeron?" my uncle said through the fog of my mind. "She tried to kill us."

"But we aren't like them." We didn't live and die to complete Missions, like Thrillers. As Fantastics, we lived and died for Adventures. We weren't shadows who infiltrated, spied, and killed objectively. We explored, fought to survive, and accepted glory and fame for our victories. Feeling dirty and corrupted, I muttered, "I want to go home."

"Same," my uncle agreed, "but I think we hit the treasure trove of computers."

Forcing myself to turn away from the dead agents, I surveyed our surroundings. This abandoned floor might have once been a storage hall or warehouse with a large open space and scattered wooden pallets. There was an office desk with a computer tower and a wall of monitors displaying black and white camera footage. Half of them showed crippled agents, while others were empty. A figure blurred past one screen and into another, disarming and incapacitating an agent before they could react. My father followed at a safe distance.

"Looks like Theo and Pansy found each other," my uncle remarked. He narrowed his eyes at a screen of agents marching in a line down a hallway. "Bullbegger, that shows a floor above us. They must have requested backup from the rooftop."

Keeping the dead agents outside of my periphery, I let the urgency of our situation demand my attention.

"Can you hold them off while I plug this in?" I asked, jamming the thumb drive into the computer tower.

My uncle twirled his short sword and created another blackout around himself. "Be quick about it."

I pulled up the hardware file, finding a single program called "Virus." I smirked but hesitated to run it. Did I have time to download incriminating evidence?

Shots echoed through the stairwell as the new agents encountered Dunstan's blackout. I clicked through the files, searching for specifics, mis-clicking in my haste. Curses! I hated feeling rushed. Finding the right folder, I copied it to the thumb drive and then ran the Virus program.

It loaded with the slow growth of a major power-up.

Meanwhile, the gunshots halted. I considered going to the door to check on Dunstan before I noticed a gas seeping beneath the door crack. Curses, had they gassed my uncle and knocked him out? I couldn't open the door without inviting the gas inside.

"Neil? Could you check on my uncle and give me a moan if he's in danger, chuckle if he's fine?"

I shuddered with chills as he floated through me. A quick check back to the computer confirmed at least another minute's wait.

My parents and uncle fought to protect me, but I was a fully grown adult with my own training. Couldn't I do something to help?

"Spirits?" I whispered. "Who's with me?"

An owl hooted in reply. Daphne or Fredrick? The owl hooted again, but not with its usual call. One long hoot followed by three short. Morse code for "B?"

A light flickered from one of the large warehouse windows, distracting my nervous tapping during the download. I studied the source of the light, but it was a mere pinprick in the distance and night.

Neil returned with a short moan in my ear. Shoot. That meant Uncle Dunstan was unconscious somewhere. I couldn't interpret Neil's moan further to know if he needed my help. No, the best help I could give would be to complete this computer work.

The download finished, and I snatched the thumb drive from the tower as the owl gave five simple hoots. H-E? Or I-S? Or simply the number five.

Movement whispered behind me. I spun around and found myself face to face with a masked agent. Curses! How had they sneaked in? A hidden door?

"We don't want to kill you," they said with a voice modifier as they gestured to my chest. Looking down, I spotted three red dots of light. Aiming markers. Only one agent stood before me, but there were obviously two others unseen. How had they sneaked up without my noticing? Was there another entrance to this floor? Probably. I suddenly felt foolish for thinking I'd been safe or trained enough to face these guys.

Swallowing, I asked, "What will you do to me instead?"

"That's not for us to decide. It will depend on how deep your attachment to Agent Moreno goes, and if she has even the smallest amount of attachment to you in return."

I stared back, measuring my breathing. "Whether or not she cares about me, she's not dumb enough to fall for any traps you set involving me."

The agent tilted their head, amused. "People in love do dumb things. We've received several sightings of her in a nearby neighborhood. We expect she fell for one of our misdirections and went to another black-site, planning to rescue you. Agents are circling her position now. After everything you did to protect her, after all you've suffered and sacrificed, you can't save her."

I gritted my teeth, hoping it was a bluff while my heart panicked for Anita. If "B" stood for Agent B—who was linked to Anita—then that would confirm her presence nearby. However, if that was the case, I took a gamble and smirked. "There are five of you, right?"

The agent tilted their head slightly, questioning.

"They that be with me are more than they that be with you. Open your eyes."

The dots on my chest wavered, and the agent standing before me fell back into a defensive guard. Without turning around, I could guess what they all saw.

Agent B could multiply herself and make herself visible among the living. Even though she couldn't do anything physically to the agents, her presence comforted me. Because if Agent B was behind me...

The glass windows shattered, breaking the silence and our standoff. Thankfully, I wasn't the target.

The agent in front of me fell to the ground as if hit on the side of the head with an invisible rock. I took the hint to duck as bullets sprayed into the room. One of the agents managed to secure cover behind a desk, but the flurry of bullets tore it apart and then pelted them. I peeked around my hiding place to spot my rescuer by the flashing light of their firing gun…more than a hundred meters away. A sniper? They weren't trying to be delicate with their shots now, but that first one had been perfect.

The bullets stopped.

Before I could wonder if my mom could shoot that far, she appeared next to me. Only two seconds after the ceasefire. She was fast, but not that fast.

"Mom?"

"Aeron! Thank the Supernaturals."

"Literally," I muttered.

"Are you hurt?" she asked.

"No, thanks to—"

"Good. Are there any left alive?"

Groaning behind a pillar told us there was at least one. My mom shifted her revolver and turned her mother-bear scowl toward the survivor.

"Mom!" I grabbed her arm before she could use her ability to speed away. "They're human, not Hauntings. They don't all need to die. Besides, we need at least one alive to return a message to Arrowhead."

"Aeron, they abducted you and your dad."

"I know, but—"

"Pansy! Above!"

I barely had time to register my father's entrance and shout from the stairwell doorway before my mom blurred into her speed ability. She shoved my arm, pushing me to the side as bullets sprayed. They originated from an air vent in the exposed ceiling. Of course, only in Thriller were those vents large and strong enough to hide an adult human.

Bullets rained down from the grated hatch. I took cover behind a concrete pillar as my mom disappeared and Father hid behind the doorway. More shots fired through the window, but the sniper's view wasn't angled toward the ceiling. I considered shooting back but knew any bullets would be blocked by the grate.

"Agent B?" I asked between the smacking bullets. "Go to Anita. Warn her to get away before they catch her. Neil? Can you distract the shooter?"

A dark chuckle replied. I positioned myself in a crouch, waiting for Neil's distraction to rush out for a better shooting angle.

"Pansy! Wait!" my father cried from the doorway.

I hesitated. When had my mom returned? Did Father see danger in her aura?

A blur ran past me with a ladder in tow. Even with her speed ability, my mom was a target directly below the agent. Two shots fired before Neil screamed from the vent, sending echoes of his haunting screech up and down the metal tunnel. The agent shouted in return, halting the rain of bullets. The vent gate swung open as a blurred figure climbed the ladder and attacked like a shark from below.

The vent choked, then went silent.

My mom returned to normal speed as she groaned and slid down the ladder, crumpling to the floor.

"Mom!"

"Pansy!" My father and I shouted and ran to her side. An entry wound in her thigh bled furiously.

She gritted her teeth and snarled, "Page three; never get between a mother and her child."

I was fairly certain that quote was under the Common Courtesy section of her brother's Haunting Survival Book.

"Pansy," Father moaned, holding her close. "You said that you had no plans to die anytime soon. That was too dangerous. Without Neil's distraction, you would have been killed."

She narrowed her eyes. "You're saying a poltergeist saved my life? I'm…not sure how I feel about that."

My father chuckled. "We both owe Neil many thanks after tonight. I may explain after you receive proper medical attention." He smiled at an empty spot—where Neil floated? Then, graced his wife with a simple kiss of love and gratitude.

"Get a room," Uncle Dunstan said, supporting himself against the stairwell doorway like he was still waking up. Blinking at the bullet-ridden monitors and computer, he asked, "Aeron, you delivered the package?"

I nodded. "And retrieved my own."

"Good. We cleared the building, but I bet more reinforcements are on their way now. We need to leave."

"Wait," I said. I walked over to the shattered window and searched the distant skyline for the sniper's light. All was dark.

I released a slow and mollified breath. Had it been Anita out there?

I had to satisfy myself with the fact that she could find me if she wanted to join me. Turning away from the window, I searched for an agent who remained breathing.

The one that had spoken to me was definitely dead, but, to my amazement, the three hidden agents weren't mortally wounded. Still, I doubted two of them would ever walk or fire another gun. One was still conscious and twitching for a weapon. A threatening look from Dunstan made his aura less dangerous, according to my father.

"Remarkable," he said. His voice-altering machine had broken, revealing a ragged masculine voice. "Even with your limited training and resources, your Fantasy abilities make you overpowering. Yes, if you help us capture the traitor, Arrowhead would still accept your alliance. We could make you unstoppable."

My father sneered. "We have more than our abilities to thank. We have our families and trust. That, you obviously lack."

"You can take this message back to Arrowhead," I growled. "My father and I don't want to fight. We fight with words until someone threatens our family. But if someone dares to threaten our family—" I glanced at my mom and Uncle Dunstan "—then they have bigger problems coming than just my father and me. So, listen closely and report my words exactly."

I grabbed him by the neck of his headscarf to snarl closer. "Back. Off."

CHAPTER 20

Thrillers have a habit of saving the day
at the very last second before the bomb
goes off.

- *Lemuel Gulliver's Travel Guide, Vol. 5: Thriller*

With the help of Prince Alun's ability to use Sci-Fian tech outside of Sci-Fi, we teleported home before the peak of the night. We rushed my mom to the magic healers of Ruezdad, who expected her to make a quick and full recovery. Exhausted in more ways than one, I collapsed in bed to visit my departed grandfather.

After a full and adventurous life, death had been a relief, nullifying his curse and renewing his energy. He still gave me an earful about taking my place as future duke, but this time, I gave him a satisfying answer.

The duke's funeral was scheduled for later that week, and my parents' coronation would be the following day. Then, I'd officially take my father's place as marquis. The idea was still daunting, but considering the encouragement and hope I'd received lately, there was a little lift to my heart at the thought. I'd be the best marquis I could be. For the sake of my people. For Anita's sake. I'd find a way to deliver her mercy despite Arrowhead's demands for deadly justice.

In the meantime, I received a call from Detective Ross, asking me about what happened. He'd seen the news: leaked camera footage of Arrowhead agents abducting and torturing a Fantasy Duke and his heir with no probable cause. (So, the reporters finally vetted my anonymous gift.) Thriller's president made an official statement of severing all ties with the private organization. Without government backing and support, I expected Arrowhead would leave us alone and struggle to follow Anita.

I smiled with that hope while standing at the windows of Ruezdad's royal dining hall, sipping tea, staring at the city below with all its people. My people. Mine to build and protect.

My glow ball and Fantastical virtual assistant buzzed with another incoming call.

"PI Spade," I answered automatically. Oops. Not anymore. "I mean, this is Earl Fromm of Margen speaking. What can I do for you?"

"Hey, Aeron."

I almost dropped my teacup. "Anita?"

"Don't let yourself get so spectacularly cornered again. I can't keep watching you through my scope."

"You were the sniper who helped me in that abandoned storage room?" I glanced around, wondering if Anita was nearby and spying on me. "I thought so, but how did you know about our abduction to Thriller?"

"Truth told me."

"How did *Truth* know? How did Truth contact you?"

I could almost hear her eyes roll. "Truth knows everything. Well, after your visit, she found an Arrowhead agent sneaking onto her parents' property and shook their hand. Then she told me what she had seen. Anyway, I'm sorry you had to go through that because of me."

I managed a small smile. "It's alright. Will you come—"

"Well, I'm glad I could help," she said.

"I am too. Where are you? Won't you—"

"I'll drop clues to my whereabouts so they'll leave you and your family alone. Please take care of yourself. This needs to be goodbye."

"Anita, wait—"

"I love you, Aeron."

Click.

I stared dumbfounded at my glow ball as its light dimmed.

Goodbye? But she loved me, and I loved her. Love was supposed to conquer all, right? I had a hard time seeing how in our situation.

In a messed-up way that I didn't want to admit, it was probably good for us to be temporarily separated. She'd said that she didn't know who she'd become without me. It was about time that she found out. I just wished she didn't need to do it while as a fugitive on the run. Besides, I had some of my own soul-searching to do.

The door opened, admitting my father in his pressed tunic and followed closely by his fairy guard.

"Ah," he said, walking over to join me at the window. "Are you enjoying the view?"

I nodded, too overwhelmed with Anita's call and my impending future to speak.

With a deep breath, he spoke, "Aeron, I hoped to comment on how well you handled yourself in Thriller. Your incident report was…enlightening, especially in regard to your commands to the spirits."

He hadn't asked a question, so I remained silent. He could thank Truth for teaching me how to file detailed incident reports, even if they were in Noir's style instead of Margen's.

"Your mother," he continued, "reminds me that the word 'duke' comes from the Latin word 'duc,' meaning 'lead.' I reckon that leading the people of Margen will be easier than what you have done in Noir, solving Cases for both the living and spirits. The people look up to you, and from what I understand of your spiritual experiences, the dead do as well. They may not have a monarchy, though you are a duke among them. A Duke for the Dead, so to speak. You understand more about being a duke than you think."

I sighed. "I understand enough to be daunted by the work. As a private investigator in Shigaqua, I only needed to concern myself with the motive, means, and opportunities of a handful of suspects at a time. I didn't need to worry about the sociologies of dozens of towns, the economics of hundreds of businesses, or the individual lives of millions of people."

"A duke's responsibility is not to do every task on his own. It is knowing the right people to delegate each task. Knowing people means spending time with them, their peers, and those they manage."

I fidgeted with my leather bracelet. "I'm well aware of interviewing tactics and observation techniques to study people, but I can't interview two million people."

Father raised an eyebrow. "When given a Case, do you interview every single citizen of Noir as a suspect?"

I frowned. "No. I study the crime scene, start with witnesses and next of kin, following the trail of clues to expand the list of suspects until all the clues narrow down to a single villain."

He nodded. "Exactly. Whenever an issue arises, consider the local lords as the 'next of kin' to learn more about the issue and follow the leads to a solution. The occupation of a duke is far from a one-man job. The lords and ladies, knights and clergy, and the everyday citizens may help you. I suspect, as an investigator, you utilized the aid of partners—fellow investigators, such as Truth and Nita and the police officers?"

"Yes," I said, wondering where he was headed with that extended metaphor. Instead of explaining, he gave me a patient stare. Curses, he wanted me to figure out something on my own…meaning it was likely a subject he didn't want to bring up or say directly.

"You're saying that I need a partner for help?" I guessed.

His nod was heavier this time. "Your biggest supporter will be one who shares your title with you. Having a trustworthy marchioness and future duchess beside you will lighten your burdens and increase your effectiveness."

Marchioness. My wife. That was a weird thought. I suddenly understood his hesitancy bringing up the topic.

"I'm not single for my lack of trying. I just haven't met anyone I felt like I couldn't live without," I lied. It ached my core to be away from Anita, but a fugitive wasn't marchioness material.

Father's nod was empathetic this time. "I understand. I was not the heir to the duchy when I first met and fell in love with your mother. As the original heir, my older brother had been arranged to marry Princess Anwen since his twelfth birthday. Your mother and I convinced my father and King Aneirin to hold off making any arrangements for you because we wanted you to marry for love as we had."

"For which I'm deeply grateful," I said. One reason I'd dated so much was to avoid marriage arrangements with King Aneirin's daughter, my second-cousin, Princess Sayer.

Father sighed thoughtfully. "If you accept your place as marquis, it would serve you well to marry a lady of the court, preferably within the next year or so."

"Next year?" I coughed, choking on my own air. I'd been dating since I was a teenager but still struggled to commit to anyone. I'd spent three years with Anita before we confessed our love for one another.

"How am I supposed to find and fall in love with a woman worthy of a title in the next year? I'm already in love, but…she's in no place to accept any royal commitments. You gave me permission to help Anita as marquis, if only as a friend. I'll have no time or desire to court anyone until she's free."

My father narrowed his eyes. "What if freedom is impossible? Even if Thriller as a whole has backed down, I can guarantee that Arrowhead will find another government supporter to fund and publicize the hunt for her head.

I swallowed back my doubts. "Give me at least six months. Six months to put everything I have into finding her master and proving him as the real villain." Of course, I hoped to resolve Anita's issues in the next month or two, but it had taken years to finally nail down Sponsor. And that was with clues to his location in Shigaqua and weapons-dealing employees. All I had for Stryker was an alias and an idea that he was in Londinium during our chase out of there.

The new duke raised a brow. "And after you resolve her issues or six months pass without resolution?"

"Then, I'll be the best marquis anyone could ever hope for."

Father rubbed the back of his neck with a light moan. "No need to sacrifice yourself for duty yet." Whipping out his calendar, he mused, "I may convince King Aneirin to hold off any arrangements until your twenty-fifth birthday. That gives you six months to help Anita, then another year after to marry for love. You missed the applications this year, though if you become desperate for a Lady, you could visit Romance next year for their courting season."

Grateful for his leniency regarding betrothal arrangements, I still shuffled uncomfortably. Would I ever find love again? At the moment, it felt impossible. I didn't even want to love anyone else. Maybe I could ask Cupid to shoot me with Love at First Sight in Romance?

The whole idea sounded contrived, but maybe, if I still hadn't found a way to resolve Anita's crimes by next year, I'd be desperate enough to patch my heart and to avoid the arrangement with my second-cousin.

I especially struggled within high society. I had a hard time imagining myself with a flouncy lady who wanted to host tea parties and talk about flower arrangements. When considering any women who interested me, I thought of Anita. The ache in my chest confirmed my annoyingly inconvenient feelings for her. What a rotten time to fall in love. She'd left me.

Seeming to notice my pain, my father slipped his arm around my shoulders. "Would a visit to the training grounds help? After seeing our abilities and being outmatched in their home state, Thriller may leave us be for now, though I would not be caught so thoroughly unprepared again."

With a huff, I agreed with a nod. "Whatever they throw at us, we'll be ready."

My father smiled and started to lead me from the room. I took one more glance out the window, wondering where Anita was. I would accept my place as Margen's marquis while searching for a solution to her condemning Case against Arrowhead. It probably meant finding her master, Stryker. As if finding Anita wasn't hard enough. I cringed to think of what could happen if he found her first.

That settled my resolve. I'd find and bring Stryker to justice. If I couldn't do that, I'd find Anita to protect her from him and Thriller. No matter where she went, I'd find her again, even if I had to search the whole world of Novel or neighboring planets of Sci-Fi.

Thank you

for reading *Spirit of Suspense: Dead and Back Again #2*. If you enjoyed it, I'd really appreciate your honest review on Goodreads, Amazon, and/or the website of your purchase. As an extra "thank you" and to help introduce the next book (the finale!) of this series, here's Anita's "A Killer Romance" novelette.

Happy reading!
   - C. Rae D'Arc

P.S. Be sure to follow my newsletter or social media to receive updates on the finale, Dead and Back Again #3.

Website: craedarc.com
Facebook: facebook.com/c.rae.darc
Instagram: instagram.com/craedarc

DEAD AND BACK AGAIN #2.5

A KILLER ROMANCE

a Novelette

C. RAE D'ARC

Chapter 1

I thought that discovering my past would give me clarity and a place in this world. Instead, I was more lost than ever. The amnesiac Nita Incog, combat specialist of Visionary Investigations in Noir, Mystery, was dead. Her life was a long-gone dream from the past. Then again, so was my actual past as double-agent Linda Moreno, traitor and mass murderer. She was the kind of person that governments erased from every file, every record, and every conversation, but still felt breathing down their necks. Even after a whole year, I flinched at mirrors and reminders of the person I'd been back then.

Instead, I'd taken on the names and lives of Anya and Nithryla in northern Fantasy kingdoms, Nicole and Angella in various Childrens counties, then Anastasia in the large town of Avon, Romance. All were struggling actresses and secretly in love with Aeron Fromm, the Marquis of Margen.

That last part stayed true for my current alias as Miss Annette Smith.

She was a middle-class actress in Pemberly, Regency, Romance; a place that smelled of damp cobblestones and powdered wigs, of roses cultivated for display, not scent. Her debut was to be Titania in "A Midsummer Night's Dream," queen of fairies, lover of fools. The irony wasn't lost on me.

The innkeeper hadn't asked questions when I paid in advance and smiled too easily. Most people didn't when the story looked right from a distance. My boarding room was narrow, the bed uneven, but it was a stage I could control. And in my line of existence, control was everything.

I told myself it wasn't a bad life. I had shelter, work, and faces that smiled back when I laughed on cue. Even people who thought we were friends. Sometimes, I almost believed it, almost forgot the sensation of squeezing a sniper's trigger with an ignorant smile on the other side, or of chucking a pulled grenade into a room of cadets who had trusted me.

I tried to push those memories away as I sat on a patio of lace and pretense. Porcelain cups balancing on saucers, sugar dissolving into shallow civility. I sat among Ladies Newman and Edwards, and Misses Northrop and Spear, playing my part as the charming Miss Annette Smith, actress and harmless ornament. The chairs were designed for posture, not comfort, forcing the spine straight and the expression mild. Perfect for a bunch of composed pretenders like myself.

Misses Northrop and Spear laughed easily, as actresses did when the scene demanded. They were Hermia and Helena offstage as well as on. Lady Edwards, all rouge and righteousness, admired her reflection in the teapot while claiming she despised vanity. Lady Newman barely spoke, likely the most honest one among us, but the quiet ones always knew more than they divulged.

The others thought they were discussing theater and gossip, but to me it was fieldwork. I measured pauses, the tremor of a cup against porcelain, and the way Lady Edwards mentioned a tutor like a name drop. Was I supposed to know his name and act impressed?

In Regency, inheritance bought influence, but beauty granted access. I sold the latter illusion on clearance.

The door into the estate swung open with a flurry of thick heels. I'd already noticed the movement on the other side of the windows and registered the disturbance as mild, but set my hand at my hips, where I kept a single-shot pistol in the folds of my dress.

The mother of Lady Newman squealed with delight as she danced toward us. "Don your best laces! We were just informed of a new lord in town in search of a wife."

"A lord?" Lady Edwards asked. "What is his title?"

"Marquis Fromm, the Haunted, from Fantasy." Countess Newman raised her eyebrows suggestively.

My blood froze. Aeron was here. He'd found me. Shoot his spirits, I couldn't hide from them. He'd been extra active in his search for me during my first six months of running. Especially in the fifth and sixth months, I'd catch wind of his approach after only two or three weeks between hideouts. I should have run immediately, but his search made me feel alive and…loved. Each time he found me, I left him a postcard before fleeing the scene. But then, he'd tapered off. I expected it was a ploy to convince me to let down my guard, and maybe I had. I'd spent two months in Avon before spotting operatives, and I was on my third month in the small town of Pemberly.

Still, there was another part of Lady Newman's announcement that confused me. Was Aeron really looking for a wife? Or was that just the story they'd been told as his cover for looking for me?

Then came a thought I couldn't control, absurd and dangerous: what if he was looking for me to be his wife?

No, that was the kind of thought that could get me killed.

Countess Newman placed a delicate but commanding hand on her daughter's shoulder. "He is boarding with our cousins, the Kenningtons, for the season."

Lady Edwards fanned her face. "I had no idea the Kenningtons had such friends. To think! Chastity and Charity have connections to Fantasy royalty!"

"Charity has mentioned her parents having friends of high status since their days at university." Lady Newman shuffled a little, uncomfortable with the attention.

"A Fantasy royal?" Miss Northrop asked. "And you said his title was the Haunted? How is he haunted? Does he have a dark past?"

"Sounds positively intriguing," Miss Spear smirked and leaned in for more gossip.

Countess Newman flipped out her own fan as if to flip away the concern. "Charity did not say the reason for his title, though revealed that his lineage is half-Horror."

Lady Edwards scoffed. "A half-breed? Truly, I do not know what to make of this Marquis. One moment he intrigues me; the next he repulses. Of what duchy is he to inherit?"

"I believe he is from Fairy."

I bit my tongue to keep from correcting Countess Newman. Fairy was the whole kingdom. Aeron was heir to half of it as the Margen Duchy. But what would a traveling actress know about that? I played my part and kept quiet.

Lady Edwards "hmmed," as if debating whether he was worth her time. "I have no interest in Fairy, though I imagine he will become a duke soon enough, and the title of Duchess Fromm does appeal to me."

I bit harder on my tongue. Lady Edwards didn't deserve Aeron. I didn't either, but at least I knew my unworthiness.

If Aeron had tracked me down, the question wasn't why; it was who he brought with him.

I cleared my throat, drawing their attention. "Does he have an entourage?"

Countess Newman replied, "Chastity said that Lord Fromm requested a new footman to accompany him since his own Fantastic valet would be 'inappropriate' in Romance. I did not understand the meaning."

I allowed a private smile. Master Bahr would have become mute in Romance, and I didn't imagine a massive bear wandering around hunting-happy Regency was a good plan. Yet Aeron had arrived without even a servant? No backup, no guards, or even a Thriller spy playing the part of a servant? Strange. Unless their people were already here, watching from the same inn where I slept.

I made a note to check the register that night. Quietly.

"Too bad," Lady Edwards mused to me. "Surely, if Lord Fromm had brought a valet, you might have had a chance for a Fantastic Romance."

I smiled sweetly back. "Surely. As it is, I haven't any reason to meet this Lord Fromm. In fact, forewarn me when he comes near, that I may make my exit as speedily as possible."

The ladies laughed too easily at my remark. Either way, I hoped they'd take the opportunity to tease me by actually warning me if he came near.

Lady Edwards and the Misses excused themselves to drift toward the gardens, their laughter thinning with distance. I stayed behind. Lady Newman lingered too, speaking quietly to her servants. Instructions, by the sound of it.

Half of my brain shouted "Run!" The other half whispered, "Hide." Flight meant abandoning everything I'd built in Pemberly; my new identity, the forged credentials, the fragile illusion of belonging. I'd spent months weaving myself into this town, becoming someone worth admiring from box seats, not someone to shoot like a hunted tiger.

Even if I ran to a nearby town, Aeron would follow. To truly lose him, I'd need to vanish beyond this county, maybe

Regency altogether: burn the identity, plant false sightings, erase every trace. I'd need to start over again. From nothing. Again.

I clenched my jaw. No, not this time. I would stay, blend in, and wait for Aeron to give up his search. If he left empty-handed, he'd stop searching here for a while and draw Thriller's eye elsewhere. That might buy me a season's worth of peace.

But peace required distance. I mentally reviewed my weekly schedule, activities, and any possibilities of crossing paths with Aeron. He wasn't boarding at the inn, but he'd visit and find the social circuit of parties, festivals, markets, and the theater. Especially the theater. He'd know to look for me there. After all, he'd been the one to suggest I try out for the stage in the first place.

"Lady Newman," I asked, "if you could do me an enormous favor, please do what you can to dissuade Lord Fromm from visiting the playhouse. See, we are performing 'A Midsummer Night's Dream,' which is very Fantastical, and I worry the mockery of events might offend him."

"Oh," Lady Newman clasped my hands, "of course, I had not even considered that! Though should we not ask for his advice to make it more accurate to Fantasy?"

"No," I said, allowing my anxiety to show as nerves, not fear. "Lord Fromm is from Fairy, correct? Well, there are fairies in the play. It simply won't do. Promise me you will keep him away from the playhouse? There are so many other activities and events around here, that it should not be difficult to entertain him otherwise."

"True," Lady Newman agreed, "though your performance as Titania is most inspiring."

"Perhaps," —I puffed up with forced pride— "but Lord Fromm came to be inspired by the *ladies* such as yourself."

Lady Newman giggled gently. "If you insist. I will do what I can to charm him away."

"You are most marvelous." I grinned and graced her with a polite kiss on the cheek.

Miss Spear and I rode back to town at dusk. The fog crept in, softening edges and carrying sound unnaturally. I thought about getting off a block early to change into my favorite black velvets that didn't belong in Regency daylight. But the stealth clothes would have drawn more eyes. Better to look ordinary. Expected.

I stepped down from the cart like any other local and let the brim of my hat and fall of my hair cover enough of my face to pass unnoticed. Inside, the innkeeper met me with his usual mix of weariness and politeness. No new guests, he said, though he did mention Lord Fromm's arrival. Aeron knew how to make an entrance.

Except it didn't make sense if his goal was to find me. Didn't he know that loud announcements and attention would only frighten me away?

I saw it then—the strategy. Noise was the point. A scare tactic. The first shot to flush prey from cover. While Aeron paraded through the center of town, agents of Arrowhead and Thriller would wait at the exits, watching the roads, ready to catch the fleeing fugitive.

Classic misdirection. That meant staying and hiding was the safest course.

That night was for preparation. Whether Aeron had come alone or with a Thriller net waiting beyond the town limits, I needed to be ready to move: fast, silent, and without a trace.

Escape meant distance, and distance meant leaving Romance behind. My fastest route out was by magic candle, but the one I'd taken from Aeron was down to its last use, and it had its limits. Magic teleportation candles only worked for places that I could vividly imagine within the realms of magic.

My first time using it on my own had been to the property edge of Truth's parents' home. Spotting agents already in wait, I'd remained hidden, recognizing Aeron's car when he came to visit. It literally ached my heart to watch them reunite without me, but I found my chance after Aeron left and several agents followed him. I knocked out a spy and flashed Truth a message from the woods for her to meet me and Read his palm.

"Shoot," she swore. "There's a plot to torture Aeron for information. This agent has been to the prepared black site. I felt him go downstairs—to a basement, based on the chill and humidity. It felt sterile, like a hospital, but also moldy and abandoned. He handled surgery and dental machinery and tools."

Surgery and dental narrowed it down to either off-grid clinics or an animal hospital.

I spared a brief moment to reconnect with the woman who loved me like a sister, allowing her to shake my hand as a parting gift. Her eyes went wide, and she stared at me as if truly seeing me for the first time.

Nervous, I asked, "What did you see?"

"You, um…huh. That was not what I expected. You might be a better match for Aeron than I thought."

I pulled my hand away, embarrassed to realize that she'd probably sensed our last kiss before I'd left him.

Despite my awkwardness, she smiled warmly and blinked as her eyes glistened. "Good job at not killing anyone this time at Arrowhead. I'm…I'm so proud of you and the choices you're making."

That was enough to warm my core and encourage my next choices to protect Aeron with my sniper rifle in Thriller and then research a bunch of Fantasy towns where I could use my candle. I hadn't expected the candle to work in Romance, but it did. Maybe because fae creatures were finding ways to cross over without losing their magic?

But I needed a new place to escape in case Aeron and Arrowhead had found me again. That meant going to the library.

What were the odds of Aeron visiting the library tomorrow? It was the kind of place he'd like to haunt, full of adventurous stories and minds. But libraries also had shelves and plenty of hiding places. I made a plan to visit in the morning.

That night, I checked my room's perimeter: thread traps still intact, floorboard markers undisturbed, and locks untampered. Nothing out of place except me.

I finally lay down, but sleep didn't come. My body stilled, but my thoughts didn't.

Aeron was here.

Was his loud entrance for me? A message and greeting, not a hunt? Part of me wanted to believe it and run to him, to the Kennington's cottage and climb through Aeron's window. I wanted him to hold me again, to hear him say how he loved me, and how he didn't care about my past sins. I wanted to hold him in return and say how much I loved him—how I'd be anyone for him.

But that was my weakness that Thriller agents counted on. The rational part of me—the part that kept me alive this long— knew better. I needed to stay hidden, and Aeron's love couldn't erase my guilt.

Chapter 2

The morning came slowly, and I didn't rush. My movements were deliberate, small, and rehearsed even in the privacy of my own room. I dressed, fixed my hair, and watched the street through the mirror's edge, utilizing the warped reflection for a wider view. People moved in patterns with their carts, shopping, and gossip.

The ordinary rhythm was perfect for camouflage. Predictable places were the easiest to blend into. I told myself I'd chosen Romance for the quiet safety, but that was a lie. Aeron was the reason.

He was the reason behind every choice I made, every alias I enveloped, and every bit of research I did in my free time. He occupied too much of my head—too much of me. My love and irritation of him were two edges on the same dagger.

Remembering my past—who I'd been—had been an unexpected blow from a larger barrel than I could dodge. As Nita Incog, the amnesiac, I'd expected to remember a normal past; a normal childhood with a normal family, normal school troubles, and normal relationships. Of course, tragedy had to strike in there somewhere when I'd lost my memories, but I fully expected to discover a past with…life.

For three years, I worked beside PIs Truth Johnson and Aeron Fromm, solving Cases, teasing, and becoming good friends. Aeron had tempted me with constant flirtations, but I could have been engaged or married with kids for all I knew. Well, I was almost sure that I didn't have kids, but I knew that remembering my past would redefine me.

And it had.

I didn't have kids. No marriage, no boyfriend, and no real family. No friends to call my own, and definitely no love. Only training and commands to follow from a man named Stryker. My life had been built in the shadows and raised for one purpose—to go undercover into Arrowhead, a Special Operations Agency. Infiltrate, learn, and then destroy the director and everyone in my way. Basically, everyone in the facility.

I completed my Mission, but it had fractured me.

I'd cried and begged Stryker for release from the horrors. My master had given me another Mission to refocus my mind, but my renewed memories hadn't returned that part. I still wasn't sure how I'd ended up on the shores of Lake Mishi and then Shigaqua's hospital with no past and no orders. Only survival.

I'd teamed up with Truth Locke as she promised to help me find my identity. Then, she brought Aeron into our circle, saying he'd challenge me and bring out my personality.

I had never known romantic love…until Aeron. After everything we went through together, after learning the truth, he still loved me. And I loved him, but shoot, love was a weird thing.

I came to Romance to gather intel. Specifically Regency because if there was a way to understand how to handle a future Duke of Margen, it would start here.

However, if he'd come to cut my personal Mission short, I needed to be ready to move. Fast.

The library was quiet that afternoon. Meant to serve the whole county, it was a single room attached to the town church. Some people took books to read in the pews, but I preferred to stay in the library with only one door and window. I scanned the travel section, which was limited and predictable. Mostly propaganda for neighboring provinces. One book stood out: The Western Wilderness: Notes on the Regions Beyond Civilization.

Thin on facts and heavy on speculation, it warranted a closer look. Lady Newman housed a sizable library that could possibly scratch my new curiosity. For now, I checked out the book and continued on my usual daily routine.

Days bled together. No sign of Lord Fromm, but his name was everywhere. The innkeeper asked daily if I'd run into him yet. His persistent inquiries led me to confess that we'd met, but "our stars are on different paths." The best lies were mostly true.

My associates weren't helpful. Miss Spear had a running commentary on every rumor tied to the foreign lord. Miss Northrop was her eager listener, contributing her own gossip and wild theories. Lady Edwards was impossibly worse, openly strategizing her way into his company, undermining anyone "unworthy" that Aeron spared as much as a glance. According to her, that was every woman except herself.

Lady Newman was the exception. Under pressure from her family, she took the lead in guiding Aeron through balls, garden parties, horse races, and other social gatherings. At first, she spoke of the events with a pale face and mortified expressions. Lately, had she seemed more comfortable. Aeron had a way of putting her at ease. Because he was Aeron.

I spied on them once from my inn-room window, catching Lady Newman laughing over some conversation. She and Aeron passed through the main square in an open-air carriage with her cousin Johnnie. Even from fifty feet away and through a cloudy window, I recognized Aeron leaning on his left arm, gesturing at the sights around him, polite yet casual at the same time—a gesture I knew all too well.

Confirmation. He was here. The truth hit harder than expected. My pulse wouldn't slow even after they disappeared around the street corner. I wasn't the only one left staring.

A month passed. Reports of his presence spread across the county. If he'd wanted to find me, there would be rumors of his search, right? Nothing. Only gossip about his search for a marchioness. Had he given up searching for me? Had he given up…on me?

Good, I told myself, even as my eyes burned with the thought. I'd told him goodbye. I'd told him to stop looking for me. I'd told him to move on and find someone who deserved his love. I told myself these things too, but…believing it wasn't as easy.

It still hurt. It hurt a lot. Yes, I wanted him to be happy, and I expected his best happiness would be with someone other than me, but…he was the only man I'd ever loved…still loved.

I'd come to Romance to analyze relationships and the historical culture, but the more I studied, the more absurd it all seemed. The people were obsessed. Engagements and alliances were suspended with hopes of aligning with the future duke. Every conversation circled back to Aeron, from the young hopefuls to fathers and brothers pushing eligible family members forward. The entire system was as dramatic as a theater production.

The longer he stayed, the more I accepted the likelihood: he was here to find a wife. Not me. All the more reason to avoid him.

The chatter only increased with time. Lady Edwards turned distant, snubbing her nose at any gatherings or conversations not related to the marquis; Misses Spear and Northrop doubled down on Lady Newman for details after every event. I heard all the gossip secondhand at rehearsals.

The theater was my cover and safehouse. Rehearsals kept me busy, and anytime someone asked my opinion or presence at an event, I found reasons to figuratively stay behind the curtain or leave early. Pretending indifference took too much effort.

Apparently, my false disinterest in the foreign lord was a double-edged sword.

Two months into the season, my fellow actresses giggled about an upcoming horse race. Aeron was a star competitor. I ignored the laughter and snuck away to put away the set pieces. Sir Thomas observed my efforts and came to help. He was a lean man of short stature with an easy and mildly awkward smile, making him the perfect actor for Robin Goodfellow—a puck.

I waved off his assistance, and he stood back, watching. Not curious. Assessing. I kept my eyes on the set pieces while guarding myself against any possible attacks.

"Miss Smith."

"Yes, Sir Thomas?"

"Will you be at the races tomorrow?"

"I was not planning to attend," I said.

"May I ask for your reason? Is it because you are otherwise preoccupied, or do you simply have no desire to watch the men try to impress you?"

Honestly? Because Aeron would be there.

Instead, I asked, "What men would want to impress me? At twenty-three, I am nearly a spinster. There are far more lovely ladies available to be courted." Technically, I was closer to twenty-six, but that age removed the "nearly" from my spinster status.

"Except they are all enamored of the Lord Fromm. Your disinterest in him and his exotic titles is... encouraging."

I pushed the set aside and wiped my hands down my dress, careful around my hidden pockets of daggers, the Fantasy candle, and vials with fillings to aid a quick getaway. "What are you saying, Sir Thomas? That you are only interested in me because I am the last woman available?"

"P-pardon?" he sputtered. "No, Miss, I merely—"

I laughed. "Now you know the real reason I'm still unattached. If you find me appealing, it only goes to show how little you know about me."

There were only two people in the world who knew everything about me and still cared: Aeron and Truth.

Oddly, Sir Thomas took my words as a challenge. He stepped closer and reached for my elbow. I had to restrain my natural instincts to guard against a simple advance or grip his wrist for a twist and threat not to touch me.

He said, "I would like the opportunity to make that call for myself. Join me at the horse races tomorrow. Root for me from the stands, and I promise you will not be disappointed."

I raised an eyebrow at him and considered my excuses. I was growing tired of my fact-lacking library book on Western. I needed Lady Newman's permission to access her library. Busy as she was with pleasing her father by shadowing Aeron, the only way I could talk with her (short of sending snail-mail) was to attend a social. Shoot.

I graced Sir Thomas with a practiced smile and small curtsy. "If you can promise satisfaction, then yes, I will cheer you on from the sidelines."

Chapter 3

I was a master of disguise. During my brief visit to Aeron's hometown, I'd bought a magical bracelet that let the wearer change their appearance like the common spell "Disguise Self." The magic item didn't work in lands of realism, but I wore it anyway because…sometimes I thought it still worked, anyway. Again, maybe the crossover fae creatures were spreading their influence. If anything, it felt like a good-luck charm.

Whether or not the magical item worked, I altered my appearance the old-fashioned way by dyeing my hair light-brown to blend in with the local Regency, Romantics. For the horse races, I curled it in the popular fashion. I hated hiding a work of art, but covered my stylized hair with a broad hat. Nothing suspicious with the bright summer sun and cloudless sky. I then added color to my lips and cheeks, something I rarely did around Aeron. I kept it subtle, since makeup was largely uncommon among Regencies. Enough to blend in without drawing the wrong kind of attention.

I rode to the grounds alone, fully aware of this stupid choice to put myself in Aeron's proximity. I'd never confess it aloud, but I wanted to see him. After months of rumors, whispers, and speculation, I wanted to spy on the man who star-crossed my love.

Finding him was effortless. Thirteen months after walking away from him, I still spotted him among the polite attendants all too easily. Aeron's darker skin tones made him stand out, contrasting with his inherited blue-green eyes and dark brown hair. He wore a simple white long-sleeved undershirt and a fitted tunic of his favorite shade of light blue.

My core tightened with physical pain. Stupid, useless, and annoying heart. It literally ached to see Aeron again. Was that a side effect of love? Why did it hurt so badly? My nose tingled, and my eyes burned with tears. It was unlike any other pain I'd suffered, which was saying something considering my physical, mental, and emotional training with Stryker.

Shoot, why was I there in the open? I needed cover. Fast.

The simplest cover was to blend into the group of women closest to him. They leaned over the railings, swooning and fixating on him as he took a brown horse through warm-up laps. He handled the animal like someone raised around them—steady posture and with deliberate control. I'd never seen Aeron ride a horse before, but with a grandfather like Duke Konrad, the Horse, of Margen, I wasn't surprised by his skills. Lean, muscled, and beautiful could describe both the horse and rider.

Shoot, he was as gorgeous as ever. My heart raced at the same pace as the horse. I could easily watch him all day.

I consciously reminded myself of my Mission and real reason for coming to this event. I was there to accompany Sir Thomas and to contact Lady Newman. I spotted the Puck actor near the rail, leading a fine grey horse. The female onlookers urged him out of the way so they could ogle Aeron. Thomas scowled at his competition until he found me—pointedly not fawning over Aeron.

"The stars bless me after all! I did not think you would come."

"After such a promise, what could keep me away? You do remember your promise not to disappoint me, don't you? Well, I will be sorely disappointed unless someone is thrown from his horse. What is entertainment if not brutal comedy?"

Sir Thomas laughed. "Surely, your idea of entertainment is too dangerous!"

He meant it as a joke. He had no idea how close he was to the truth. He couldn't be laughing if he knew my favorite forms of entertainment included moving unseen through alleys, setting traps, and protecting my friends while they chased criminals and murderers.

I responded with an innocent and harmless expression of wide eyes, relaxed posture, and the kind of look that convinced people I was exactly what I appeared to be.

He accepted the simple lie without question. "We have suffered without your presence at too many gatherings of late. I would implore your disinterest in the Lord Fromm to become contagious."

"Beat him in this race, and you will cause the spread yourself."

He bowed. "I plan to do as much with ease. Will you grant me luck?"

"Perhaps." I shrugged. "Though I can't promise whether my luck is good or bad."

"Hah! Then keep it. I shall win by merit and my own determination to recapture these ladies' attention."

"Let's keep our goals realistic, why don't we?" I said just as Aeron happened to pass during his cool-down walk.

Shoot! That was exactly the type of response I used after Aeron's "If I told you, I'd have to kill you." I angled away to let my hat cover my face right as Aeron snapped toward me. Through the fabric holes of my hat's brim, I watched his silhouette search the crowd for whomever spoke those familiar

18

words. To add to my disguise, I slipped into my acting role, and said to Sir Thomas, "Yea, see your horse, 'Though she be but little, she is fierce!'"

Sir Thomas frowned for a second before he caught the reference. Then he chuckled and gestured to the line of women watching Aeron. "'Cupid is a knavish lad. Thus to make poor females mad.'"

With a nod, he mounted and moved to the starting line. Aeron positioned himself second from the outside, and I cursed my exposed seating. He could easily spot me if he looked long enough. Thankfully, he was distracted by his horse. He stroked the horse's neck fondly, leaned in to whisper in its ear, then straightened with a quick pat. The other riders teased him, and Aeron answered with a confident smile.

The starting shot fired. The racers launched forward.

Aeron claimed the inner ring before the first circuit finished. Sir Thomas stayed close, pushing his mount hard. The other riders became irrelevant by the second cycle. The third and fourth cycles continued with the same order: Aeron in the lead and Sir Thomas sweating to keep on his flanks.

It shouldn't have bothered me, but it did. Aeron always won. He always excelled. Always so shooting perfect. Always infuriating.

The crowd cheered politely around me. I stood from my seat, marched to the railing, and removed my hat. Then I fixed my stare directly on Aeron. Shoot his perfections. I shifted my expression into Aeron's lost partner, Nita Incog: lost, yet determined, and a little dreamy-eyed in Aeron's presence.

Aeron rounded the final curve and finally sensed my target. His focus tore away from the track to find his hunter. His eyes locked on mine. Recognition lit his face. For one glorious second, my heart swelled with simple and pure joy. Even in my Regency costume, Aeron saw me and knew me. He gaped and let his horse slow. Sir Thomas inched ahead.

Aeron's focus snapped back to the race, but it was too late. Sir Thomas won by a nose. Aeron's irritation at placing second was minimal compared to his frantic search among the crowd. I'd already replaced my hat and moved to sit several feet away from the spot in question. Instead, I was close to the finishing area, close enough to hear Aeron and Sir Thomas talk as they brought their horses down from the run. Their words carried easily with Aeron's breathing still uneven and Sir Thomas's triumph.

Sir Thomas laughed heartily. "You gave us a good run! Never before have I been so close to losing!"

"Second place is hardly losing," Aeron said, frowning. "Forgive me for not giving it my all. I was distracted."

Sir Thomas hunched a little, as if playing his fairy role. "'If we shadows have offended, think but this, and all is mended, that you have but slumbered here while these visions did appear.'"

"Visions, indeed," Aeron mused, then tilted his head. "'A Midsummer Night's Dream?'"

"Yes!" Sir Thomas straightened with pride. "You know it?"

"Of course." Aeron smirked. "Its setting is based in Fairy, written by the most successful playwright in history. He exaggerated a few things, but it still makes for a fantastic play."

Sir Thomas puffed out his chest. "I have the role of Robin Goodfellow—a puck. Consider yourself personally invited to our opening night."

I internally screamed while the disaster was locked in place. My mind calculated the fallout and raced for exits—any excuse from performing opening night, any tactic to keep Aeron out of my playhouse. I had three weeks until the first performance.

It was enough time to plan and set something in motion if I moved fast.

While weighing every contingency and angle, I spotted Lady Newman among the viewers. She was my ultimate plan of escape. I approached her without hesitation.

"Oh, Miss Smith!" She beamed. "How good it is to see you again. You have been far too busy with that play as of late. Pray tell me that this exciting race has convinced you to join us for more wondrous social events."

I smiled back, surprised by her energy. This wasn't the same shy woman who had carefully befriended me only with the help of Lady Edwards. The woman before me could hold her own conversation and speak louder than a silencer shot.

"Lady Newman," I curtsied, "you are too sweet. I must say how much you've transformed in these last two months."

"Two months?" she gasped. "Has it truly been so long? Oh dear, I have missed your enlightening company. I heard you came to support Sir Thomas today? How delightful that he won the race! How would the two of you like to join Lord Fromm and me on a picnic to the evergreens next week?"

"You're going on a picnic with Lord Fromm?" I asked. Uncomfortable and unjustified jealousy brewed in my stomach.

"Lady Edwards and Lord Norrington will join us also," she said, continuing to beam like the sun.

Meanwhile, I squirmed. "I fear my relationship with Sir Thomas isn't that intimate, and we would be outclassed by the presence of so many wonderful lords and ladies. I will have to decline."

"Pity." She slumped a little.

"However," I added, "I was hoping to stop by your manor sometime soon. I hear you have a marvelous library."

"Oh, yes." She grinned again. "My mother loves to boast that we have the largest collection of tomes in the regent."

Perfect. I secured an appointment for later in the week and held my position until Aeron was swallowed by his circle of admirers. Once his attention was diverted. I gave Sir Thomas a quick congratulation and slipped away from the grounds.

With the contingency set, one crisis was contained. But the larger problem remained: keep Aeron away from the theater or find a clean exit for myself. How many more crises would threaten to expose me before Aeron left me alone?

Chapter 4

As for the library at Newman Manor... well, it was adequate. I'd operated in larger spaces, but that was an unfair comparison; Aeron's palace/castle library had skewed every metric. Still, Newman Manor had a different advantage—hopefully, something I could use.

"Never before," I said in awe, "have I seen so many handwritten and special leather edition books. How did your mother acquire such a collection?"

"Not on her own, by any means." Lady Newman giggled. "My grandfather taught my grandmother to read. Of course, in the beginning, it was not a woman's place to read; thus, my grandfather would buy custom-made books to bring home for my grandmother to read in private. Our family's desire for stories has only grown fonder with each generation. With such a love of books as tradition, many friends and family have gifted us with books. Also, whenever my father travels, he buys two books as souvenirs: a history for my mother, and a fictional tale for me."

I smiled. That was exactly what I wanted to hear. "Has he traveled far? I would love to see the histories from other places."

Lady Newman guided me through the room with enthusiasm toward a wall of volumes sourced from every corner of the world. Their material from Western was thin—a single shelf—but it was enough. One book detailed the shifting conflict zones as Sci-Fian influences pushed deeper with each passing year. The Newman collection included maps, grainy photographs of isolated towns, and useful intel. Perfect.

"May I borrow this?" I asked.

"Of course," Lady Newman said, setting down a history titled <u>The Robber Bridegroom.</u> The small book was labeled from Margen, stirring my curiosity.

"What's that you're reading?"

"Oh, this?" She blushed and placed her hands over the cover.

"<u>The Robber Bridegroom</u>?" I asked. "Is that from Margen? Why, Lady Newman! Are you researching Lord Fromm's homeland?"

Her blush deepened. "The history of his homeland can be quite grotesque."

"You should try picking up a horror book." I grinned and nudged her.

"Miss Smith," Lady Newman said, so quietly that I barely heard her, "may I confide in you?"

"Of course," I said. "What's on your mind?"

She lifted a handkerchief and worked it between her fingers, tension rolling off her in quiet waves. Her teeth pressed into her lower lip.

A cold worry cut through me. Had she uncovered the truth of my identity? Her gaze wasn't fixed on me or anything else; it drifted, unfocused, as if she stared through the room rather than into it.

No, whatever she fought to say, it wasn't about my cover.

I moved to the sofa, sitting close enough to steady her without crowding her, and closed my hand over hers. Her pulse trembled against my palm.

"What is it, m'lady?" I asked.

"'Tis about the marquis," she whispered as her cheeks blushed.

"Lord Fromm?" I asked.

She nodded with her lips pinched between her teeth again.

"What about him?" I urged. As much as I needed to avoid Aeron, I desperately wanted to know anything and everything about him.

"He…he is a very generous man, is he not?"

Why would she ask me that? Did she somehow know about my relationship or past partnership with him? Hoping to clarify, I asked, "I do not follow?"

She met my eyes for a brief second, then looked away with a small huff. "Surely, you are not ignorant of the rumors. That he is the first man to pay me such attention, and he pays attention to me more than any other lady of the area."

I locked my jaw and calculated the heat spike in my chest. None of this was news, but the jealousy flared before I could tamp it down.

I disciplined my emotions not to betray me. Aeron wasn't mine to claim. I couldn't allow any desire to keep him for myself: I could only allow desire for his safety and happiness. If he was drawn to Lady Newman, she was hardly the worst choice in Pemberly. She had a pure reputation and a keen mind. But I couldn't shake the question of whether she could keep pace with him.

Would she support his drive to solve Cases? Stand beside him when the work turned dark? Challenge his intellect and push him through his fears? Would she…brave his haunted living quarters and share his bed while surrounded by ghosts?

Maybe she could. Maybe she'd fold. But none of that changed the truth of my outsider perspective. I needed to stop evaluating her against the partner I imagined for Aeron—the partner I wished to be.

Lady Newman fidgeted more with her handkerchief. "He has… He proposed—"

"What!?" My stomach dropped like a dead man and my heart burned. Tears even threatened to blur my vision.

My outburst shocked and confused Lady Newman. "Yes, he—oh! Oh dear, my dear, you did not allow me to finish." Lady Newman flustered. "Did you think he proposed marriage to me?"

"I—you mean he didn't?"

"No, good heavens." She flipped out her fan to wave at her flushed face. "He proposed to escort me to the next ball. I haven't a clue what I would say if he proposes marriage. I suppose I would be a fool to say no, though honestly, I know not what to think of the man."

"Really?" I asked. "You've spent the most time with him."

"True, true." She continued to fan herself. "He is a charmer, yet he carries the heart of one star-crossed lover. His duchy is in a land of magic, yet he is familiar with contemporary advancements such as handguns and automobiles. His duchy reflects a time even older than Regency, yet he speaks Contemporary slang with such an odd accent. He says he is only five years my senior, yet at times he seems decades beyond me with his stories and experiences."

"You can blame his parents." I smirked. "His dad's a Duke of Fantasy, and his mom was a Horror commoner, right? Then he went to school in Mystery, so I'd say it's actually a surprise he turned out as normal as he did."

Lady Newman shuddered. "His blood is half Horror. As kind and gentle as he is to me, a part of me is terrified of him."

"Because he's half Horror?" I asked, confused.

She leaned in to whisper, "Because he is the Haunted."

"Oh, you mean his ability? Yeah, it's quite odd, but all his spirit friends are just that; friends. Even his wild poltergeist assistant."

Lady Newman stared at me wide-eyed. "You know about his ability? And his…assistant?"

"Doesn't…everyone?" Shoot, shoot, shoot! Did I just spoil my cover by revealing too much about Aeron?

"Perhaps he is better known in the bustling city of Avon." Lady Newman blushed. "No one else here knows. In fact, the lord confided in me that he felt relieved to come to a place where people do not already know of his many skills and achievements. Yet he also confessed to feeling distant and forlorn because his assistant and many Fantastic friends could not abide properly here. Did you know that he has a bear as a guard? To think! A walking, talking, and clothed bear!"

"Yeah, it's strange." I smirked. "Did you say his assistant isn't in Romance then?"

"No, he says his spirits are here." She shivered. "However, they and his demon spirit have limited power in this land. Thank the heavens. I forget about his eerie ability entirely until he makes some side remark to the empty air, as if he sees them. I tremble in his presence when reminded that he is regularly surrounded by ghosts. Such contradictions. He is a fine gentleman, but to keep such frightening company is beyond me. Is this why you have avoided him all this time? I feared I was losing your friendship, but have you distanced yourself from most social gatherings because you know how…he is?"

"Um, yeah," I said, grabbing onto whatever story she'd believe. "He's well-known where I'm from."

Lady Newman hunkered down with me, conspiratorial gossip lighting her eyes. "What else do you know about him? Tell me all."

"All?" I repeated. "That might take a while."

She giggled like a gossiping schoolgirl. "Now I must know. Surely, the most eligible royal bachelor of Fantasy has more stories than he tells."

"Oh, does he ever," I laughed. Shoot, it felt good to talk overtly about Aeron. It almost felt like I was back with Truth in our shared Noir apartment, talking about wild Cases and the ways men irked us. "You should ask him about how he gets along with the Noir detectives."

"The detectives?"

"Yes." I smirked. "They can't stand how young and successful he is. They break their backs to solve Cases, and all he does is take a nap, talk to the spirits, and voila! Case closed."

"Truly?" She set down her fan in disbelief.

"Truly," I laughed. "But in Fantasy, everyone adores him. The poor man can't even enjoy a meal in the market without young girls squealing over him."

A smile crept in before I could stop it as my memory struck fast and clean; Aeron and I slipping through a Fantasy market, ducking beneath cloaks and charm-laced hats, playing at misdirection like it was second nature. One of the many near collisions where a kiss hovered between us, close enough to feel its gravity. I should have taken every one of those chances instead of pushing them away like a coward.

I drifted through the moments I did take in his ghost-filled bedroom and on the edge of Fantasy's borderlands before I'd walked away. I became lost in the heat of his mouth, the stolen breath, his urgent grip and tight chest against mine, the way he held me as if our pasts couldn't trap us…

"Miss Smith?"

Lady Newman's voice yanked me back into the role I'd chosen—this carefully crafted Regency shell and lie that I'd never loved, worked with, or even met Aeron Fromm, Marquis of Margen. I shrugged. "At least that's what they say in Avon. How did you respond to his proposal?"

"I agreed." She picked up her fan to wave it at her face again. "As conflicted as my feelings are for Lord Fromm, I shan't reject a gentleman's offer. Enough about him, though. Tell me more about the proceedings of the playhouse."

"Well, our opening night is in a couple of Saturdays." I still needed to find a way to keep Aeron from attending.

"How wonderful—oh dear, did you say Saturday? I must ensure the next ball is not during your opening night. After accepting Lord Fromm's proposal, I cannot excuse myself, even for a delightful play starring my favorite actresses."

"Of course, I would understand that your prior commitments take priority."

And that was when the outline of a reckless, probably ill-advised, but clear plan snapped into place.

Chapter 5

Dearest Lady Edwards,

You must know how deeply I miss your companionship during this Season. I understand much of your time of late has been preoccupied with the dashing Lord Fromm, and mine with my playhouse. Thank goodness our opening night will be soon. I do hope to share an afternoon with you before then, as Lord Fromm is arranged to return to Fairy soon after, and it is doubtful he will take any other woman with him except your ladyship.

If I may beg a single request from you before we part ways, I would be forever in your debt. With each passing day of preparing and rehearsing for our opening night, I am overcome with extreme anxiety. I have heard such excitement for the show that I worry so many people may come. As much as I wish this play to be a success, I also cannot bear the thought of a large audience watching my performance. Please, I beg of you for help, and offer a solution that may benefit you as well as myself.

I ask only that you arrange a grand ball on the same night as the opening performance. Arrange it in Lord Fromm's honor as a farewell party, to be sure of his attendance, and many others to lessen the crowd for my first performance. This is all I ask.

Your dear friend,
Miss Annette Smith

Dear Miss Smith,

What a superb idea! Thank you for your suggestion to host a farewell ball in honor of the visiting Lord Fromm. He continues to pretend that I mean nothing to him, but I think that by giving him one last chance to appreciate my beauty and graciousness, that he will set aside his aloofness and confess his love to me at last. This is the least I could do to aid your plight.

As you have been so ingenious in making this suggestion, please come to my estate on August 20th, at noon, that I may ask for your opinions on certain matters.

Your dearest friend,
Lady Edwards

Chapter 6

My true thoughts about visiting Lady Edwards' estate were simple: I didn't want to set foot anywhere near it. But she was my cleanest way to keep Aeron far from the playhouse when the curtain lifted on opening night. That made the trip necessary.

I hired a small cart to carry me toward the Edwards property. The estate rose up out of the countryside like a monument to excess. Smaller than Aeron's castle/palace, yes, but somehow far more pompous.

His archaic castle with its worn stone walls and medieval decor never struck me as gaudy. It had history, weight, and a strange calm in its corridors. Peace? I remembered the unexpected ease I'd felt while walking through those hallways with Aeron as my guide. Even the guards trailing us had carried themselves with a protective courtesy instead of the stiff suspicion that usually clung to armed men around me. The tapestries, rugs, and magical fairy lights had drawn me in, inviting me to spend hours studying their intricate threads of detailed history.

And the family…they'd been the real reason behind the warmth and welcome. The Duke and Duchess of Margen deserved their respectable titles. Powerful, charismatic, and sharp, they'd somehow known not to trust me entirely, but they'd offered me kindness and grace I hadn't earned. Aeron's younger sister, Samantha, had opened up to me immediately, shy and tender like a fawn. Maybe Aeron gravitated toward Lady Newman because she echoed some of Sam's gentleness.

None of that existed at the Edwards' estate. This place was a study in sterile wealth; gold vases with no craftsman's love, white walls too polished and cold, and even the air felt curated.

I kept my expression neutral, working to hide my instinctive grimace. I smiled graciously as the butler led me through a maze of pristine cleanliness and filthy richness until arriving at a drawing room.

Lady Edwards was mid-performance with a violin tucked under her chin. The piece was beautiful enough to inspire reflection and study, but too demanding and intricate to allow it. I stayed by the door, waiting. She didn't acknowledge me, didn't look up, simply pressed through to the end of the page. Her bow stuttered as the intricacies increased. After a measure of blunders, she tore out a screech against the strings before she lowered the instrument with a tight breath.

"Bah! This would be the perfect piece to impress Marquis Fromm if only I could master this final section. What do you say, Miss Smith? Should I cut it short at the ball, or play another piece?"

A real friend would've been honest and told her to stop wasting her time. Aeron didn't care for displays crafted to dazzle a room. He respected talent and skills, yes, but only when they reached past the performer and touched someone else's life. If she wanted to impress him, she'd need more than precision and flourishes. She'd need a purpose. She could perform at a charity fundraiser, teach children who had nothing, or—knowing Aeron—put her bow to unconventional use by turning it into something sharp enough to stand between civilians and a threat. He admired honest courage more than applause.

A real friend would've told Lady Edwards that much.

"You should keep practicing," I said instead. "Surely, you will learn it in time."

"It will not be enough to simply learn it," she complained. "It must be perfect. Everything about the ball will need to be perfect for Marquis Fromm to finally realize that I will make the perfect Duchess of Fairy."

I held back my intuitive correction. Aeron's wife (if ever he chose one) would become the Duchess of Margen, and I couldn't imagine him tolerating a partner who dissected every detail as if preparing for forensic review. Precision he respected, not pettiness.

Unfortunately, that was exactly where Lady Edwards steered us for the next two hours. Flowers, ribbons, music, performers— every variable laid out as if the fate of the regency hinged on her choices. I answered only enough to stay useful, nodding at the right intervals, keeping my voice even while my patience thinned to the wire.

By the time we'd dissected hairstyles, gowns, and jewelry arrangements, I was seconds from dropping the façade entirely and walking out with a blunt farewell.

"What about my outfit today?" she asked. "My hair has fallen limp since this morning, and I wonder if I should wear a hat for this afternoon meeting with Marquis Fromm. If I wear a hat, we will need to take our tea outside, though the wind has been blustery today."

I internally panicked. "You have an afternoon meeting with Lord Fromm? Today?"

"Of course." She wiggled her shoulders as if pleased with herself. "My father arranged for Marquis Fromm to join us for tea to discuss the details of the ball in his honor. Will that not be wonderful?"

"Tea?" I checked the height of the sun. How much time did I have to escape? Did it matter? I needed to leave. Fast. What would my excuse be?

"Dear heavens," I said, allowing my anxiety to show only in the most proper manner. "Is it tea time already? I hate to cut my time with you short, but I have an appointment in town to make."

"What kind of appointment? Can it not wait? What could be more important than fawning over the most handsome and eligible lord?"

Not dying when that lord spotted me and inadvertently alerted the cavalry.

"I didn't know you invited Lord Fromm for tea," I said. "Otherwise, I wouldn't have made my previous arrangements. Even if he is well beyond my station, I would bask in the mere opportunity to chaperone the two of you together."

Lady Edwards giggled mischievously. "Oh, of course, though before you go, I must ask you about one more thing. 'Twas the main reason I invited you today."

I tried to remain calm, though I hoped that some of my flustering would encourage a quick discussion. "I suppose I can spare a minute."

She squealed with delight and pulled me by the hand to the dining room.

"What appetizers and drinks do you suggest for the perfect banquet?" She gestured to the table. I stopped short at the sight laid before us. Platters of food covered every square inch of the ten-seater table. "I asked my chef for a sample of every option available to his limited mind. I have an idea of my favorites, but since we will host every eligible maiden in the regent, I thought to ask someone without a refined palate. What would you say?"

Each dish was excess masquerading as simplicity. I pitied her kitchen staff. Lady Edwards insisted I taste everything, then taste it again to confirm whatever verdict she expected.

I braced myself for the next forced bite when movement at the door triggered an instinctive jolt. Black shoes, dark trousers, and a sharp silhouette coiled my muscles, ready to spring for cover under the table.

Only a footman entered. He bowed and announced, "M'Lady, Marquis Fromm has arrived."

"Send him in," Lady Edwards said, sealing my doom.

"Lady Edwards," I said as the footman bowed out. "I really ought to go. I think the cheese tea sandwiches will be perfect. Now, if you please, I dare not intrude on your opportunity to speak with Lord Fromm. Excuse me."

She giggled and waved me goodbye. "You truly are a gem. Farewell."

I managed to escape, slipping my way to the back exit as light steps entered the room behind me. How did I ever mistake the heavy stride of a footman for Aeron's genteel swagger?

"Who just left?" Aeron asked. Shoot his sensuous voice. How I missed him and his odd mix of accents. His voice layered with the polished cadence of his Fantastic upbringing, the hushed edge of a Horror survivor, and the curious rise of a Mystery's questions. I pressed my back to the wall, listening, holding still and holding on to the sound of him. Part of me wanted him to follow me, to find me.

"Give no thought to her," Lady Edwards said, her tone sharp enough to chip glass. "She is an upstart and unworthy of your attention."

Shoot Lady Edwards. She couldn't have misread him more. He rebelled against arrogance, enjoying the thrill of proving pompous people wrong. Her discrediting my value and calling me an "upstart" would only increase Aeron's interest in me.

"Are you sure?" he asked, footsteps heading in my direction. "Because I thought she was 'truly a gem.'"

Shoot! I bolted, bunching my skirts up to run faster from the servant's hallway and to the freedom of open air. I didn't dare risk a glance behind. If he caught sight of my face now, my whole charade would collapse. I ran as fast as my cumbersome historical dress allowed, putting distance between us before my resolve betrayed me.

Chapter 7

My plan to keep Aeron clear of the playhouse ran like a clean operation…right up until it detonated. One week before opening night, the director burst in, wild-eyed and breathless, carrying chaos like a contagion.

"No one is coming! We have sold a total of four tickets for our opening performance! The entire region has been invited to Lady Edwards' ball, and because it will be Lord Fromm's last before he returns to Fantasy, it has been widely rumored to be the event where he will announce his betrothal! We have been upstaged!"

Misses Northrop and Spears shared a plotting glance, then Miss Spears spoke out. "Let us open another night. Move our opening performance to next week, and then we may attend the ball as well."

"Oh, will you?" Miss Northrop added. "Let us not compete with the event of the year."

"Nay, let us contribute to it!" Sir Thomas said, shifting our director's expression from doubt to interest. "What say ye about a teaser performance at the ball? We perform the first two acts to introduce every character and the twisted love plot. Play to the desires of men and women wishing to cast love spells at the ball as Robin does to the characters. After they spin and toil their dreams to a man who can only choose one, we will fill their heartbroken souls with fantasies and wishes come true!"

"Hah!" our director laughed. "That is a splendid idea! Northop, Spears, and Smith: you all know the hostess? Volunteer our performance as entertainment. We shall tease them with the first two acts, then schedule our opening night the following week!"

I stood frozen, stunned, as the cast erupted with excitement. The vote was unanimous; everyone wanted to perform at the ball.

I hadn't voted. I couldn't risk objecting; any resistance would only spotlight me and spur questions I couldn't answer.

Misses Northrop and Spears sprinted off directly to petition Lady Edwards for the opportunity. I prayed she'd refuse, thinking it would disrupt her perfectly immaculate agenda. But the answer came the next morning: approval. They even flattered it as a "tribute to Lord Fromm's homeland." The others cheered. I groaned and considered how to escape as the other actresses rushed to secure gowns for the event. They expected to change out of their costumes after the performance.

Shoot. What were my options? Perform at the ball and hope Aeron didn't recognize me… or disappear from Pemberly before nightfall? Titania wasn't a pivotal role. They could replace me without too much hassle.

But…it would be another betrayal. Memories of my deeper betrayal—of blasting bombs and igniting fires across Arrowhead—haunted me. This wasn't the same. Not even close. But the guilt still tightened around my ribs.

No, if I was going to run, I would've done it the second Aeron stepped foot in Pemberly. I'd stayed, and I would see this through. Besides, I could be a master of disguise.

Titania's fairy queen costume was a Regency's interpretation of Fantasy, filtered through lace and imagination. Her long gown fell in loose folds to the floor, its panels shaped like oversized royal-purple flower petals layered over green leaves. Her paper wings were cut in a butterfly silhouette but patterned and colored with the bold eyes and iridescent colors of peacock feathers. The costume was topped with a crown of flowers and winding vines that dipped over my brow, softening the angles of my face.

In the days before the ball, I analyzed every element for adjustments, adding textures and strategic shading to distort my features. I practiced other methods of misdirection and posture, dimming and amplifying various parts of myself to appropriately embody Queen Titania. Would it be enough to escape Aeron's familiar gaze?

When Misses Northrop and Spears arrived to share the cart to the Edwards' estate, they took second looks with squinted eyes to recognize me. I counted that as a win.

"Miss Smith?" Spears gasped. "I feel that I ought to bow before the queen of fairies. How do you plan to dance in that after the performance?"

"I don't," I said. "I abhor crowds. The only reason for my attendance tonight is to support the rest of you."

Miss Northrop let out a soft, adoring coo and pulled me into an unexpected hug. I willed myself to return her embrace—accepting it, accepting the comfort, and accepting the reassurance that staying had been the right call, even if every instinct warned otherwise.

When she stepped back, her eyes were wide and misty with the kind of romantic optimism that I struggled to imitate. "Then you'll support us when Lord Fromm chooses one of us and whisks us away to the land of 'your people'?" She smirked with an added point at my fairy costume.

I forced a smile, though my pulse kicked hard at the possibility of Aeron choosing a wife that night. I didn't exactly want it to be me—I wasn't ready for that kind of commitment—but the idea of the biggest flirt I'd ever known binding himself to someone else? My blood chilled at the despair of living and dying alone.

No, I'd been the one to walk away. I'd told him to forget me. A whole year had passed since then. His love would forever haunt me, but (unlike me) he'd loved before. He'd love again. He deserved joy and stability with someone as magical and elevated as himself.

The Edwards' estate was as extravagant as ever: beautiful, immaculate, and impersonal. The sheer number of guests actually worked in my favor. A crowd this dense was usually perfect cover. Usually.

When someone bumped against my wings, I realized the mistake of my disguise. Titania stood out. She was too bright, too colorful, and too noticeable.

Better to vanish into an unused room until the performance.

The ballroom was packed with bodies jostling for the dance floor. Windows fogged, and people apologized often around the perimeter, giving the dancers in the center space to twirl. I held close to the walls, scanning for Aeron to plan my escape route in the opposite direction.

My Aeron radar spotted him standing near the back. I edged sideways, hiding around a corner. From behind my shelter, I watched him move through the crowd. He greeted lords and ladies with a practiced smile and worn eyes. No one else probably noticed the cracks in his composure, but I had spent far too many hours stupidly studying his gorgeous features. He practiced diplomacy the way some people endured the rain: resigned, detached, and simply waiting it out. He smiled, but his heart wasn't in it.

His gaze started to sweep the room in my direction. I ducked into the hallway before it landed.

What was I doing? This was reckless, the kind of fire I should've been running from, not circling like a moth with a death wish. I needed to hide. Fast.

I pushed through the crowd, murmuring apologies as I checked room after room—disrupting servants and interrupting couples who glared or shrieked. Finally, I found a small storage closet occupied only with luggage and boxes of letters. Spears agreed to fetch me before the performance, parting with a pitying look.

Thirty minutes crawled by. I kept my ear to the door, tracking muffled conversations and footsteps, one hand gripped around a dagger. Old habits and training that refused to retire—just in case. When Spears' laughter and swishing Helena costume drifted down the hall, I returned the blade to its hiding spot.

She opened my closet door with a nervous squeal and chimed, "It's time."

I followed her to a waiting room to the side of the ballroom and cycled through various breathing techniques—grounding, focus, dissociation, reconnection—until my pulse obeyed me. Act 2, Scene 1 began, and it was my turn to enter the makeshift stage in the ballroom. Hearing my cue, I went undercover as Titania and strutted onto the stage.

My Aeron-radar pinged instantly. He sat dead center in the front row. Of course. His jaw dropped slightly at my entrance. Hopefully in amazement of my costume, not in recognition of the face half-hidden behind a draping crown and shaded with makeup to transform my features.

Time to test whether this disguise would hold.

I lifted my chin, shifted into the airy cadence of a Fairy Queen, and pitched my voice into a higher vocal range to address Titania's acting husband. "What, jealous Oberon?"

I delivered my sixty-nine lines with my best performance yet, finishing with, "If you will patiently dance in our round, and see our moonlight revels, go with us. If not, shun me, and I will spare your haunts." I couldn't help glancing at Aeron in that last line, wondering if he had shunned me yet as I'd avoided his haunts. His eyes narrowed suspiciously.

Oberon replied, "Give me that boy and I will go with thee."

"Not for thy fairy kingdom," I said. "Fairies, away! We shall chide downright if I longer stay."

The moment after delivering my final line, every survival instinct in me detonated—*Abort-abort-abort!*

I made my exit with as much regal glide as Titania required while every nerve screamed to sprint. I felt Aeron's eyes tracking me, his familiarity giving his perception check an advantage against my disguise.

Shoot! One scene left. Eight more lines. Breathing drills and wishful thinking kept me from lighting my candle to escape.

Sir Thomas exeunted, queuing the final scene of our teaser and my return to the stage. For this particular performance, I turned my back to the audience as I lowered myself into a staged sleep. Safer that way. No eyes on my face. I remained on stage until the scene wrapped, then rose to bow with the others while our director announced our play schedule.

Aeron's seat was empty.

Good. Or terrible. Where had he gone?

I was the first to break from the bowing line, whispering an excuse to Northrop that I felt unwell. My flushed face and damp skin sold my lie well enough.

I hurried offstage, weaving through the side door to our temporary waiting room, finding Lady Newman beaming to congratulate me.

"Miss Smith." Lady Newman approached and took my hands. "Your costuming is positively Fantastic! Oh, dear, are you alright? You look terribly flustered."

I needed to escape. Fast. No time for pleasantries. No time for Lady Newman's praises or questions. I pivoted toward the next door and collided directly with Aeron.

So much for my Aeron-radar.

For the first time since seeing him buried in the dull manners of Romance, his eyes snapped fully awake.

"Anita!"

Shoot! That single name could ruin my whole cover! One slip, and all of Thriller would tear through the borders with grudges strong and guns loaded. I dipped into a bow and angled to escape, but he caught my arm.

"Anita? Wait, is that you?"

I turned my hesitation into confusion, speaking with Romance's airy cadence. "Forgive me, kind lord. You must have mistaken me for someone else."

He narrowed his eyes with an analytical expression I recognized from his PI days in Noir. I could practically feel him exchanging my costume and makeup for my usual black stealth clothes, reconstructing the woman underneath. He blinked and shifted his eyes to recognize the scene we created as the rest of the cast funneled into the waiting room behind me.

With that, the investigator inside him stepped aside for the marquis.

He bowed his head slightly, masking his revelations with the etiquette of Regency. "No, sorry, the fault is mine. Please accept my apologies with this next dance."

"Oh, I couldn't—"

"Please?"

I couldn't refuse him without creating a bigger scene. Already, Lady Newman made way like she could read our history. Miss Spear tapped her fan against every nearby shoulder to point out our situation.

I gave the smallest of nods. Aeron smiled and reached for my crown. "If I may assist you, I believe this might be cumbersome while dancing."

"Yes, yes," my director ordered. "Remove the wings too. We cannot have them rip before opening night!"

I cringed as Aeron unveiled me, petals brushing my temples. His smile broadened as my revealed face confirmed his suspicions. Miss Northrop swooped in to take my wings, leaving me flightless.

Aeron offered his arm to escort me, and, clenching my teeth to remain stoic and composed, I slid my hand into the crook of his elbow.

We reached the ballroom floor before the next piece began. I used those breaths to reconstruct my poise, vertebra by vertebra. When I dared to meet Aeron's eyes, his intensity was too familiar, too sharp, and too much to hold.

The minuet began—measured, elegant, and inescapable. Aeron bowed. I responded with a curtsy, then our hands met in the center, fingers brushing. The contact weighed heavily with every unspoken question and explanation between us.

"I realized," Aeron said, "that I don't know your name."

"Miss Annette Smith."

His eyes squinted with a hint of a smirk. "Of course it is."

With a turn of the dance, his smirk vanished, replaced by conflict. Even after a year apart, I recognized the layers of emotion within his features. His tight mouth wove a thread of pain, frustration, and tenderness. His eyes wrapped around something softer, like the longing for an impossible dream. I'd hoped he might be happy or relieved to find me. Foolish wish.

The minuet pulled us apart and brought us together in rotating patterns, switching between partners, but Aeron's gaze never wavered. Not once. Shoot my ears trained to catch whispers behind walls and to infer conversations between snippets. I picked up the swell of gossip rippling outward. Even if the other guests couldn't guess our exact relationship, Aeron's focus on me painted a picture of our intimate history.

The music began to close without more words exchanged. I'd spent all this time afraid he'd expose my alias by saying too much. I hadn't expected his silence to worry me more. What was going through his head?

In the final pass of the dance, he leaned in—quick and subtle enough to hide his sensual whisper from watching eyes.

"Greenhouse in ten."

I kept my face casual as the last note fell. We polished the dance off with smiles, a curtsy, and a bow. We parted to separate sides of the ballroom as if all was normal. He didn't seem thrilled to see me, but at least he was willing to talk.

I lingered near the front doors, waiting for a moment to slip out. After slipping into the night, I was tempted to flee back to the inn. My instinct screamed to escape, away from Aeron and Romance, toward safe anonymity. But he'd likely chase me until I answered his questions. Besides, I'd missed him too much to leave him without saying goodbye. I could spare a few minutes for the man who broke past every wall I'd built.

In the shadows of the late summer night, I snuck around the estate to circle toward the greenhouse.

On the off chance that it was a trap, I arrived early. Apparently, Aeron had still beaten me to the punch. The little sneak had abandoned his own ball.

He sat on a white wire bench with his back to me, posture relaxed but alert, shoulders square, and weight balanced. He straightened as I neared. He couldn't have noticed me…could he?

"So, it is you," he said, standing. "Only Anita could sneak up on me like a ghost. Thank you, Neil."

Neil. I grumbled. His poltergeist friend had alerted him to my presence. Confirming the area to be empty and safe (enough), I stepped into the open.

"What are you doing here, Anita?"

"You asked me to come—"

"What are you doing here, in Pemberly? Now? Did you come just to torture me?"

I rocked back. I thought he believed in my change of heart. Did he think I'd torture him because I'd killed all those people so long ago? Did he find me repulsive after all?

"I was here first," I defended. "What are you doing here if not to find me and take me in?"

He narrowed his eyes suspiciously. "Then you were at that horse race?"

"Yes," I confessed. "You didn't answer my question. Why are you here, Aeron?"

His eyebrows wrinkled with confusion. "Were my intentions unclear when I first arrived three months ago? This very ball is supposed to be where I make my decision."

I swallowed back my emotions. He really had come to find a wife. A small part of me had still hoped he'd come looking for me.

He sighed heavily. "You say that you were here first? Where have you been all this time? Avoiding me? Then why come now? Truly, you torture me."

"How am I torturing you?"

"You play with my heart!"

I stared back, unsure how to respond to the hypocritical irony. After all those years of his flirting, dating, even tempting me for kisses again and again, he accused me of playing with his heart?

Then again, I wasn't the only one who'd changed this past year. While I'd been running and dodging Thriller, wrestling my past and memories, Aeron had accepted his place as Margen's Marquis. His speech had sharpened: more formal, more measured, every word weighed before release. And I… I'd honed my own skills to bend emotions and manipulate conversations to steer them for my own purposes.

We both carried new armor, new caution, and new burdens.

In my silence, he dragged his fingers through his hair, a sound escaping him like a suppressed groan: raw, frustrated, and too honest for his public mask. "I tried, Anita. Those first six months, I exhausted every resource to find you and your master, pulling favors, dragging Detective Ross into the research and putting his job in jeopardy to obtain files. But you didn't destroy Arrowhead; you simply revolutionized it. What other Missions did he give you? Are they connected in a way that could hint at his end goal?"

"Please, Aeron," I said, struggling not to beg. "Don't make me relive my past, and stop searching for my master. He's dangerous. I can't protect you from him. He could have destroyed Arrowhead on his own if he'd wanted."

Aeron's brows constricted. "Wait, how would you know that? Has he done it before?"

I clamped my mouth shut and exercised my right to remain silent. I'd said too much. I couldn't feed Aeron's drive to find Stryker. My former master would kill my former partner without a thought of regret.

My muteness made Aeron's shoulders slump. "It's probably too late, anyway. Six months was the time limit they gave me. I failed to find your master and find mercy for you. And after six more months of failing to forget you…" He huffed and gestured to our Regency surroundings.

A cold chill spread through me. That explained his frenzied searching and then sudden disinterest. He'd had a deadline. He hadn't come to Romance simply to find a wife. He'd come to *forget* me.

I stayed silent as he studied my remaining costume and makeup, looking at me while still avoiding me. "Since I couldn't run away with you, I couldn't continue running after you. Being the marquis is a lot of work, and everyone says the duties are easier with a marchioness to help shoulder them. Coming here was supposed to help me find love again."

But if my mere presence tortured him…

"Do you still love me?" I whispered.

He met my eyes, tender and frustrated. "Of course. But until I find a way to free you from Thriller agents, our lives are incompatible."

Until he found a way? He still looked to clear my name? Even though I knew it was a lost cause, he still fought for me? That was enough to encourage my next words.

"I came to Regency, Romance, because my master never taught me how to love without lies. I came to learn… how to properly love a Marquis of Margen."

I didn't promise him anything, but I offered hope. Even if it was the truth, it was the wrong thing to say. Hope was a cruel gift, because it trapped him in my poisonous embrace. As long as there was hope for us, he would reject others, even the sweet Lady Newman.

To confirm this thought, Aeron closed the distance between us in a single stride. He wrapped one hand around my shoulder and the other around my neck, yanking me to him. His lips hit mine, sharp and insistent. I responded equally.

His explosion and my implosion of emotions hit all at once—the pull, the need. It wasn't desire. It was a necessity. Our breathing became a shared rhythm, pulses racing to keep up with our craving for one another.

My heartbeat quickened even as our intensity slowed. Whatever fear or need drove our desperate kisses calmed. Arrowhead wasn't there to break us up or take me away. This wouldn't be our last kiss. We allowed ourselves to linger in each other's arms.

Aeron's touch became a gentle caress, and I savored each moment. Savored it…because it couldn't last. I hated to be the voice of reason, but one of us needed to be. I forced myself to lean away.

"We shouldn't be doing this," I said, my voice steady and forced. Not an argument or plea, but a simple fact. "This is a mistake."

"I disagree." He kissed my cheek. "Even if it is—" my jaw "—this is a mistake I want to make—" beneath my ear "—over—" my neck "—and over—" my collar bone "—and over."

With that, all reason fled.

Our embrace shifted as we began to timidly explore each other. His hands crept down my back, pulling me closer, and I nibbled on his ear. He shivered and chuckled with excitement.

Footsteps cracked sharply against gravel around the corner. Right, even though Arrowhead wasn't an immediate threat, my alias as a Pemberly spinster was in danger. I needed to hide before someone spotted us together, especially in this Contemporary embrace.

I twisted free before two female ball guests appeared behind the greenhouse glass. Except Aeron's hands remained on my lower back, and I guessed the heat in our faces was equally incriminating.

The two women caught us and froze for a split second, then squeaked and retreated. Aeron's face snapped toward the glass, his expression hardening as he assessed the situation. No words. No panic. Only investigation and resolution.

"You've blown my cover." I sighed. "I can't go back among those people if they all know I'm intimate with you. They'll ask questions that I can't answer and treat me differently."

"I should say sorry, but it would be a lie," he whispered and brushed another kiss across my lips. "I can't believe I found you. Of all the places in Novel, we both ended up here."

He buried his face in my hair and breathed me in. I wanted the moment to never end, but reality nagged me.

"I can't stay," I said. "These people tolerated me and accepted me as a talented actress, but they'll hate me for stealing your attention."

Aeron moaned softly and pulled me tighter. "Please don't disappear again." He kissed me again with a delicate tenderness, as if he feared too much would break me. Except I was already broken.

I bowed my face away to ask, "Will Arrowhead forgive me?"

"Arrowhead?"

"Yeah. Do they still want to see me executed for my crimes? Shoot, I deserve to be—"

"No, Anita. Please stop condemning yourself." His thumb grazed across my cheek to wipe away a loose tear. "I *will* find a way to clear your name."

"You can't clear me, Aeron. I'm guilty." Another tear dropped.

"And reformed," he argued. "What about the man who raised you? The reason you killed those people was because he demanded it of you, right? What if we found a way to make him confess?"

"We'd need to find him first. If you think I was difficult to locate, how will you sniff out the person who taught me everything I know? I don't even know where he is, and I'm probably the closest thing he ever had to a daughter."

"I will find a way," Aeron repeated. "I can claim you as a refugee in Fairy, I don't care—whatever it takes to keep you safe from Thriller."

"I am safe from Thriller," I said, looking up and into his eyes. "As long as they can't find me. But now that you've found me and spoiled my cover here, they won't be far behind. I can't stay."

"No, not again. Please don't—"

"I'm not leaving right now," I said, though he continued to hold me tightly. "I need to gather my things. Will you escort me home?"

His jaw clenched, a flash of painful frustration passing before he masked it and nodded. He extended his arm, and I looped mine through, exiting the greenhouse all composed like a proper couple. As if we hadn't ravished each other between the flowers.

He guided me to the carts, but held me back from climbing on.

"This is where we part," he said. "My reputation is already questioned from hiding in the greenhouse with you. I must stay to give my excuse and proper goodbyes. I may excuse you too, if you wish."

"Yeah, thanks," I said, and met his eyes—pained and sorrowful. I didn't want to say goodbye at the carts, but I knew parting ways would only be harder at the inn or in my room. I didn't want to say goodbye at all. I wanted to convince him to stay the night with me, then vanish together in the morning.

We'd make good use of the last bit of my Fantasy candle, fleeing to the borderlands of Western, far away from anywhere anyone would think to look for us.

No, Aeron had responsibilities. He was a marquis with obligations. People relied on him, and I was a complication.

I wanted to embrace him with my passion and pull him into the cart with me, but I restrained my affections as I graced him with a simple but lingering kiss. I cut away as soon as Aeron tried to deepen it.

I forced myself to turn and climb into the cart. After giving the driver directions, I dared to glance back. Aeron remained at the side of the cart, watching and waiting.

The reins snapped, and I whispered, "Goodbye, Aeron."

"I will find you again," he said. "I love you."

"I love you too."

Afterword

I found Anita. After six months of mad searching and six more of pretending she didn't matter to me, I found her. And she was gone again. I watched her cart drive away until it disappeared down the street. That was perhaps the strangest part of all this; I let her go. The feel of her lips still tingled on my own. With every breath, I continued to inhale her scent. I drowned in the memory of her as I wandered back to the ballroom.

One fact was confirmed from this trip: I could no longer pretend I wasn't madly in love with Anita.

I walked inside and the change of atmosphere was as drastic as going from Fantasy to Mystery. Twenty minutes ago, all the women in the building had swooned in my presence, vying for my attention. Not unlike the parties in Fantasy I attended. Now, the eyes and whispers turned guarded against me. Not unlike the police in Mystery.

Go figure. I had acted like a love-sick Contemporary at a Regency ball. Such passion was considered improper.

But the whole purpose of this season had been to help me find someone to marry. And I found Anita. I was a fool in love with the impossible.

I chuckled to myself, wondering at the odds that she'd be here. After all that time of searching for her, I had run into her by accident?

People cleared the way before me, keeping their distance as if my Contemporary manners were contagious. Everyone shied away except the shyest person of all.

"Lady Newman." I stopped, and offered a small bow.

"Lord Fromm," she replied with a curtsy. "I heard the most troubling rumors concerning you and Miss Smith."

I chuckled lightly and glanced at the guests giving me a wide berth. "I suspect the rumors are even more scandalous than the truth. Still, I returned to apologize. The company of you and the Kenningtons has been most valuable and enduring. However, I hope you understand when I say that we would struggle to give each other long-term happiness."

"I—" she stuttered with baited breath, "—agree." Then she smiled, surprisingly relieved.

I bowed again in farewell, then made my way to my hosts, ready to apologize again for my behavior. Viscount Edwards seemed surprised to see me. His daughter fumed silently behind him, glaring fire at me. I ignored her as easily as I had ignored her throughout the Season.

I bowed to my host. "Please forgive me, Lord Edwards. I must confess that I cannot stay any longer."

He laughed like I'd spoken the understatement of the year. "When the Bennett sisters came in from the gardens with such gossip of your secret meeting, I had not expected your return for apologies. What was the maid's name again?"

I straightened myself and blinked in surprise. "Miss—er—Smith," I said, catching myself from blundering her alias. "She begs her pardon as she has already departed. We previously dated—if you catch my modern phrasing. At the sight of her, I acted rashly and irrationally."

"Dated?" Lady Edwards shrieked. "What about *manners?* After all the work I slaved over to give you the perfect—"

Her father cut her short with her first name and a glare far more menacing than any stare my father gave me.

"As it is—" the viscount frowned "—you have shamed our house and this event. I must ask you to leave now."

I bowed to show as much gratitude and respect as they would accept.

I had no reason to remain in Romance, and considered my return to Margen. There was no use hiding the truth from what happened tonight from my mom and father. They would find out soon enough anyway. I was determined to tell them myself; I was a condemned star-crossed lover.

I loved Anita. She loved me. But I was a future duke, and she was a fugitive. At least until I could save her from Thriller. Then, I'd find her again and find a way for us to be together.

The End

(for now)

ACKNOWLEDGEMENTS

I began this book with no intentions of publishing it, but this particular story was my favorite procrastination project. I had half of the book drafted since Nov. 2023, but it required a *lot* of edits. I also had no idea what would happen in the climax until I really dug into the thriller genre. I grew up loving the combined genres of action, mystery, and romance. I also want to thank Traci Hunter Abramson with her Guardians, Royals, and Saint Squad series to provide romantic-thriller ideas. Particularly, "Safe House: Guardians #2/Saint Squad #8.5" (the first book I read by her). Kade's off-grid truck/home inspired unhealthy research into tiny homes that I "justified" with Anita's getaway van.

I'd like to thank my first eyes, Julie Carpenter, for helping me to believe that the story didn't suck, but was, in fact, an entertaining thriller.

My amazing Alpha Readers include the incredible authors, Jim Doran and R.A. Cheatham. Thank you for helping me to kill some darlings (three chapter's worth) in Fantasy to help Aeron and Anita get to Thriller faster.

To my Beta Readers: Bruce Tracy, Bettilee Hunt, Jazmin, and Marla Summers. Thank you for taking time out of the hectic holiday season to read 72,000+ words. You all have my heartfelt thanks.

Then, to my editor from Enchanted Quill Press; thank you for correcting all my mistaken word combinations. I wrote this paragraph after your proofread, so sorry if this includes punctuation errors.

There isn't a "THANK YOU" big enough for my Alpha (and partial Beta) reader, Michael. So much of this book wouldn't exist without your "storm-braining." I still laugh at the time I attempted to ask AI for brainstorming ideas, and (despite its in-depth analysis and suggestions) your solution was much better. (Who's surprised?)

Finally, I thank God for helping me to put all my crazy ideas together and make them work. Even if I'm not preaching non-fiction, He still helps me with my goals. My beliefs in second chances and opportunities for mercy are 100% rooted in the gospel of Jesus Christ.

ABOUT THE AUTHOR

C. Rae D'Arc has been involved in every stage of a book's life. As a writer, editor, retailer, reader, and reviewer, she once worked four part-time jobs simultaneously. Thankfully, one of them actually paid her. She received her Bachelors in English from Brigham Young University and now lives in the Tri Cities of Washington with her husband and Aussie dog.

PS. To save you from hiccups, D'Arc only has one syllable.

Learn more about books by C. Rae D'Arc on
her website: craedarc.com
Facebook: facebook.com/c.rae.darc
Instagram: instagram.com/craedarc

She stared at me with shimmering eyes, on the brink of tears. Curses, I'd made her cry.

"You left me."

"What? No! I'd never leave you."

"But you did. When I needed you most, you abandoned me."

"I needed more information. I needed to know what happened."

"You'd know soon enough! You didn't need to skip ahead of the story—to the *last* page—and betray me like that!"

She turned away, biting back her anger. "Go back. I don't want you here."

My heart broke. If only I'd been more patient, this would have ended differently.